In her youth, award-winning reimagined the Regency rom now she loves writing her own. Although living in Canada, Ann visits Britain every year, where family members understand—or so they say—her need to poke around every antiquity within a hundred miles. Learn more about Ann or contact her at annlethbridge.com. She loves hearing from readers.

Also by Ann Lethbridge

Rescued by the Earl's Vows
The Viscount's Reckless Temptation
The Wife the Marquess Left Behind
A Cinderella to Redeem the Earl

The Widows of Westram miniseries

A Lord for the Wallflower Widow
An Earl for the Shy Widow
A Family for the Widowed Governess
A Shopkeeper for the Earl of Westram

Discover more at millsandboon.co.uk.

COURTING SCANDAL WITH THE DUKE

Ann Lethbridge

MILLS & BOON

All rights reserved including the right of reproduction in whole or in part in any form. This edition is published by arrangement with Harlequin Enterprises ULC.

This is a work of fiction. Names, characters, places, locations and incidents are purely fictional and bear no relationship to any real life individuals, living or dead, or to any actual places, business establishments, locations, events or incidents. Any resemblance is entirely coincidental.

Without limiting the author's and publisher's exclusive rights, any unauthorised use of this publication to train generative artificial intelligence (AI) technologies is expressly prohibited. HarperCollins also exercise their rights under Article 4(3) of the Digital Single Market Directive 2019/790 and expressly reserve this publication from the text and data mining exception.

® and TM are trademarks owned and used by the trademark owner and/or its licensee. Trademarks marked with ® are registered with the United Kingdom Patent Office and/or the Office for Harmonisation in the Internal Market and in other countries.

First published in Great Britain 2025
by Mills & Boon, an imprint of HarperCollins*Publishers* Ltd,
1 London Bridge Street, London, SE1 9GF

www.harpercollins.co.uk

HarperCollins*Publishers*, Macken House, 39/40 Mayor Street Upper, Dublin 1, D01 C9W8, Ireland

Courting Scandal with the Duke © 2025 Michéle Ann Young

ISBN: 978-0-263-34534-6

09/25

This book contains FSC™ certified paper and other controlled sources to ensure responsible forest management.

For more information visit www.harpercollins.co.uk/green.

Printed and Bound in the UK using 100% Renewable Electricity at CPI Group (UK) Ltd, Croydon, CR0 4YY

Chapter One

Spring 1817

The start of the London Season

Rain pitter-pattered on the roof of the carriage. Rain mixed with snow if Barbara wasn't mistaken.

'What a dreadful evening,' Barbara's Great-Aunt Lenore moaned from the recesses of her corner of the carriage. 'Are we to ever have some decent weather?'

While not even the glow of a street lamp pierced the gloom inside the carriage, Barbara did not doubt the dissatisfaction pasted on the older woman's expression. She also sensed her fingers restlessly twisting her handkerchief.

'March in England,' Barbara said coolly. ''Tis only to be expected.' She pulled her indigo velvet cloak closer about her person. Rain. It could not have worked out better.

'I hope you remember all that I told you, Barbara,' her aunt said anxiously. 'The rules.'

The rules of Almack's were strictures that every young lady new upon the town must obey or for ever be ostracised. Her aunt had a reason to be anxious. She knew Barbara's lack of fondness for regulations. In the darkness, it was easy for Barbara to hide her glee. 'I have them memorised.'

It would not do to show that inside she was bubbling with resentment and anger and... Well, a kind of naughty anticipation. 'Let me see.' She counted the items off on the fingers of her gloved hand. 'Do not dance until you have been approved by a hostess. Do not dance with the same gentleman more than twice. Do not—'

'I think you should not dance more than once. Not on your first visit, at least.'

'Isn't dancing the whole purpose of Almack's? Would it be so scandalous to dance more than once?' Barbara asked, grabbing for the strap as the carriage lurched around a corner.

Her aunt raised her walking stick and banged on the trapdoor. 'Slow down!'

The carriage's speed reduced to a crawl, no doubt to the annoyance of every other conveyance on the street.

Barbara swallowed her urge to laugh.

'Not scandalous, no,' Aunt Lenore said. 'But there would be no reason you should. After all, you do not know any gentlemen. We will be lucky if any of them ask you to dance tonight. I think it is most unfortunate that your father has kept you out of England all these many years. Following the drum. I ask you.'

'Good gracious, Aunt, you have me sounding like some round-heeled washerwoman.'

Her aunt gave a little squeal. 'Barbara. I implore you. Do not use such language. You are a lady. Act like one, for heaven's sake.'

'I must add that to your list of rules, Aunt. No unseemly language.'

'That is not a rule. It is common sense.'

'Hmm. What else? Oh, act modestly. Debutantes wear white.' Barbara's ostrich feathers were white. Married ladies could wear other colours, muted greys and so forth. Her aunt hadn't thought to mention widows. 'Speak when spoken to, especially with regard to the hostesses. Will I know who they are?'

'Of course you will. Did I not say I would introduce you? Indeed, your father insisted upon it. As soon as possible.'

Her father insisted upon a great many things. 'Did he indicate when he would be in London?'

'Not to me. I thought he might have written to you of his plans.'

'Ah. Plans.' Father's plans were like dandelion clocks. They blew thither and yon in the slightest wind. Never seeming to settle anywhere. Until they did. Barbara was always the last to know. But this time she'd had advance warning of one of them. Foolish of Father in the extreme, as it turned out.

'I did mention,' her Aunt went on, 'did I not, that you are not dance the waltz with anyone?' Aunt Lenore said. 'Not on your debut.'

'Several times, Aunt.' Barbara hoped she sounded suitably meek. 'I don't know why you are making such a fuss. I'm not some miss fresh out of school. I have been married. Twice. A widow can do more or less as she pleases.'

'Pish posh. You were married to foreigners. On foreign soil. It is not at all the same. And besides, your father is very keen for you to make an excellent match. This Season. His wishes were very clear. It is very important.'

Father be hanged! Barbara cared little about his wishes. Her own wish was to remain steadfastly unwed until she reached twenty-five years of age in a year's time. That was when she would have access to the money left her by her first husband instead of having to rely on whatever Father decided to dole out to her. As long as she could avoid marriage.

If she did marry, on her twenty-fifth birthday, the money would automatically be handed over to her husband instead.

Barbara had no such intention. Never again would anyone bully her into marriage. She was going to make sure of it.

The carriage pulled up.

Aunt Lenore leaned forward to peer out of the window in the door. 'Hah. Right outside. Well done, John Coachman. Come, Barbara. A few steps and we shall be out of this terrible weather.'

A footman opened the door and let down the steps.

He held an umbrella over them as they made their way into the building.

In the cloakroom a throng of women were changing into dancing slippers and shedding wet cloaks. Aunt Lenore handed over her outer raiment and sat down to allow a maid help her on with her slippers.

Still in her cloak, Barbara squeezed onto a bench as far from her aunt as she could manage. She fiddled with the fastening of her shoe.

'Barbara, are you ready?' Aunt Lenore asked a few minutes later.

'My buckle is caught. Go ahead. I will catch you up.'

Aunt Lenore hesitated. Then nodded. 'Very well. I will present our tickets. Do not be too long. They will close the doors promptly at eleven.'

Other ladies were also hurrying. It wanted only a few minutes to eleven. The rain had made travel slower than normal. There were very few minutes to spare.

Perfect.

She slipped on her slippers and handed her cloak to the waiting maid.

The girl gasped.

'Something amiss?' Barbara asked, knowing very well why the girl looked as shocked as a lad with buckshot in his britches.

The girl swallowed, her eyes wide. 'Nothing, miss.'

'Milady,' Barbara corrected. 'Dowager Countess of Lipsweiger and Upsal, to be precise.' Father had been so pleased about the title. Much good it had done him.

The girl didn't seem the slightest bit impressed, but

then the British were notorious for their scorn of anything foreign.

She went to the mirror and tucked the two curling ostrich plumes she had sheltered from the rain inside her cloak into her elaborately dressed coiffure. 'Perfect,' she said and sashayed up the stairs to her waiting Aunt.

It was all going swimmingly.

She tried not to laugh.

Rules.

Pish posh.

From now on, they were for other people.

Xavier, Duke of Derbridge, regarded the company at Almack's with cool uninterest.

No matter how he tried, he could not seem to summon up any enthusiasm. They were all so…dull.

Duller than ditch water.

Duller than a rainy day in March.

Duller than a blade used to cut bone.

Duller than a sermon.

Duller…

What on earth was he thinking? They were all absolutely perfect wife material.

He rolled his shoulders and hid a wince at the pain from a bruised rib. His sparring partner had caught him a witty castor, as pugilists liked to say. It had been a good fight. At Jackson's saloon, he was just another fellow who liked to box. No one there cared that he was a duke.

It provided him with all the excitement he needed. That and his horses.

The last thing he needed was an exciting wife. His father had married a woman the *ton* had admiringly called the Daring Duchess shortly after Xavier's mother had died. Her recklessness had led his father to his death, leaving Xavier alone. A duke at twelve years old.

No, he certainly did not need that sort of woman in his life.

Oh, he had liked his stepmother well enough when he had first met her. He recalled thinking her pretty the first time Father introduced them. Father had gone to London on business and met her at a ball. Everyone who knew them said it had been love at first sight.

Xavier had liked her at first, and not only because his father said he should, but because his father said she was going to be his new mother.

He hadn't realised he wanted a mother until then. He scarcely recalled his own mother. He and his father had been so close, he had never felt the need for anyone else.

As soon as he was old enough to ride a pony, he had accompanied Father on his tours of the estate, or out shooting for the table, or sailing in the bay. More often than not of an evening, he and Father had sat beside the fire, Father reading aloud from his newspaper. They had discussed things, man to man. Or so it had seemed to Xavier.

But he had noticed other boys' mothers. How nice they were. Sort of gentle and sweet.

Sweet didn't describe Lady Leticia. She hadn't been

interested in shooting, or newspapers, or, it seemed to Xavier, small boys. Those things weren't fun.

She liked to ride fast. And because Xavier's pony was too slow, she and Papa had stopped inviting him to go along. Papa said it was because Leticia was young and liked a bit of excitement. He said she made him feel young.

And besides, if he didn't do what she wanted she would get very upset. Father didn't like it when she cried.

Great-Uncle Tom, when he came to visit, muttered in his beard and said she was reckless and had addled Father's brain. He used to say the moment Leticia saw him, she had decided to catch him.

As time went on, Father had spent more time in London, going to balls and parties. With her. And only came home in the summer, when they'd invited lots of guests, and because adults did things a lad of Xavier's age wouldn't be interested in, according to his stepmama, he was better off in the schoolroom with his governess or tutor.

Happier, she had assured his father.

Only he hadn't been.

So, they had sent him away to school.

Xavier shoved thoughts of the days before his father died aside. The memories of how they'd gone off sailing without him that summer always churned up the anger he had tried to bury along with memories of his childhood.

No, he definitely did not want a wife like his stepmother.

He wanted a nice quiet female who would give his son, or sons, a warm and comforting upbringing.

Unlike his own.

To be certain, his Great-Uncle Thomas had done his best, but he'd been a bit of a martinet. As old-fashioned and irascible as they came.

His best friend, Julian Pettigrew, nudged him. 'What the devil are you doing?'

'Nothing.'

'Yes, you are. You are glowering. I thought you wanted to meet a few of this Season's debutantes, not scare them out of their dancing slippers.'

'Nonsense. I am not glowering.' At least not any more than usual.

'You are. At everyone. At least one of those little misses fainted at the sight of that frown of yours.'

The Derbridge frown. His grandfather had been famous for it, so Uncle Thomas had said. Was it his fault that he had inherited his family's well-known heavy brow and thick black eyebrows that drew naturally together over shockingly blue eyes and an equally prominent nose? Certainly, no one had ever accused him of being handsome.

'If a frown is all it takes to make a girl faint, she is clearly not the woman for me.' Though, since he had decided this was the year he would wed, *one* of these delicate debutantes had to be the perfect woman.

Which was why he had come to Almack's.

'By the way,' Julian said. 'Thank you for your advice on that race at Newmarket. I never would have picked that horse to win. I recouped most of my losses from Epsom.'

'Which you incurred because you went against my advice and bet on the favourite.'

Despite his renowned expertise on racehorses, Xavier very rarely gave tips on races any more. He'd done it to gain friends at school, only to realise they were fair-weather friends at best. Now he offered advice only to those closest to him. And only if pressed. He never advised on races in which he had one of his own horses running, because in the past rumours had spread that he had somehow fixed the results.

'It was a nice-looking beast. How could it not win?'

'All show and no go.'

A ripple of interest over by the entrance caught Xavier's attention.

Like the seas parting, a space opened between him and the door. His jaw dropped. Red. The lady was wearing red.

He snapped his mouth shut.

'Oh, my word,' Julian murmured. 'That has set the cat among the pigeons.'

And an exceedingly exotic feline it was to be sure. Walking with a sinuous grace, she entered in the room, taking in her surroundings. Her dark eyes sparkled, her full lips curved in the hint of a smile and her hair was a sleek as a panther's fur, except on one side where it fell to her shoulder in a riot of ringlets. And she was wearing the tallest ostrich plumes he had ever seen. On such a tall woman, they towered above all around her.

Confidence—and something else he could not quite name—exuded from her every pore.

Stunning. Startling. Shocking.

The ennui that had been washing through him a few seconds before dissipated in a heartbeat. 'Who is she?'

He could not believe he had asked the question. He could not recall the last time he had enquired about a woman.

'No idea.' Julian chuckled. 'Some poor hick from the country I would imagine, if she thought that colour was acceptable.'

Red? Or crimson? Perhaps scarlet? It was brighter than the large exotic-looking rubies in the jewels at her throat and ears. Whatever the shade it might be called, it was most definitely the most daring gown he had ever seen. Cut low across her generous bosom, it missed her shoulders altogether; mere wisps of fabric clung to her upper arms, apparently in an attempt to stop the gown sliding to the floor.

At any moment.

Like him, every other gentleman in the room seemed to be holding his breath. Questioning. Hoping. Would the gown slowly slide over those curves to the floor?

Annoying. 'A veritable country bumpkin,' Xavier pronounced.

Several bystanders within earshot closed their mouths and turned away from the vision in red.

A hint of his disapproval was all that was needed.

The buzz of conversation picked up again.

Yet for some reason, he could not resist the temptation to look again. A casual glance. His gaze drifting past where she was now engaged in animated conversation with an elderly grey-haired woman wearing a dreary grey gown. The older woman did not look happy.

The woman in red flicked open her fan, a black lacy affair, with feathered edges. She hid the lower half of her face, but there was no mistaking the amusement in those dark eyes. Almost taunting.

A gentleman approached, clearly intent on asking her to dance.

'You are doing it again,' Julian said.

Xavier dragged his gaze from the tableau playing out across the other side of the room and glanced down at his friend. At six foot two inches, he looked down on even the tallest of men. 'If you are unhappy with the way I look, old fellow, perhaps you should find someone else with whom to converse.'

Julian laughed. He knew Xavier too well to take offence. 'Perhaps *you* would prefer to play cards?'

'Only old men play cards at Almack's.' He had come here to view candidates for marriage, to identify those suitable to be his bride, if at all possible. He certainly wasn't about to let some hussy in red distract him from his purpose.

The woman he actually had been seeking was now standing near the orchestra—Lady Cowper, one of Almack's Lady Patronesses. 'Lady Cowper promised me some introductions this evening.'

Julian grinned. 'I bet a shilling to a pound you end up dancing with her.'

He didn't have to say who the *her* was that he meant.

'Nonsense.' Whoever the woman in red was, she was beyond the pale as far as Xavier was concerned. He didn't have to meet her to know that she was one of those sorts of women who did anything to get attention.

Like his stepmother.

And look how that had turned out.

'What on earth were you thinking?' Lenore's fingers fluttered at her throat, touching her necklace, then flew to her waist. Like little sparrows, her hands never stilled, and it was worse when she was anxious.

Oh, my. Aunt Lenore was more agitated than Barbara had ever seen her before. She hadn't actually thought it was possible.

'What do you mean?' Barbara asked. She knew, of course, but she could play the innocent with the best of them. When needed.

'Red. I know I told you to avoid red at all costs.'

'Red?' Barbara set her face in a picture of puzzlement.

'Your gown. It is red.'

'Nonsense. The dressmaker assured me that this gown is geranium.'

Fingers twisted her fan. 'Geranium *is* red,' Aunt Lenore hissed, her glance darting hither and yon, clearly fearing they would be overheard. 'Whatever are we to do now? You are quite ruined. Your father will never forgive me for allowing you to make such a spectacle of yourself.'

'Oh, dear.' Barbara tried to keep her smile pleasant, but she could not help feeling a little spurt triumph. Goal one, accomplished. She had put herself beyond the pale as far as capital *S* Society was concerned and could now relax and enjoy London exactly as she pleased. The real world awaited.

The gentleman who had glared at her when he first saw her, a man of imposing height and strong features of around thirty, was once more glancing her way. Not boldly. Not covertly either. A passing cold stare from icy blue eyes, pausing for little more than a fraction of a second. A tingle ran across her shoulders. In recognition? No. For she did not know him. But something about the way he looked at her seemed to cause a visceral reaction on her skin.

He had said something as she entered room that had made people standing near him turn their backs on her.

He clearly did not like what he saw.

Well, she did not think much of him either.

Too stern, in a striking sort of way.

Too judgemental.

Too cold.

Too…attractive?

How could such a stern looking man be attractive? But then given her own lofty height, she did like a man who was tall.

Fluttering fingers curled around Barbara's wrist, drawing her attention back to her Aunt. There was kindness in those muddy greenish-brown eyes. Sympathy.

Guilt washed through Barbara. Aunt Lenore had tried her best, after all. She snapped her fan shut, quite happy to make a rapid retreat and save her Aunt from further embarrassment, for this entrance of hers was not about Aunt Lenore. It was about Father. And his interminable plans. 'I am sorry. I seem to have made a mess of things. Let us go, and quickly.'

Aunt Lenore's grip tightened. 'Certainly not. We Lowells have more gumption than that.'

Barbara stared at her, astonished by the unexpected bravado. And the opportunity was lost. A gentleman in the regulation black tailcoat, starched white neckerchief and satin knee breeches was bowing to her aunt.

'Miss Lowell. How delightful to see you here at Almack's. You have not graced us with your presence for some considerable time.'

'Mr Elton, how kind of you to remember me,' Aunt Lenore said. 'May I present you to my great-niece, Dowager Countess of Lipsweiger and Upsal. This is Mr Paul Elton, my dear. A great friend of our Prince Regent.'

That accounted for the little man's look of self-importance, but not his revoltingly coloured waistcoat, a rather sickly shade of green which emphasised the red in his nose.

Barbara inclined her head as if to a lesser mortal, and she felt her aunt's hand quiver then drop away.

'Your great-niece?' Elton beamed. 'Then you must

be March's daughter. I heard your arrival was expected imminently.'

Her aunt had been touting her arrival for several months, apparently. Building expectations as it were. Advertising her attributes. The main one being her fortune inherited from her late husband, part of which she was currently wearing around her neck. At least, that was what Father had written in his last letter.

Ugh. She allowed a brilliant smile to cross her lips. 'Indeed.'

Elton raised his hand to his mouth, leaned in close and lowered his voice. 'Your gown is magnificent. You carry it off to perfection, but if I may mention the... colour.'

Barbara raised her right eyebrow and looked down her nose at the little fellow. It had taken many months of practice looking in the mirror to achieve a perfect expression of incredulity. As usual, it achieved the desired result.

The gentleman flushed. 'I am known for my s-sartorial expertise,' he stuttered.

Barbara did not move a muscle.

'Red is such a difficult colour,' he mumbled.

'It is geranium, not red.'

'Yes, yes. Geranium.' He pursed his lips and tilted his head a fraction as if considering her words. A small sly smile curved his lips. 'Well. I should think geranium will be all the rage within the week.'

Not at all what she intended.

'How can you say so?'

He waved a deprecating hand. 'I am told your dowry is vast.'

Dash it all. Surely the *ton* could not possibly be shallow enough to ignore her faux pas, simply because they thought she had wealth.

'W-would you care to dance?' he asked.

Beside her, Aunt Lenore's smile brightened. 'Oh, yes. Do dance with Mr Elton, my dear.'

She did not need her aunt's permission. But dancing with this little fellow, the top of whose head barely came above her ear, would likely serve as yet another cause for ridicule.

And she would be dancing before she had been introduced to one of the Lady Patronesses.

Hah! Sin upon sin.

'I should be delighted.' She gathered her skirts, and he escorted her onto the dance floor. A reel. A shame it wasn't a waltz.

She would have loved for it to have been a waltz.

The tall glowering gentleman was part of their set. He was taller than any other man in the room. Exceedingly tall, up close.

One of the few men in the room she had to look up at to see his expression, she realised as their hands met in the circle of four.

Her fingers tingled at the brush of his fingertips. Perhaps because he so clearly did not approve of her. Did he feel it too? Not if his distant expression was anything to go by.

The pretty young lady with him, a blonde, wore the

uniform of a first Season miss. The modest white muslin gown with little pink flowers in her hair, at her bosom and on her hem, identified her as an inveterate follower of the rules.

Her glowering partner was clearly an ogre who would eat the young thing alive. And still be looking for more.

Barbara could not but feel sorry for the child and flashed a smile at the ogre.

His expression remained…disapproving.

Now, who on earth could he be, to be so overtly disapproving of anyone?

They returned to their respective places in the set and moved down the line. She sent him a teasing glance.

His shoulders stiffened almost imperceptibly. She stifled a giggle. He really did not like her.

Of course, she did not look at him again during the dance. That would have been too obvious. But she was aware of *his* glance from time to time. His haughty, disapproving glance was like a physical touch brushing her cheek. Or her shoulder. A tingle ran down her spine. Very odd, since obviously he was a man who thought his opinion counted for a great deal.

Perhaps she could find a way to use him to her advantage.

Now, wouldn't that be perfect?

Chapter Two

Xavier deftly relieved a footman of the two glasses of ratafia he had promised to fetch for his last dance partner and her duenna. The girl had turned out to be the best of the bunch, so far. Quiet and calm, if a little shy and rather plain as far as looks went.

And not dressed in red.

'I know who she is,' Julian said, over Xavier's shoulder at the refreshment table.

Xavier's heart skipped a beat. The glasses of ratafia wobbled.

'Who?'

Julian nudge his arm and Xavier cursed under his breath as he once again barely saved the nasty sticky stuff from spilling.

'You know who,' Julian said.

He glanced at his friend. They'd been friends for years. Since school, where Julian had been small for his age. As had Xavier. They had stuck up for each other and fought for each other against bigger boys. Julian was the only person who knew how Xavier had felt when his parents died. Right now, Xavier considered planting him a facer. Fortunately, he had his hands full.

'Very well, I know. So?'

People cleared a path as Xavier carried the drinks across the room with Julian on his heels.

Close on his heels.

Julian chuckled. 'She is the Countess of Lipsweiger and Upsal.'

'A foreigner. That accounts for it.'

'No, no. She only married a foreigner. Two of them. Did away with them in pretty short order too. At White's they have started calling her the black widow.'

She sounded as dangerous as she looked. 'Never heard of her.'

'Yes, you have. She's Ambassador March's daughter. Barbara. The fellows at White's are taking bets on who will be her next victim.'

While not foreign, she clearly didn't give a damn what people thought. Reckless in the extreme.

He handed a glass to the petite blonde Miss Simon and another to her mother. 'As promised,' he said with a bow.

Both dipped curtseys and expressed their gratitude before he moved on to watch the dancing.

It would not do to show too much interest in the Simon girl. Not until he had met all the young ladies on the list. It wouldn't be fair to get anyone's hopes up until he had come to a decision. Lady Cowper had been right though. She seemed like a very good prospect indeed. Reasonably good family. Reasonably good-looking. Reasonably well-mannered. Reasonable.

Unlike the lady in red.

'Would you like an introduction?' Julian asked, his grey eyes twinkling. Clearly teasing.

'Why not? Obviously, you are not going to be happy until I meet the wench.' His pulse picked up speed. Damn it. He wanted to meet her.

Julian's jaw dropped. 'I was jesting.'

'I called your bluff.'

'Er... I don't actually know her.'

Xavier gave him the look. The one designed to shrivel a lesser mortal to a shivering jelly.

Julian grinned. 'You win.'

Disappointed, Xavier turned away. Disappointed? How could that be? She was the last person in the room he wanted to meet.

He glanced around the room and found Lady Cowper standing with a group of older ladies near the orchestra. Neatly dressed in the latest fashion and her hair artfully arranged, as a Patroness, she was a model for what the young unmarried ladies in the room ought to aspire to become. He caught her eye. She had said she had one more prospect for him. He might as well meet them all and get it over with. Then he could leave.

She trotted to his side. 'What did you think of Miss Simon?'

'As you described.'

Perfectly adequate.

It didn't matter if she wasn't perfect as long she had

all most important attribute. A nice biddable nature. Why not give up the search and make do?

'Oh, I am so glad.' Lady Cowper fluttered her fan. 'I am so sorry. I thought there was one other young lady I would present to you this evening, but it turns out...' She coloured. 'She is not quite what I expected.'

His palms tingled. His heart picked up speed. He knew exactly what she was going to say next. It was like a sixth sense.

'You mean the Countess?'

Embarrassment shone in Lady Cowper's gaze, and she grimaced slightly. 'I had no idea. Lenore Lowell completely misled me about the girl. And to think she made me promise to introduce you. So awkward. Naturally, I shall not. I am sure there will be other, more suitable girls in the weeks to come. It is early in the Season.'

Briefly, he held up a hand. 'My dear Lady Cowper. Do not cause yourself anxiety. You have been more than helpful, and if it will ease your burden, I will meet the Countess.'

He could not believe he had said those words.

Lady Cowper's jaw dropped. She stared at him. 'Meet her? I mean, I should...' she spluttered into silence. Gathered herself. 'You are teasing me.'

Despite his inner turmoil he kept his smile calm. 'Not at all. I should be delighted to be of assistance, if it will save you embarrassment.' More than delighted. His blood was humming with anticipation.

Damn it all. What he needed to do was give this

woman, this countess, a set-down and send her back to whence she came.

'Very well,' Lady Cowper said with the air of one about to escort him to the gallows.

He tucked her hand beneath his arm. 'Take courage, my dear. I am certain she cannot be nearly so bad as she looks.'

Lady Cowper tittered. 'Do not be so sure.'

Aunt Lenore's eyes widened.

What now?

Barbara lifted her chin and turned her head slightly to see what could have made her aunt look so surprised.

Aunt Lenore twitched at Barbara's glove above her elbow. 'Don't look, but I think… Lady Cowper.'

One of the patronesses.

'Oh. Is she coming our way?'

Aunt Lenore had pointed her out as the only Lady Patroness present this evening. And when Barbara had suggested they go introduce themselves, her aunt had flatly refused. Far too dangerous given the red gown.

To risk a cut direct. Unthinkable.

'I doubt it. Pretend not to see her.'

Having caused her aunt enough grief for one evening, Barbara did as she was bid and smiled into her aunt's worried face. 'Do not fear. I shall deal with Papa. He had no business…'

'Miss Lowell.'

Aunt Lenore looked ready to faint. 'Lady Cowper.'

Astonished, Barbara turned to meet not the gaze of

Lady Cowper, but the arctic blue eyes of the tall disapproving gentleman.

Her heart missed a beat. Her stomach fluttered.

'And here is the niece you told me all about,' Lady Cowper was saying.

'Yes,' Aunt Lenore said breathlessly. 'Indeed. May I introduce the Countess of Lipsweiger and Upsal?'

'Dowager Countess,' Barbara said with a smile which she made sure encompassed the gentleman at Lady Cowper's side.

His expression did not so much as flicker.

'I am pleased to meet you, Lady Cowper,' Barbara continued. 'My aunt informs me you are one of the leaders of this venerated institution.'

'I am one of the patronesses, yes,' Lady Cowper said stiffly. 'Miss Lowell, Countess, it is my pleasure to introduce you to His Grace the Duke of Derbridge.' She didn't sound pleased in the slightest.

Aunt Lenore's fingers twitched.

Amazingly, she kept them where they were.

Barbara sank into a curtsey. Aunt Lenore followed suit.

'Your Grace,' they said in unison.

'Miss Lowell,' the Duke said. 'I believe we met last year at Lady Crome's picnic.'

'How good of you to remember, Duke.'

He turned his gaze on Barbara. 'You are new to town. How are you finding it so far?'

Barbara gave him a bright smile. 'A little chilly.'

Did he take her meaning? Or would he see it as a comment on the weather?

'Those unused to London's rarified climate can find it so.'

No dolt then. But arrogant.

'Yes, the climate on the Continent is far more welcoming.'

'My niece was recently in Paris,' Aunt Lenore said brightly. 'Her father, the Ambassador, is expected back in London any day now.'

'Ambassador March,' he said.

'Indeed,' Barbara answered.

'I do not know him personally, though I have heard of him of course. He was of great assistance to Castlereah in Venice, I am given to understand.'

Barbara was a little surprised. Most of her father's activities remained in the background. Much to his personal disappointment. 'Your Grace has a finger on the pulse of diplomacy, then?'

'I am interested in all matters affecting our country. Would you care to dance, Countess? I believe we are to be treated to a waltz. Isn't that right, Lady Cowper?'

Lady Cowper looked startled.

Aunt Lenore tugged an apparently wayward ringlet at her temple into place.

Barbara narrowed her gaze on the severe expression of the Duke. What was Derbridge playing at? Was this a good thing or a bad thing?

Bad. It had to be for Lady Cowper to look so frazzled. Excellent.

'L-let me check with the orchestra.' Lady Cowper bustled away.

The Duke stared at Barbara. The sort of critical inspection one might give a horse at a fair.

She lifted her chin. 'Well?'

He blinked. 'Well, what?'

'Do I pass muster?'

Aunt Lenore gasped.

The Duke looked bored. 'It depends on one's expectations.'

'Mr Elton believes geranium will become all the rage by next week,' Barbara said carelessly.

He glanced down at her gown. 'Then no doubt you will be certain to wear primrose, or gentian.'

This man was frighteningly perspicacious. 'Shall I take that as your advice?'

The band struck the opening chord of a waltz.

She gave him an arch smile. 'It seems you are also gifted with foresight.'

His lips twitched.

A smile? Surely not.

More likely irritation.

Or a figment of her imagination. Likely the latter the gentleman did not seem prone to showing any sort of emotion, except disapproval.

Such a lovely tall gentleman, too. A rare find.

She took his offered arm and they strolled towards the dance floor.

Barbara kept her face equally impassive.

Why on earth had he asked her to dance?

Why on earth was she pleased that he had asked her to dance?

It wasn't hard to imagine the glee with which Aunt Lenore would relay the information to her father.

It had all the makings of a potential disaster. Which she could use to her advantage if she was clever.

If it wasn't all too good to be true.

Nonsense.

It didn't matter why the Duke had asked her to dance. What mattered was what she did with the opportunity.

He twirled her under his arm and brought her around to face him.

The expression on his face remained cold.

Had he wanted to dance with her? Or was something else going on behind the mask?

Other people on the floor were looking at them askance. As were those looking on from the sidelines. Was this duke about to embarrass her in some way?

Whatever it was, she had the feeling it boded her no good.

Which might well serve her purpose.

He bowed. She curtsied. They moved into each other's arms. A sense of being enveloped within a fortress, protected from the outside world, almost shattered her composure.

She neither needed nor wanted anyone's protection. She had learned early to look after herself. Relying on anyone else for anything only led to heartache.

She was tired of heartache.

Within the circle of his arms, she drew closer than

she should. Glanced up and challenged him with a knowing smile. Dared him to accept.

Seeming not to notice, he somehow managed to keep her at an almost proper distance. Almost.

Not close enough to be scandalous. Not quite far enough apart to be completely proper.

Challenge accepted.

The large, gloved hand enclosing hers was satisfyingly warm. His height and breadth a definite advantage as they travelled around the floor, twirling and gliding in and around other couples as if they did not exist.

No one existed, beyond him and his powerful presence. And her.

The intensity was nigh overwhelming.

For such a big man, he moved with elegance and grace. She had noticed that before, hadn't she? He seemed to have no difficulty matching his steps to hers and yet he made it seem perfectly natural.

'What has brought you to London in such a chilly season?' he asked after a few moments.

'My father,' she said, hoping she sounded as nonchalant as he.

'And yet there is no sign of him in London.'

'As yet,' she agreed. 'But as Aunt Lenore said, he is expected any day now.'

'He was in Paris, I gather.'

Her heart stilled. Was? 'So far as I know he is still there.'

'No. He is in Lisbon.'

How would he know? And why?

'Oh, dearest Papa,' she said gaily, hiding the hurt that once more her papa had jaunted off without a word to her. 'Forever dashing off to some place or another on behalf of this country of ours. No doubt I shall hear from him that he has been commanded to meet some potentate or other at a moment's notice.'

Hearing anything from Father would be little short of a miracle. Unless there was some instruction or other he wanted to give her. His last round of instructions was clear and, as far as she knew, completely unchanged.

'Find a husband from among the British nobility.'

Pah!

The composure of the woman Xavier held in his arms was surprising and pleasant.

Most of the young ladies he had danced with this evening had been nervous, which meant they'd danced stiffly and giggled at everything he said.

Except Miss Simon, of course.

She had been shy, true, and somewhat stilted in response to his conversation, but had been generally agreeable, even if her nose was too large and her chin a little receding. She was clearly not the sort of girl to be going off on mad starts. A well-brought-up English young lady from a good family.

Ideal wife material.

And as boring as a pet fish. The thought came into his mind from nowhere.

Completely irrational.

Everything would be fine once they got to know each other better. With that in mind, he had asked her to drive out with him later in the week.

She'd been charmingly grateful.

This woman, this countess, was a horse of a different colour. A bold hussy. An exotic orchid, compared to a daisy. A short-lived comet, compared to a star's steady pinprick of light. A flash in the pan.

Possibly out to catch herself a duke.

Who would soon discover she should have stayed in Paris.

Passing beneath his arm and joining her hands with his in the promenade, she once more closed the distance between them, an inch closer than was acceptable, while catching his eye with a sly glance. Goading him?

His hip grazed hers. A sensual slide of gossamer fabric again the satin of his breeches. To say he felt her touch through his clothes would be ridiculous, but he did sense the whisper-soft brush, the slight drag of air and fabric.

As did she, from the gleam of mischief in her gaze.

Playing with fire.

Was she a tease who would recoil from the heat or was she really prepared to go up in flames?

Based on the way her gown barely clung to her full breasts, tormenting every man in the room with imminent disaster, he thought she would brave the inferno—if she thought it might get her what she wanted.

He had been the target of ambitious women for too many years to be taken in at this point in his life.

Rather than let her rule the roost, he made sure to maintain a proper distance, resisting any attempt she made to get closer. 'You normally travel with your father, the Ambassador, I understand?' he said to fill the weighty silence.

'It is kind of Your Grace to take such an interest in my habits, but you are right. I have visited most of the capitals of Europe with my father.'

Take an interest? Was that how she interpreted a casual enquiry? Or was she being sarcastic? He decided to ignore the comment.

'And with your late husbands, I assume?'

'My first husband never left his estate. His health kept him at home. My second was a soldier assigned to Metternich. We travelled a little but were mostly in Vienna.' A brilliant smile curved her lips and held him mesmerised for a second. 'While there, I believe I was of some assistance to the cause.'

So, she would take credit for saving Europe? Incorrigible.

'I am sorry for your untimely losses.'

'No need for sorrow, Your Grace. My first husband was at death's door when we wed. My second, no great loss. To me, at any rate.'

Startled by her flippancy, he gazed at her. 'I see.' He could not keep the stiffness from his voice or his disapproval.

She laughed. 'You are shocked. You should not be.

I believe in calling a spade a spade, don't you? And now I seek a third. Do you know any good prospects?'

She twirled away, and they were arms' lengths apart, making conversation impossible. When they came together again, he had recovered from his surprise.

'Your prospects are limited,' he said, intending to repress any sort of idea she might have in his regard.

She gave him an arch look. 'Indeed? I believe my dowry will pass muster.'

'Is that what you desire? A fortune hunter?'

'Desire?' Her voice caressed the word, gave it lascivious meaning.

His pulse tripped. This woman was dangerous indeed.

'Should desire enter into it?' she asked.

'One should have goals, certainly.'

'Are they the same? Desires and goals?'

Again, his gut tightened at the way she spoke of desire. Such boldness.

She was a widow, he reminded himself. Knowledgeable with regard to matters of the flesh. A widow twice over, in truth.

'Desires are ephemeral, changing with the wind, today you desire a hat, tomorrow a necklace. Goals, being more logical, and more important, ought to be achievable, measurable. So, no. Not the same.'

'To me, desires have a more physical connotation, somehow.'

He gritted his teeth at her obvious ploy to continue to shock him. 'It depends on the object of the desire.'

'Indeed.'

Her agreement gave him no pleasure, no sense of having won the argument, since it was more of a challenge than an acquiescence. She was sparring with him. Testing for weakness. She need not bother.

As they traversed the width of the dance floor, he noticed her aunt watching them with an anxious expression.

'Your aunt worries about you.'

'No. Aunt Lenore worries.'

'Isn't she concerned for your reputation? I understand you are the subject of speculation at White's.'

She laughed. A low, husky chuckle that sent a pleasurable shiver down his spine. Quite deliberate, of course.

'London must be terribly boring if people have nothing better to do than speculate about me.'

'Speculation is a pastime here. Apparently, they are betting how long number three will last beyond the wedding.'

She rolled her eyes. 'I heard they call me the black widow—after a rather unpleasant spider. Apparently, after mating, the female kills the male. To me, it sounds like an excellent arrangement.' She seemed quite pleased with the idea.

Shocked, his jaw dropped. 'Is that a warning?'

A sly little smile touched her lips. 'That would be telling.'

The woman was reckless in the extreme. To admit to liking the idea of doing away with a husband, having already… Well, not done away with them. He was certain there would be a perfectly reasonable explanation for their deaths or she would have been arrested. But to be pleased that they were dead, and admit to it, was rash in the extreme.

As the dance drew to a close, he wasn't sure if he should be pleased or sorry.

He was definitely intrigued.

Clearly, this widowed countess was to be avoided in future.

Chapter Three

The morning after their visit to Almack's, Barbara popped her head into her aunt's chamber. Originally, the room had been Barbara's, but Aunt Lenore had discovered the noise from the street at the front of the house had disturbed her sleep, so Barbara had been agreeable to exchange it for her quieter room at the back of the house.

Good morning, Aunt Lenore,' she said cheerily. 'I shall return in about two hours.'

Aunt Lenore peered at her from amid her pile of pillows, her cap slightly askew and a cup of chocolate steaming on the night table beside her bed. 'Where on earth are you going at this ungodly hour?'

'It is nine in the morning,' Barbara said. 'Hardly ungodly. I am going riding. I understand that if one wants a good gallop it is the only time of day when it is possible.'

'Ladies don't gallop in Hyde Park,' Lenore said.

Barbara raised an eyebrow. 'This one does.' Or perhaps since she had no wish to be thought of as a lady, she should have given a different reply. Still, she didn't want to completely ruin Aunt Lenore's morning.

'What do you think of my riding dress?' She'd had it made in Paris.

Aunt Lenore gazed at the fitted riding dress that had been tailored like a man's but fit Barbara's shape to perfection. 'It's…unusual. A little severe, perhaps. But unlike the gown you wore last night, at least it is perfectly respectable, I suppose.'

Barbara slapped her top hat against her hip, causing it to open up, and popped it on her head. 'I will see you later.'

'Barbara!' She could hear her aunt's voice as she continued on her way downstairs. 'That hat…'

Yes. It was a man's top hat. And one of the tallest to be had. The milliner had added a bit of netting to it as a nod to a veil. Not at all the sort of thing a fashionable young lady would wear to go riding in London. She had worn it in Paris to great acclaim.

'Good morning, Countess.' Outside the front door, the stable master held a gelding ready at the mounting block.

'Good morning, Soames. How are you this morning?'

'Well, my lady. Thank you. Unfortunately, I cannot say the same for this hack.' He shook his head.

She looked the horse over. A rather rangy, big-boned animal. 'It was the best to be had?'

'Yes, Countess. Might I recommend postponing your

ride until I can find something more suitable for a lady? It's as bad-tempered a horse as I have ever come across.'

It certainly wasn't anything like the dainty little mare she had borrowed in Paris. And in that regard the horse was just right for her purposes. 'Nonsense, Soames. He looks fine.'

'Very well, Countess,' Soames said, looking resigned. 'But if you'll take my advice, you'll steer clear of his hind quarters. He bit Jack when he got too close this morning.'

Jack, the groom who would accompany her this morning, was already mounted and waiting on the only the only riding horse in her aunt's stables. A rather elderly mare who looked as if she should have been put out to grass some time ago. Fortunately, it wasn't used to carrying a ladies' saddle. A lucky escape for Barbara.

She had thought to dispense with a groom's services, but had changed her mind when the stable master had talked of riff raff and criminals and streets she should definitely avoid. It would be better to get to know London before she started riding out on her own. She might be contemptuous of Society's rules, but she wasn't stupid.

'I will remember your advice.' She walked around the front of the horse to the mounting block and Soames helped her up. The horse remained still. 'He seems calm enough.'

She moved off at a walk, and the horse responded as he should. Perhaps he wasn't quite as perfect as she had thought. Oh, well. She would make the best of what she had. As usual.

Hyde Park was only a mile from her residence, and the streets were busy with tradespeople going about their business. Not unlike Paris. Or any of the great cities she had visited since she was fifteen. Traipsing along behind Father had been an education. She was a woman who had seen a great deal of Europe.

But oddly, this was her first visit to London.

And now she was apparently supposed to snare some unsuspecting Englishman.

Not if she had anything to do with it. Two marriages were enough for anyone. Her first had been a marriage of convenience. To help her father with his debts. Mr Twickenham had been rich and a confirmed bachelor, until he realised he needed a nurse in his old age. When she had discovered the financial arrangements her father had made with the autocratic old gentleman, she had been furious. She was unable to touch a penny of the money from her first husband until she was twenty-five. Still a year hence.

Then, she had let her heart rule her head, and married Helmut, Count of Lipsweiger and Upsal. He'd broken her heart with his philandering ways. But at least she'd been left with a fortune in jewels for her pains.

The jewellery from Helmut was going to be her salvation. She hoped. From what she had gathered, Father intended to use it as the dowry for her next marriage. She had other plans. But to sell it too soon would give her away.

And she needed to find the right buyer.

Which was why she had worn part of the set to Almack's. To generate interest. Helmut. So handsome, debonair and charming, he had swept her off her feet and into marriage. Only after they'd wed had she discovered he'd had a string of mistresses.

Everyone else had known. Including Father. But as usual he had seen Helmut as a valuable conduit to his ambition to become Ambassador and hadn't said a word.

How they must all have been laughing behind her back.

Men. It was all about what *they* wanted.

From now on she would please herself and Society could go hang.

Which meant she really had to put herself beyond the pale as quickly as possible. Hopefully before Father turned up.

As she passed through Hyde Park's gate, she took a deep breath of sooty air and glanced around.

As she had been informed, the park at this time of day was quiet, with only a few gentlemen out for their morning exercise. She glanced at Jack. 'Let us put him through his paces, shall we?'

Jack looked about to argue, but she urged the animal into a canter and then a full-fledged gallop.

Oh, my lord. The horse had seemed placid enough up to now. But given its head, it took off like a racehorse. Never in her life had she ridden a horse with such an awkward gait. It bounced her all over the place and she was hard put to keep her seat.

From out of nowhere, another rider appeared at her side and grabbed the reins, as well as put an arm around her waist to steady her.

Immediately she knew exactly who had his hands on her from the way her body tightened.

'Your Grace,' she said. She thought she spoke, but the feel of that iron hard arm around her waist made her feel weak. Hot.

He brought both of their horses to a standstill.

Breathless and flustered, because of her struggle with the horse, she told herself, she glared at him. 'What the devil do you think you are doing?'

Derbridge gave her a considering look. 'Stopping you from making a complete cake of yourself.'

'I had no need of your assistance.'

At that moment Jack arrived looking hot and anxious. Realising the situation was under control, he drew back to a respectful distance.

'Your groom didn't seem to think so,' the Duke said mildly. His gaze narrowed. 'Whatever possessed you to ride such an abomination?'

Barbara glanced around. Several gentlemen were watching them with interest. They were making a scene. Not quite the one she had planned for, but equally as good. And he still had his hands on her reins.

'Remove your hand.'

He drew back as if stung. Then something changed

in his expression. He looked…annoyed. 'You did that on purpose.'

She tried to look affronted. 'What are you talking about?'

His gaze narrowed. 'You set that horse galloping on purpose. Once more you would be the talk of the town.'

She lifted her chin. Oh, dear. Could it possibly be that the Duke saw too much? Surely not. 'I have no idea what you are talking about.'

'Do you not?' His face was grim.

'Certainly not. I merely came to Hyde Park to get some exercise, which I am informed is the only place one may find to ride out in London.'

'It is not the only place. Allow me to escort you home.'

'My groom will—'

'Your groom is useless. Or rather, his horse is useless. Come along.'

As he moved off, to her surprise, her horse followed.

And since there was no more to be gained from arguing, she allowed it. After all, she had, as he had pointed out, successfully made a cake of herself.

There were more carriages on the road now and progress was slow.

'What did you mean when you said there are other places to exercise a horse?' she asked. 'And if there are, why do you not avail yourself?'

'It is a matter of available time. I have to be in the House today.'

For a moment she was not sure what he meant. 'Parliament?'

'Of course.'

Did he have to sound so supercilious? 'What is so important that it needs your presence?'

He raised an eyebrow. 'As to that, I will have to check with my secretary.'

'Your secretary? Don't you know for yourself?'

'There are a great many demands on my time. I rely on him to keep my schedule.'

Odious beast.

'I beg your pardon?'

Oh. Had she said that aloud?

She must have.

His frown deepened.

And they had arrived at her aunt's house, there was little more to be said. 'Thank you for your escort.'

'Come riding with me later in the week,' he said, in a manner that was more a command than request.

She stared at him in astonishment.

'I will provide the horse.'

'Oh, but—'

'I will send round an invitation to you and your aunt shortly.'

'You will?' she snapped. 'Or your secretary will? Assuming you don't have some other pressing engagement you have forgotten?'

'My engagements can always be rearranged.'

He spoke with such assuredness she immediately

imagined the docket for Parliament being altered at his whim.

'I believe I am otherwise engaged,' she said. Dash it, she sounded missish, instead of chilly as she had intended.

He raised a brow. 'You haven't received the invitation yet, so how can you know?' He bowed and, having handed her horse's reins to Jack, rode off, no doubt with every expectation she would accept his invitation when it arrived.

Damn his arrogance.

She stopped on the doorstep staring at the footman who had opened the door. What a strange turn of events. What on earth was this duke about?

'Milady?' the footman said.

'What? Oh, yes. I beg your pardon.'

She stepped inside.

Perhaps she would accept the invitation after all.

Was he mad? Assailed with the sort of doubt he hadn't experienced since he was at school, Xavier stood in the foyer of the small manor house he owned halfway between Mayfair and Hampton Court. A strategically placed home by way of one of his ancestors to be at the ready for any royal command. It was one of many estates owned by the duchy, and it was here he trained his racehorses because of its closeness to Ascot.

What the devil was he doing? Here he was, supposedly pursuing this Season's crop of eligible debutantes, girls who would accept a proposal in a heartbeat, and now for some reason inviting a most unsuitable woman to ride out at one of his estates.

Be honest.

He had always been honest with himself—why change now? Very well. He would admit that the widow fascinated him far more than the debutantes. At least so far. Fascinated, but not in a good way. She caused him to want to do things that under normal circumstances he would reject without a moment's thought as being ridiculous. Foolish. Even reckless.

He was never reckless.

Watching her wild gallop along Rotten Row the other day had made him want to gallop alongside her, to feel the wind in his face, to feel—free. She looked like she was enjoying herself, despite her obvious difficulty controlling her ungainly animal.

He tried to recall the last time he had enjoyed a good gallop for the pure joy of it. One exercised one's horse and one's self when in town. It was a duty, not a pleasure. It was done with the intention of meeting likeminded men and, more often than not, he had used much of the time discussing parliamentary business, not riding.

There was nothing enjoyable about it.

He preferred another form of exercise to keep his body fit. And not only that, sparring at the gymnasium allowed him to let off steam. Something a man with his responsibilities needed from time to time. And it was better than letting his temper get the better of him and engaging in fisticuffs with his peers when they angered him.

He'd discovered that at school when he'd been about fifteen. He'd fought a couple of boys who had been bullying a weaker lad. He'd stepped in and fought them. And been beaten badly. But in the aftermath, some of the anger and confusion he'd been feeling about his father's death had faded beneath the pain of his bruises.

It had been a welcome relief.

The master who had separated them had suggested that if Xavier wanted to fight, he should take up boxing. And so he had.

Perhaps the Countess had been similarly afflicted, that day in Hyde Park. Maybe she too needed a release for anger or frustration. Nevertheless, it had been his duty to put a stop to the Countess's hoydenish behaviour before she ruined her reputation or suffered a terrible accident. Hadn't it?

Of course it had. It was the duty of any gentleman to protect the life and reputation of any lady. Even if *she* did not seem to give it a second's thought.

That was the reason he had invited her here today, was it not? To allow her to enjoy a day of riding, without fear of censure.

Which she seemed to invite wherever she went.

Lady Cowper had whispered just before she introduced him to the Countess, that she had been seen shopping in Bond Street after midday with only a maid to carry her parcels.

Shocking! It was time someone took the lady in hand or she would be utterly ruined in the eyes of Society.

Her aunt should know better, Lady Cowper had said.

Xavier had the feeling that the aunt had little influence over the headstrong young woman.

Someone needed to explain the rules to her. In an avuncular manner, of course. Kindly but firmly, the way his Uncle Tom had explained everything to him.

This was why he had decided that an invitation to Woodburn House would be the perfect opportunity to speak privately, with only her and her aunt present.

Though why he had decided he should be the one to impart the rules, he wasn't quite certain, even if it had seemed to be a good idea at the time.

Fortunately, the day he had chosen had turned out to be a bright spring day, perfect for what he had planned.

He loved this house. He rarely shared it with anyone. It was one of the few places he really felt comfortable. Perhaps because it was one of the last places he recalled his real mother and father spending time together, and the memory was a happy one.

For some odd reason, he wanted the Countess to like it.

His stable master had arranged for two ladies' mounts to be ready at the appointed time, and his housekeeper would provide a collation fit for a queen after their expedition.

The sound of wheels on the gravel drive at the exact moment his guests were expected to arrive, brought a smile to his lips. His coachman was nothing if he was not punctual.

He nodded to the footman who opened the front door and went outside to greet his guests.

Like a well-oiled machine, his household slipped into motion—a groom ran out to take the horses' heads and another to let down the carriage steps.

As orderly as clockwork.

Exactly the way he liked it.

To his surprise, the younger woman, the Countess, alighted first. She looked magnificent in her riding dress. The same one he had admired in Hyde Park. It was elegant and, though bright, the colour suited her to perfection.

He stepped forward to greet her, glancing into the carriage, expecting the other lady to emerge—

What the devil! 'Where is your aunt?'

The Countess gave him a mischievous smile. 'My aunt is indisposed.'

Taken aback, for a moment he could only stare at her. 'Then you should have sent a message to postpone the engagement.'

She glanced around at the house, at him, at the sky. Finally back to him. 'And waste such a beautiful day, when it has rained for weeks, and after all the trouble you have gone to? Certainly not.'

Damn him for an idiot. Because he wasn't exactly unhappy at the absence of the woman's aunt.

He should put her back in his carriage and send her on her way.

And yet...

Perhaps this would be a perfect opportunity to school her in the way of the *ton*. Perhaps she would listen to him, if she would not listen to her aunt regarding the niceties of London Society. No doubt she had been misled into thinking that widows were not bound by the same strictures that applied to unmarried women and wives.

Perhaps she did not realise that behaviours such as hers would eventually lead to her being thought most dreadfully fast.

Beyond redemption.

But the laughter in her eyes—those lively dark brown eyes with a golden sunburst at the centre that you only saw close up—was a worry.

Because that twinkle gave him the feeling that she knew exactly what she was about.

'So—do we ride out? Or not?' she asked.

There was an element of dare in her voice.

A challenge.

'We ride out,' he said grimly.

She laughed. That same chuckle he'd heard on the night that they'd met, a light amused sound emanating from the back of her throat.

He wanted to smile back but he frowned instead. No point in encouraging the reckless female. 'Something amuses you?'

'You look as if you are headed for the gallows.'

Did he indeed.

'You should not have come without a companion,' he said repressively.

'Why? Are you unable to keep the line?'

The question took him aback. 'I am a gentleman, madam.'

'Then there is nothing to worry about. No one would assume such a strait-laced gentleman as yourself would get up to mischief. Therefore I see no reason to concern myself with such nonsense.'

Her words irritated him for some reason. He was perfectly capable of 'getting up to mischief.' He simply did not choose to do so. His position made it beneath him.

And nor was he a Johnny Raw. He knew better than to spend the day alone with an unmarried lady. That problem he could easily solve.

'The stables are this way. Unless you need to freshen up after your journey.'

'Three miles is hardly a journey,' she said, smiling. 'Let us be off. I haven't ridden out in the country for weeks and weeks. I cannot wait. I hope you have a decent mount for me and not some sluggard that likes to dawdle.'

He gritted his teeth. He was known for the quality of his horseflesh.

'I do not think you will be disappointed.' He took her arm and escorted her around to the stables.

As they entered the courtyard in front of the stable block a few yards from the main house, two grooms emerged from the barn with three of the most beautiful animals Barbara had ever seen.

Two with ladies' saddles and one for riding astride.

'We will not require Galahad, Paul,' the Duke said. 'One of our guests has not arrived.'

The groom called to a lad who took the smallest of the three horses back inside.

Another man took the other with a side-saddle to a mounting block.

'This is Kemp, my stable master and Lucky Lady.'

'Mr Kemp,' Barbara said, and greeted her horse with a stroke of her nose. 'She is lovely.'

'I am glad you think so,' the Duke said in his usual grim tones. 'Allow me to assist you.'

She stepped up, and he easily boosted her into the saddle. Unlike most men, he did not struggle to lift her somewhat large frame—and his fingers did not dig into the flesh of her waist. Indeed, he hoisted her up without effort.

His firm strength made her feel as light as a feather. A unique and rather breathtaking sensation.

Lovely, in fact. An odd sort of weak feeling took her by surprise. And right at that moment, despite some earlier reservations before she left home, she knew she would enjoy the day.

As she settled into the saddle, he guided her foot into the stirrup and glanced up. 'How is that?'

'Perfect.' And it was. The saddle needed not the slightest adjustment, which was unusual as most times there was a lot of fiddling about to lengthen the stirrup.

Once they had even had to change the saddle because she was too tall. Talk about embarrassing.

Today, it was if he had somehow taken her measure and judged her needs and passed them along to his staff. Did that make him too fussy or just caring?

Maybe the former. What need had he to care?

He made a slight adjustment to the girth.

She forced herself not to be taken in by his solicitude. 'I assume you have some grass over which we can gallop and streams we can jump, to make my journey worthwhile.'

A look of satisfaction crossed his face. 'I will do better.'

Such arrogance. But before she could ask what he meant, he left her side and went to speak to Kemp, who had joined the groom holding the Duke's horse. There was some muttered conversation between the two men.

The stable master glanced her way with raised eyebrows then bustled off on some errand.

What was that all about?

The Duke mounted up.

Barbara could not help but admire his athleticism as he swung up on to the large gelding, seemingly without effort. Or how manly he looked on horseback. As if he and the horse were one.

The horse sidled a bit, showing the whites of its eyes, but the Duke soon brought it under control, firmly but gently. No jabbing at the bit or sawing at the reins.

All in all, an impressive sight.

Yes, the Duke would be a challenge. But an enjoyable one.

'Before we give the horses their heads,' he said, riding close, 'let me show you a little bit of the estate. It has been in my family for many centuries.'

To her surprise, as they left the stable, a mounted groom emerged from the stables and followed them.

'Observing all the proprieties, are we?' she asked. The gossips were right, this duke truly was a stuffed shirt. Dour-bridge. An apt nickname.

According to another, he was as toplofty as the King himself. He certainly seemed that way.

He needed taking down a peg or two.

Perhaps Barbara was the one to help in that quarter.

The Duke gave her a dark look in answer to her question. Oh, yes, as arrogant as they came. Well, she had suffered under arrogant men in the past, but not this one.

Her horse seemed eager to be off at a gallop, but Barbara held her in check. She did not know the lie of the land hereabouts and would not put the horse in danger.

They rode around to the front of the house. It was a small manor house in a rather plain style, little more than a farmhouse really.

'This house has been in my family for seven hundred years,' the Duke said.

She forced herself not to roll her eyes. 'How interesting. It doesn't seem grand enough for a ducal seat.'

'No, it is not the Derbridge seat. It is only one of many properties.'

Barbara's father didn't even own a property. As the younger son of a younger son, he had spent all his life climbing the ladder of the diplomatic corps. Always seeking a title, even if it meant climbing over the corpses of his rivals.

'I suppose its closeness to Parliament is the source of its attraction.' She could not imagine why else the Duke would keep it for his own rather than rent it out.

'Partly.'

Having a conversation with this duke was little better than talking to a rock.

She glanced over at him, to discover he was watching her intently. As if seeking her reaction to…something.

She stared back. Waiting for him to say more.

He turned away with a wave of his arm. 'The estate is bounded by Hampton Court lands on that side.'

'How nice. Are we hacking out or did you bring me all the way here for a geography lesson?'

If possible, his expression seemed grimmer than ever. 'This way.'

To her disappointment, they turned not in the direction of open country where they could likely find open fields, but towards a small copse down the hill from the house. It seems they were going to take their horses for a walk after all.

The Duke led her down a narrow, rutted path and the groom followed behind. It was so dull.

Dull as ditch water.

Dull as—

'Oh, my,' she gasped as they emerged from the trees.

She came up alongside the Duke and gazed at the sight of a race track. The mare she was riding pricked its ears forward and back and skittered around. Barbara brought it under control.

The stable master she had met earlier was waiting at the rail with an older, grey-haired woman in the severe attire of a servant.

'You own a racecourse?' she asked.

The Duke looked down his nose. 'Certainly not. I own racehorses. This is where they train.' An expression of satisfaction crossed his face. 'Nothing like a track for providing a safe good gallop. That is what you wanted, is it not?'

A small smile curved his lips.

It was the first time she had seen even the hint of a smile, and the effect was devastating. It brought warmth to those icy blue eyes and a sparkle that made them dance like sunlight across water.

Her heart skipped a beat.

What could she say? 'It is of all things, the most marvellous.'

Chapter Four

More pleased that he should have been with her delighted response, Xavier turned to the groom and dismissed him. He'd brought him along in case she preferred not to use the track and wanted to ride across country instead.

They joined the group at the rail. 'Allow me to introduce Mrs Barker. My housekeeper.'

The woman dipped a curtsey. 'My lady.'

He nodded at Kemp to show his approval. Mrs Barker was the best person he could have asked to serve in place of a chaperone.

'Do you ride in races?' the Countess asked as they made their way through the gate his stable master was holding open.

'No.' It was too dangerous. He was the last of his line. Should an accident happen to him, the title would go into abeyance.

She nodded in a way that said she wasn't surprised, and it annoyed him.

'I rode them when I was younger but now I am too

heavy.' Damn it. Why did he feel the need to explain? Should he also tell her, like some schoolboy eager to please, that she was the only woman he had ever invited to ride on the track? Not likely.

'Oh, indeed. I see what you mean,' she said with a hint of laughter in her voice. 'I have heard other ladies refer to you as enormous.'

The comment, said with such sly innuendo, caused his body to tighten, and it was only with effort he forced it back under control. He could not recall when a few well-chosen words by a woman had had such an effect on him. And he could not help but wonder at her purpose.

Well, if she thought to catch herself a duke, she was out of luck.

They entered the track. 'The ground is soft because of the rain. It will be slow going,' he said. 'We will start at a trot, move to a canter, then gallop the last furlong. You will see the marker.'

She moved easily into the trot, and he was pleased to see that the mare she rode was responding beautifully and moved into a nice easy canter when asked. His own horse followed suit.

They rode side by side, and when she glanced over at him, her eyes were alight with pleasure and her cheeks reddened by the wind. Small wayward curls escaped from beneath her hat.

His heart picked up speed at the sight of such beauty.

Nonsense. She was not at all the type of woman he

preferred. He liked small blonde females with perfect manners, the sort who would never be caught dead hurtling around a race track.

At the last marker, she urged the mare into a gallop. His larger gelding kept up easily, but he remained a fraction behind. He did not want her to think he was trying to beat her to the finish line. Therein lay the path to accidents.

At the finish line they slowed and walked the horses a few yards down the track.

She half turned in her saddle to look back at him. 'That was splendid. I think I should like to be a jockey.'

His jaw dropped. 'A jockey?' He came alongside her. 'Ladies do not become jockeys.'

She laughed. 'In whose opinion?'

About to say *Everyone's*, he bit his tongue. She was goading him.

'I doubt you would find an owner willing to hire a woman.'

She made a face that showed what she thought of such owners.

He wanted to laugh. The urge shocked him more than her idea of becoming a jockey. He quelled his amusement. 'We weren't racing, you know.'

'I know,' she said airily. 'You would have beaten me easily, but this little lady was champing at the bit to go faster. Do you race her?'

'Not any more. She earned her retirement at Newmarket a few years ago and has had three really nice foals since then, of whom I expect great things. The latest is a yearling. If you want to see him.'

'Oh, I would love to.'

Her interest in what was not just a hobby for him, but a life's work in the making, pleased him. Of course, it was likely all a sham. Lots of people feigned interest in him to curry favour because he was a duke.

And if he thought she wasn't one of those, he was likely acting like an idiot.

'Then we shall.'

They rode back to those waiting by the gate. The Countess, once dismounted, took a few minutes to see that her horse was comfortable and to pet it before the grooms took both mounts in charge and led them back to the stables for a good rub down.

'The colts and fillies are in the lower meadow this week. I hope you don't mind a bit of a walk.' He guided the Countess in the opposite direction to the house. He hadn't planned for this, but he was pleased to see that the housekeeper fell in behind them. While it wasn't an ideal arrangement—her aunt would have been the more appropriate chaperone—it did protect him from being accused of anything untoward.

'Not at all. Having been cooped up in London these past few weeks, I am delighted to get some exercise.' She glanced over her shoulder. 'I am not sure I can say the same about your housekeeper.'

Mrs Barker was indeed trudging along behind them with an expression of misery.

'Unfortunately, she is the only woman in my household available to serve as a chaperone, in the absence of your aunt. I am sure she would much rather be preparing for our luncheon than traipsing out to the fields.'

'Oh,' she said. 'I did not…'

'You did not what? Did not think I would need to provide an alternate? Or you did not think I would care to protect your reputation?'

Her already pink cheeks darkened to rose. 'I did not think you would be so unkind as to ask such an elderly woman to accompany us. A groom would do just as well.'

'You must think me a Johnny Raw, madam, if you think I would for one moment assume a groom would do.'

She shot him an angry look. 'I find I do not care to see your yearlings. Let us return to the house.'

'As you wish.'

They turned about and walked back the way they had come. He could not help but notice the relief on Mrs Barker's face as they informed her of their intentions.

To say he was surprised that the Countess would have asked him to turn back would have been an understatement. He had not expected her to give a damn about the servant.

But by doing so, she had managed to put him in the wrong, which had likely been her intention.

Blast the woman.

And he was disappointed also, he realised.

He had wanted to show off his horses.

* * *

An exceedingly youthful maid was waiting to assist Barbara in the room the housekeeper had prepared for her and her aunt during their visit.

But apart from removing her hat and making use of the necessary, Barbara was in little need of assistance. She did pin up the tendrils of hair that had escaped during her ride before heading downstairs to the breakfast room for luncheon.

The house, which had looked rather modest from the outside, was sumptuously decorated and carpeted both in the halls and the breakfast room. It had bright chintz wallpaper and large windows overlooking an expanse of lawn. The table was set for two, seated so they could each look out on the vista beyond a set of double French doors.

Standing by the window looking out, Derbridge, with his prominent nose and high forehead, looked every inch the Duke and not one to be trifled with. He was—exceedingly handsome in a stern kind of way.

He was also exceedingly arrogant, she forced herself to remember.

'What a delightful prospect to be sure,' she said.

He swung around with a quizzical expression as if he sensed her underlying meaning. He was no fool, this duke, and she would be wise to remember it.

'Countess,' he said and bowed. 'I have to admit a fondness for this property and the countryside hereabouts.'

'The view is lovely. I had forgotten how beautiful the English countryside can be—when it is not raining.'

'You have been away a long time?' he asked, coming to take her arm and escort her to the table. A footman she had not noticed stepped from the corner to pull out her seat. It seems even in this small house the Duke needed to stand on ceremony. A way of reminding everyone of his importance, she supposed.

Helmut, her second husband, had been the same, snapping his fingers at servants if they were too slow, demanding instant attention no matter the hour.

She smiled her thanks at the footman and sat down.

'I haven't been in England since I left school.' She'd been almost sixteen and had been thrilled that Papa had finally called for her presence.

Oh, he always promised to send for her to visit him, wherever he was, in the summer holidays, but something more important always came up.

Some years, she had visited a school friend if there was time to make arrangements, or was hustled off to Aunt Lenore if there wasn't.

One year, she had spent the whole of the summer vacation at school by herself, waiting for him to send his carriage for her, with only the cook and the gardener for company. The realisation that he had forgotten her had been devastating. It was then that she had lost all faith in him and his promises.

A tap at the door heralded two more servants, one with a tureen of soup, the other with a tray of cold meats, cheese and bread.

'I hope you do not mind,' the Duke said, 'but I do not keep a chef, as I entertain here very little and luncheon tends to be a rather informal affair.'

'Three footmen serving two bowls of soup and a few sandwiches hardly seems informal.'

He frowned and she awaited some sort of male indignation at her temerity.

'No,' he said. 'It doesn't.' He turned to the young man who had helped her to sit. 'I think the Countess and I can manage from here, Green. If you can remain within call, the other fellows can return to the stables unless Cook has need of them.'

Green bowed. 'Yes, Your Grace.' He ushered the others out of the room.

'You asked your grooms to serve as footmen?' she asked.

'It was either that or ask my butler and footman to travel down from London. The fellows here don't mind it. It makes a change.'

'You asked them?'

'Naturally.'

But could they actually say no?

'They have done it before,' he added. 'When I have a buyer interested in looking at a horse, I feed them. It is a matter of good business. Kemp says the grooms used to draw straws for the privilege of serving the luncheon, but because some are luckier than others, it was causing friction, so he has set up a rota and they take it in turns.'

She frowned. 'Why would they be so keen?'

He raised a brow. 'Footman get paid more than grooms.'

She should have known that. Why did she not know it? It seemed her education was sadly lacking in some departments. But then she had never really had a home of her own to run. She had always lived at school, or with her father and his extant mistress, of which there had been many, except for a very short time, when she married her first husband. And even then, there had been barely time for the ink to dry on the marriage lines before he cocked up his toes.

She had never been more relieved in her life to return to live beneath her father's roof. But then she had been shockingly young. Little more than seventeen and a widow. And then it was off to take shelter with Helmut. Another arrogant man.

'May I help you to some soup?' the Duke asked.

'Yes, please.'

The soup, cream of asparagus, tasted delicious. 'My compliments to your cook,' she said.

'She will be delighted that you are pleased, Countess. I shall be sure to let her know.'

'Thank you for this morning,' Barbara said.

'I am glad you enjoyed it. It is...' He hesitated. 'It was my pleasure.'

That was not what he was going to say.

'To be honest,' she said. 'I wasn't sure if you would make me turn back to London when you saw I was alone. The reason I did not bring my maid is because she reports everything back to my great-aunt, who I am terribly fond of but whose chaperonage I find quite stifling.'

'You should not chafe at your aunt's trying to protect your reputation,' the Duke said stiffly.

Such a stuffed shirt, this man. And so much fun to tease.

'Nonsense. I have no need for a chaperone. I have been married twice, Your Grace. I am not some schoolroom miss without a shred of knowledge of the world. I do as I wish.'

'I see that.'

'With whom I wish.'

'I would advise caution.'

'Caution.' She laughed. 'Why would anyone embrace caution? How dull. And to what end?'

'I think you will discover English Society is a little different from that on the Continent. If you should wish to marry again—'

Oh, yes. She had teased him about seeking a third husband. 'I am beginning to wonder if I would derive more enjoyment remaining as a widow.'

He looked startled. 'I understood from your aunt that you hoped—'

'My aunt does not speak for me, Your Grace.'

She finished her soup and put down her spoon with a gesture of finality. 'In the meantime, I have every intention of enjoying my visit to London.'

'Your visit? Do you not plan to stay?'

'If London is as dull as I have observed so far, I think I would far rather live in Paris.'

'I see.'

'Unless you have some notion of how London might be made more interesting?'

His eyes as he gazed at her sparkled for a brief moment. 'Is that a challenge, Countess?'

'Take it however you will,' she said, lifting her chin.

He rang the bell. Green entered and collected their soup bowls.

His Grace began slicing the bread. 'I shall have to see what I can do.'

Heavens! Did that mean he was accepting her *challenge*?

Given his very strict sort of notions about Society, she hadn't expected him to give in so easily.

But perhaps he assumed she was incorrigible, therefore not worthy of saving from her folly.

Whereas she ought to be delighted, she felt just a little let down. Which was nonsense when it looked as if things were going exactly the way she wanted.

'Help yourself to meats and cheeses, Countess. And here is bread, or there are rolls if you prefer.'

With a feeling of pleasant surprise, Xavier watched the Countess eat the simple luncheon fare with a gusto, unlike most women of his acquaintance.

Mostly they picked at the food put in front of them.

He suspected that some of them ate before attending an event so they did not appear to have any sort of appetite.

He buttered his bread, then enjoyed the sweetness

of the butter in contrast to the sharpness of the cheese. The Burgundy wine he had ordered to be served with the meal complemented the flavours.

The Countess sipped appreciatively from her glass. 'Very nice,' she said.

'I am glad you approve.'

'Are you?'

Again that provocative glance. Always testing and teasing.

'I do not say things I do not mean, Countess.'

She raised a brow in what could only be described as an expression of incredulity.

'You doubt me?' he asked.

'Everyone says things they do not mean, if only to be polite. Particularly men, in my experience.'

Did he? Of course he did. 'I see no reason in being rude for the sake of it. However, when one's guest offers to complement an item that was carefully chosen for their enjoyment, why would there be any need to prevaricate?'

'Then why be glad, when you knew that the wine was perfect? You did not need my approval.'

He was exasperated and…well yes, somewhat entertained…perhaps even amused… 'My gladness stems from the surprising pleasure of having lunch with a woman who has the sense to recognise a good thing when she tries it.'

She gasped. And then laughed. A wholly pleasing sound to his ear. *'Touché.'* She lifted her glass in toast and her elegant throat moved as she swallowed a mouthful of wine.

He had the urge to place his lips against the tender white skin and discover if it tasted as delicious as it looked. He picked up his own glass. 'Your health, Countess.'

She proceeded to demolish another slice of bread and some more of the cheese.

'The cheese is a local variety, renowned for its sharpness,' he said.

'Do you make it here?'

'No. We do not keep cows. Only horses. Cook knows all the local farmers hereabouts.'

'I am sure they are delighted to obtain your custom.'

'I doubt if I am here often enough to make much of a difference.'

'Your staff is, though.'

'Indeed.'

She put down her glass and finished the last of the bread and cheese on her plate.

'More?' he said, offering her the plate of cheese.

She shook her head. 'Not another bite. I ate more than I should. It truly was delicious. Thank you.'

The genuine smile warmed him far more than he could have expected.

'Would you care to see the gardens before you depart?' he asked. 'They were planted by my mother before I was born. She loved to garden and this was the only place she was permitted a free hand.'

'Permitted?'

Another challenge. It seemed every time he opened his mouth he put his foot in it, as far as she was concerned. Did she have to be so suspicious? Clearly, she was one of these new bluestocking types who questioned any man's opinion. He would do well to be shot of her.

'The gardener at our seat in Dorset was and is most particular about adhering to the original design. Apparently, my grandfather laid out a small fortune on it.'

'I see. Yes. I would love to visit the gardens. And then I really must go before my aunt starts to worry.'

He hadn't thought she cared a fig about what her aunt thought. He decided not to pull her up short, even though it was obviously just the sort of polite excuse she had decried only moments ago.

'Then if you are ready?' He assisted her with her chair and they stepped through the French doors onto the balcony whose steps led out into the garden.

In front of them there spread a large square of lawn, but around the corner was his mother's favourite place to while away some time on a fine day. The few memories he had were of her sitting here reading to him sometimes, or to herself while he played with a ball.

He led the Countess down the steps and through the arch into an area bounded by hedges on all sides.

'Oh, how pretty,' she said. 'Primroses. What a surprise.'

'If you look carefully, you will also find violets and campions. It is a garden of English wild flowers. There were daffodils earlier and snow drops and later there will be buttercups and marshmallow.'

'In other words, it is full of what most people would call weeds.'

If she hadn't been smiling with such delight, he might have taken her words as a criticism. That genuine smile of approval gave him a warm feeling in the region of his chest. 'I know. Grandmother called it Mother's folly, but I wouldn't let them change it.'

'I'm glad,' she said, looking up at him.

He gazed back into her velvety brown eyes and knew the words were not said for mere politeness. For a long moment they gazed at each other. His heart drummed in his ears.

Without thinking, he reached out to take her hand, and their fingers intertwined. Her lips parted and curved slightly, anticipating…

He leaned forward and brushed his lips against hers, tasting wine and inhaling a subtle, fresh and slightly floral scent that was all her own.

Without hesitation, she stepped closer, and he deepened the kiss, lost in a heady sensation of desire, lost in a sense of longing, as if lost in a mist.

Wholly unlike him.

Wholly wrong.

He stepped back. 'I—'

She smiled at him blithely. 'What a perfect end to a pleasant afternoon. Now I really must be on my way.'

She headed back towards the house and he followed her, feeling thoroughly off balance.

His mind was playing tricks on him. For her the kiss had been nothing more than a quick little peck, a sort of thank-you.

Hadn't it?

Chapter Five

Barbara awoke at some hour in the early morning to the sound of her aunt's cries of terror.

She leaped out of bed, grabbed her robe and dashed out into the hallway.

The corridor was full of servants peering in through her aunt's chamber door. Her aunt was still crying out in distress.

'What is going on?' Barbara demanded, pushing her way past the upstairs maid and a couple of footmen.

Her aunt was sitting up in bed, her cap askew and her hands over her face while she continued what Barbara could only describe as howling. Her maid stood next to her, wringing her hands and looking helpless.

Barbara went to the bed, put her arms around Aunt Lenore's shoulders and patted her back. 'Shh. It's all right. I am here now. Shh.'

It took a few minutes to get the poor dear calmed down enough to speak.

'There was a man.'

Barbara stared at her. 'A man?'

Her aunt pointed a trembling finger towards her chest of drawers, which Barbara realised were all open with items scattered all around.

And the bedroom window was wide open.

'A man. In here. He was digging around in my clothes.'

'A burglar?'

'I th-th-think so.'

'Good heavens.' Barbara went to the window and closed it. She looked at the maid. 'Rakes, did he steal anything?'

The maid hurried to the dressing table. She moved things around. 'There was some jewellery left here last night…a ring and a necklace. They are gone.'

'Oh, no,' her aunt cried. 'They belonged to my mother. Why was I too tired to put them away?'

Barbara's heart ached for her aunt. She had treasured those pieces.

'Perhaps we can find them. We can hire someone to go around the pawn shops and look for them.' It would probably cost more than the jewellery was worth, but it would be worth it to make her aunt feel better.

Aunt Lenore sniffled. 'If we had not switched rooms, it would have been your jewellery that would have gone missing.'

Barbara stared at her. That would certainly have been a disaster.

She set about calming her aunt and setting the servants to tidying the room. She also asked the butler to make sure the windows were secure. All of them.

It was almost well past noon by the time she had the household settled down and back to its normal smooth running. And an afternoon of needlework in the drawing room, accompanied by fortifying cups of tea, had settled Aunt Lenore's feathers, especially after Barbara suggested her aunt's maid sleep in the adjoining dressing room for the time being.

As Barbara dressed for her evening, she could not help but feel a little amused by the day's events. London was certainly providing her with a surprising amount of excitement, everything from riding a racehorse to a burglary. Hopefully tonight would be equally entertaining. If things went as she had planned, they should be.

When Aunt Lenore came bustling into Barbara's bedchamber, she seemed completely revived. 'Is this the gown you are wearing this evening?'

Watching from where she was seated at the mirror, Barbara could only see her aunt's back, not her expression. 'Yes. Is there a problem?'

Her aunt lifted the gold tissue gown from the bed and held it up. 'My dear, it is beautiful. Sumptuous, but surely a little too magnificent for a minor ball? More of the sort of thing one might wear at Carleton House.'

She turned to face Barbara's back with a frown. 'It does seem a little…' She lifted the fabric and let it fall.

'A little…?' Barbara required.

'Gauzy? Transparent?'

'It is an overdress,' Barbara said. 'All the rage in Paris.'

'Do not think of damping your petticoats,' Aunt Lenore said with a wag of her finger.

'Certainly not.' A good thing Aunt was not asking about her footwear.

Aunt Lenore parked herself on a small seat beside the dressing table while the maid continued to pin Barbara's hair in the style she preferred.

'I am surprised we have heard nothing from the Duke since the day you rode out with him,' Aunt Lenore said, sounding disappointed. She fiddled with the buttons on her gloves.

'Why would you be surprised?'

Aunt Lenore pushed a grey ringlet back from her face then tugged it forward. 'Oh, I don't know. I would have thought at the very least he would have attended our at home the other day. I sent him a personal invitation.'

The at home had been the most boring event possible. 'I am sure he has many more important matters requiring his attention than an afternoon at home.'

'I have it on good authority that he is looking for a wife.'

'Oh, my dear aunt. How could you even think that a man such as the Duke would be interested in a twice-married widow? It is beyond the realm of possibility.'

'He danced with you at Almack's. He invited you to go riding. What a triumph it would be if he should actually—'

'I have it on good authority that he is courting Miss Simon.'

Aunt Lenore frowned. 'What authority?'

'Your friend, Mr Elton. He seems to know everything about everyone and is happy to gossip about it too.'

'Mr Elton. Pah. That man knows nothing but what people want him to believe. You mark my words, if you play your cards right, you could find yourself a duchess before the year is out.'

'It being every woman's wish to catch the Duke,' Barbara said. 'Or rather every woman except me. I have absolutely no wish to marry again. Not even if the Prince of Wales were to ask me.'

'We will see what your father has to say about that, my dear.'

The maid stepped back with an enquiring expression.

Barbara nodded. 'Perfect as always, Marion.' She got to her feet and smiled at her aunt. 'If you don't mind, Aunt, I will finish my toilette and meet you downstairs.'

'Very well.' Lenore eyed the dress on the bed then gave a shake of her head, clearly knowing better than to argue about it. 'The coach will be at the front door in half an hour.'

'I will be ready.'

Once her aunt left, Barbara slipped out of her dressing robe, already attired in stays and petticoat. Marion helped her into the gown. It had been made by one of the foremost seamstresses in Paris and fitted her to perfection. It shimmered gold as it caught the light and floated around her as she moved. It was indeed sumptuous.

And she had it on good authority that the Duke would indeed be present this evening.

While he had been rather stuffy about her showing up to his racing stables without a chaperone, he seemed to have accepted her explanation, something she had not expected. And to boot, he had made sure her reputation remained unsullied.

After thinking it over, she had decided that he must have thought she was setting her cap at him. Trying to trap him into marriage by being alone with him, then crying foul.

A man in his position must experience that sort of thing from ambitious women all the time. In this case, nothing could be further from the truth.

Clearly if she wanted his disapproval, she would need to create enough of a public stir to cause him to vilify her, thereby causing Society to turn their backs.

And she could not be too obvious about it either, or Father would see through her ruse.

After listening to her aunt talk about Society and what was acceptable and what was not, she had decided to start with small things and work up to one large faux pas—that would be the icing on the cake.

She stretched out a foot, admiring her golden sandals and red painted toenails.

Yes indeed, it was a very good thing her aunt had not enquired about her footwear. And thank goodness, for once it was not raining.

She smiled with satisfaction. The red dress had been a start. These sandals would raise an eyebrow or two. And she would eventually figure out the one thing the Duke of Derbridge absolutely would not tolerate, and she would be out on her ear.

Once he, the leader of London Society, pronounced her *persona non grata*, the *ton* would never accept her again. Only then would she be free of Papa and his *ideas*.

A footman rapped on the door. 'The carriage is waiting, my lady.'

'I will be right there,' she called out.

'Your wrap, my lady,' Marion said.

'Thank you.'

When she heard her aunt's voice in the street below, she tripped lightly down the stairs and into the street. Aunt Lenore was already ensconced in the carriage.

'Sorry I am late, Aunt. A wardrobe malfunction slowed me down.'

'Nothing serious, I hope?' Her aunt looked her up and down.

'No. Not serious. Marion handled it.'

As usual, her aunt's carriage crawled to their destination. Fortunately they did not have far to travel, and when they arrived, Barbara made sure her aunt was always a few steps ahead so she could keep her feet out sight.

Inside the Earl of Bourne's grand townhouse, a line of the nobility snaked its way up the staircase to the ballroom on the first floor.

From above came the muffled voice of the butler shouting names as guests entered the ballroom.

Every few moments, the line shuffled up a step or two.

'Oh, dear,' her aunt said. 'Perhaps we should have come earlier.'

'Perhaps we should not have come at all,' Barbara said.

A gentleman ahead of them turned at the sound of their voices. '*Mein Gott!* Barbara, is it you?'

Barbara stared at the blond man in astonishment. 'Charles. What are you doing here?'

Her dead husband's brother grinned. 'Waiting to be admitted to some infernal ball,' he said. 'I arrived yesterday in London. I planned to send around my card tomorrow to ask if I could call on you. But here you are.'

He moved around the person standing behind him and to join them.

'Aunt Lenore, let me introduce Charles, the Count of Lipsweiger and Upsal. My departed husband's heir.'

An attractive smile lit his face. 'Such a pleasure to meet you.' He took Aunt Lenore's hand and bowed in the Continental fashion.

Aunt Lenore blushed and fluttered her handkerchief.

'Surely you didn't travel all the way to London to attend this squeeze?' Barbara said.

He winced. 'No, my dear. I am here on business. Financial matters. For my family. But I am delighted to see you here and looking beautiful as always. I have missed you.'

Financial matters were always a problem in his family. No wonder he sounded tense. 'As I have missed you.'

Charles had been in Vienna and had often accompanied her to various events when Helmut had been too busy. Which was nearly all the time. It was only after her husband's death that she discovered he had not been occupied with important matters of state but rather busy with his mistress.

While she could not blame Charles for her husband's unfaithfulness, she had wished he had informed her what was going on instead of trying to shield her from embarrassment, as he'd told her afterwards. He had been most apologetic when she'd confronted him about keeping her husband's secrets.

But then he and her husband were family and Barbara was an outsider. She shouldn't really expect anything else.

They reached the top of the stairs, handed over their cards and the butler introduced them. They walked into the ballroom together.

'I hope we will see something of you while you are in London,' she said.

'Try keeping me away.'

She laughed. He had always been full of flirtatious nonsense, but it had meant nothing. They had never been more than friends.

'I mean it,' he said with an intensity that took her

aback. 'I have never seen you look so beautiful. It must be the English air.'

'The English rain, you mean,' she said lightly, to hide her discomfort.

'I am surprised you are not wearing the Upsal parure.'

The Upsal parure, a set of rubies and diamonds, some of which she had worn to Almack's, had been the only item she had inherited from her second husband.

'I thought this gown dazzling enough,' she said.

His tilted his head in agreement. Then laughed. It sounded a little forced, she thought. 'I hope you did not sell them?'

'Certainly not.' At least not yet.

For some odd reason Charles looked relieved, but the expression was gone in a moment so she could not be sure that she had read it aright.

Against his will, Xavier glanced from his perusal of the dance floor towards the entrance upon hearing announcement of the Countess of Lipsweiger and Upsal.

An animated smile wreathed the Countess's expression.

His heart stumbled at the sight. The reason for her smile was a blond-haired gentleman with as fine a set of whiskers as Xavier had ever seen, who was escorting her in.

The warmth of her gaze on this stranger caused an odd tightening in Xavier's chest.

Nonsense. Yet he could not look away as the Countess picked her way delicately through the crowds at the doorway with cat-like grace, her gold tissue gown clinging to her curves with each sinuous step.

Stunning yet unusual. Lovely yet not pretty. Brash yet... Enough.

A stir around her caught his attention. Whispers rippled through the assembled company as gazes turned her way.

What now?

Lord North was standing nearby. His wife came dashing up to the peer's side and whispered in his ear. 'Good Lord,' North said with a chortle.

Xavier raised his eyebrows in question.

'She's painted her toenails,' Lady North said in scandalised tones. She lowered her voice. 'Not even a member of the demi-monde would be so daring, I am told!' Both shock and outrage coloured her voice.

As usual, the reaction of the *ton* to anything that they thought not quite the thing surfaced swiftly. Clearly none of them had been to Paris recently. Xavier had been there a few months ago, and painted toenails had been quite the rage, and no doubt it would be here before long.

Fashion. Such fickle nonsense.

A spurt of anger on the Countess's behalf surprised him. Devil take it. The woman was none of his concern. He simply didn't like injustice, that was all.

Lady North scurried off to join a group of matrons who looked to be in high dudgeon.

North smirked. 'Now that has stirred up a hornets' nest.'

And someone was likely to get stung, and badly. He felt a surprising pang of sympathy for the lady in question and cast a bored glance in her direction. Perhaps his apparent lack of condemnation might stem the tide without his actually having to do anything about it. 'I cannot think why what the woman wears would be of any interest.'

'Can you not?' North said. 'I would say it is because she is so extraordinary and none of them can hold a candle to her.' He moved off to join another gentleman, who was staring at the Countess through his quizzing glass.

North had more brains than Xavier had given him credit for.

A little space had formed around the Countess. One of those voids that could ruin a reputation.

The *ton* did not like unique. They liked conformity to rules of their making. If the woman seemed oblivious to the mores of London Society, it was none of his concern.

To him, she was forbidden fruit. Not the sort of woman he would ever, could ever, consider as a wife.

More the sort of woman a man would enjoy as a mistress. His mind went to the cottage in Chelsea he had been discussing with his secretary that morning. The previous tenant had moved on and it needed renting out. His secretary had joked that it was so quaint, it would make a perfect love-nest. Xavier had quelled Perry's amusement with a chilly glance.

The thought of the place and the Countess had been accompanied by a surge of heat in his blood that had shocked and appalled him.

It was as if he had learned nothing from his father's disastrous marriage.

He had learned. He knew exactly what he needed to do to ensure the Dukedom continued in good order for another one hundred years.

He needed to wed a woman who would bring honour to his name and an heir and a spare into the world.

He strolled across the room to Miss Simon's side, the young lady he was beginning to think might be his choice. As he approached, he realised she was gazing wide-eyed at the Countess. A little brown mouse gazing at a predator.

She was the one who needed his protection, not the exotic Countess.

'Good evening, Miss Simon.'

'Your Grace,' she said with a blush and a shy little smile.

'Will you do me the honour of this next dance?'

She glanced at her mother. The plump matronly woman nodded her approval while her expression showed her delight.

Xavier led Miss Simon to the nearest set to the opening bars of a country dance.

'How are you enjoying your Season so far?' he asked

smiling down at her, feeling her nervousness in the flutter of her fingers and wanting to set her at ease.

'Very well, Your Grace. Though of course they say this ball is a bit of a squeeze.'

Parroting the words of her acquaintances.

The sort of woman who would parrot the words of her husband and who would never have an opinion of her own.

Exactly the sort of woman he needed. Wasn't she?

Damnation. Why on earth did this sense of dread fill him every time he decided on the perfect woman? For three seasons now, he'd been dithering on the brink of making an offer.

And each time he'd hung back. It wasn't like him. He knew what he wanted. All he had to do was take the plunge.

The orchestra struck up a tune as they took their defined places in the set. Just as he would take his defined place as a husband and a father.

The idea used to give him a feeling of contentment, but now there was a sense of loss, as if he was missing something important.

Rubbish.

Everything was exactly as it ought to be.

Aunt Lenore had stopped to greet a friend while Barbara and Charles had wandered closer to the dance floor.

Charles leaned close. 'Are you indeed seeking a third husband, my dearest sister?'

'Some people think so,' Barbara said lightly.

Charles narrowed his eyes. 'Your Papa, perhaps?'

She had bemoaned her father's ambitions to Charles not long after she had married his brother Helmut. Charles had been sympathetic to her plight. And after his brother's death, he had been most solicitous.

'And what do you think?' he asked.

'I have not given it an iota of thought.'

He chuckled, shaking his head. 'You should. Not every man is a dilettante like my brother. You are far too young to take the veil.'

'Take the veil? What can you mean?'

'If you do not wed, what will you become? A nun? Or close to it.'

The picture he painted was hardly enticing. But the alternative was less so.

'I expect I will remain in my father's household, for the time being.' At least until she managed to sell her jewels and found a place to live. She had hired an agent to find her something far from London and given him an idea of her budget. Now all she could do was wait and avoid being coerced into marriage in the meantime.

'And you will be his hostess, influencing politics while you sit at his table, perhaps? I know you have an interest in what goes on in the world. But will he allow that?'

Unlikely.

She certainly did not trust her father to have her best interests at heart. Like most men, he cared only for himself.

So many times she had pinned her hopes on her father and been let down. She never wanted to have to rely on him or anyone else again.

She gave him a cheerful smile. 'Who can foresee the future? Are you in London to seek a wife? An heiress, perhaps?'

'I cannot deny Helmut left things in disarray and that I am hoping to set things to rights. If I must marry to do it, I suppose I will.'

'I am sorry,' she said.

She was. Her husband had been a spendthrift and a bit of a blackguard.

'I shall come about, never fear.' He frowned. 'It seems as if you have committed some sort of faux pas. You have everyone looking daggers.'

'Do I?' She forced herself not to smile.

Charles gave her an enigmatic stare, held a second too long. 'What sort of game are you playing, my dear?'

'Game?'

'I know you to be an intelligent and socially astute woman. You could hardly be otherwise with a papa like yours, yet here you are committing some sort of folly like a gauche newcomer.'

He was right, she was already drawing frowns and dark glances. It seemed it did not take much to break London Society's rules.

She briefly toyed with the idea of letting him in on her plan, but that would require giving him her trust.

The very idea sent a cold chill down her spine.

'You are talking in riddles.'

Charles gave her a knowing smile. 'As you wish. Would you care to dance?'

'Only if it is a waltz.'

He gave her a quizzical look. 'Have you been approved to dance the waltz?'

It seemed even he had been briefed about what was acceptable. 'I have.' More was the pity.

Perhaps if Charles danced with her more than the proscribed two times, it might help her cause. Unless he knew about that rule also.

On the other hand, perhaps she had done enough? Certainly, there were no other men seeking to ask her to dance.

'Then waltz we shall,' Charles said. 'If they play one. And I shall take you to supper, if it is permitted?'

'I shall certainly permit it.'

Her aunt joined them. Her smile was tight and anxious.

Charles, likely sensing she wanted to speak to Barbara privately, muttered a few platitudes about seeing an old friend and left.

Barbara couldn't help admiring his quick understanding, a sort of second sense of when to leave and when to stay. She had noticed before how attuned he was to the needs of others. In particular, her needs after she had married Helmut.

Perhaps she was wrong not to trust him with her worries.

Aunt Lenore watched him join a group of gentlemen. 'What a nice young man the Count is.'

'Yes, he is.'

Aunt Lenore glanced at the backs turned in their direction. 'I fear—' she glanced down at Barbara's toes '—we have made a miscalculation regarding what is proper.'

'We have?' Barbara said, putting a good deal of surprise into her voice. 'You did not think so when I showed you this gown.'

Her aunt plucked at her skirts in little nervous movements. 'Not your gown. Your footwear.' She moaned softly.

'Sandals? I admit it is a little early in the year, but surely—'

'Feet,' Aunt Lenore gasped. 'Toes to be exact.'

'But one cannot wear sandals with stockings. It looks terrible.' Her poor aunt looked so miserable she could not keep up the pretence of confusion any longer. 'Oh! You mean the varnish.' She glanced around her. 'Is that why everyone is giving me the cold shoulder? It was *de rigueur* in Paris, I assure you.'

'I wish you had mentioned it before we left,' her aunt said. 'Paris is not London.'

'Clearly.' And Barbara did not mean it as a compliment. 'So do we retreat in good order, or hold our ground?'

'I wish you wouldn't use such language. You are not a soldier.'

'My husband was a soldier.'

'But—oh, I do not know what to say. Your papa is like to murder me.'

'Of course he won't.' She would make sure Papa understood it was none of her aunt's fault.

Barbara's gaze fell upon the dance floor, on Derbridge.

The Duke and his partner, a small blonde-haired miss, were traversing the centre of their set hand in hand. The Duke smiled down at his partner with a sort of condescension that caused Barbara to grit her teeth. The child gazed back at him in wide-eyed awe. Was that what he wanted?

That sort of naive, unthinking adoration? How...disappointing.

An odd sinking sensation surprised her.

She turned away. Who the Duke danced with was of no concern to her. None at all.

'Oh, dear,' said Aunt Lenore, fanning herself wildly. 'Derbridge seems very taken with the Simon girl.'

Like a wolf would be taken with a rabbit. 'Why does that warrant an "oh, dear," Aunt?'

Aunt Lenore pulled at a stray curl and twitched her fichu. 'I thought perhaps after Almack's, when he was so generous as to ignore your faux pas... Well, it is of no consequence. Not now.'

It was what Barbara had wanted, but somehow, she felt strangely saddened. She moved closer to her aunt. How odd that she had no acquaintances or friends among the company. In Austria and Paris, she had known nearly everyone at any event she attended.

The country dance ended, and a few moments later the orchestra struck up a waltz.

She looked around for Charles, but he was nowhere to be seen. It seemed he had also decided that discretion was the better part of valour.

How could she blame him? She had no wish to see him ostracised.

Chapter Six

Seeing the Countess standing like an island in an unfriendly sea infuriated Xavier.

London Society was ridiculous at the best of times, but at its worst it was downright destructive.

The Countess was putting a brave face on it, seemingly unconcerned by the cold shoulders pointed her way, but he did not believe for a moment that she did not feel like an outcast.

And for what?

Because she had worn a fashion that was all the rage in Paris?

As North had said, Society was eager to find something, anything, to put someone they considered a beautiful intruder in her place.

Especially one that outshone them all. He cut that thought off. She was lovely, to be sure, but there were many lovely ladies in London. Including the one he was thinking of making his bride. They were lovely in different ways.

The thing was, while he had little sympathy with stupidity, or recklessness, he could not abide injustice.

Purposeful strides brought him to the Countess's side before his ire had a chance to subside.

Startled brown eyes gazed back at him. He had forgotten how her height meant she only had to raise her gaze a fraction to look him in the eye.

It was an unusual sensation for one as tall as he. Unusual and pleasing.

'Your Grace,' she said, sounding slightly breathless.

Beside her, her aunt's mouth dropped open. 'I...er... Oh.' She dipped a curtsey. 'I—'

'Good evening, ladies,' he interjected swiftly. The older woman was gasping like a landed fish. 'Countess, would you honour me with this next dance?'

Her eyes widened.

'Yes,' her aunt said, apparently finding her voice. 'She will.'

The Countess hesitated for a second then gave a small, smothered chuckle, a low attractive sound that had him wanting to grin. 'Thank you, Your Grace.'

He took her hand and walked her onto the dance floor. He felt a surge of pride as she walked by his side, as if he had won the prize of a lifetime.

Why not? Any man would be proud to partner such a lovely woman. He wasn't made of stone.

She gracefully followed his lead as they joined the dance. It was as if they were made for each other. Usually, when he danced, his partners were so much shorter than he, he could see little more than the tops of their heads, except when they strained their necks to look up at him. He also usually had to be careful with the length of his stride or risk lifting his partner off her feet and unbalancing them both. Not so with the Countess. Their steps matched perfectly.

It was delightful. He had never enjoyed dancing more.

'Will your reputation survive partnering with me?' she asked after a few seconds of twirling and gliding around the floor.

Talk about taking the bull by the horns. 'Why would it not?'

'Apparently, I have once more broken one of Society's silly rules.'

'You think rules are silly?' he asked repressively. His stepmother had ignored the rules about not sailing out in a storm and taunted her husband, his father, to do likewise.

Neither had survived.

'I think silly rules are silly,' the Countess said in decided tones. 'Rules intended to keep one safe, or to not hurt others, are worth obeying, but not those imposed for ridiculous reasons.'

Hard to argue with that. 'And what rule is it that you think you have broken?'

She glanced downward, then frowned. 'I'm not exactly sure what the rule is, but it has something to do with painting one's toenails, which I might add was all the rage when I left Paris a few weeks ago.'

'I am aware it is all the rage in Paris, since I was there

not long ago. But might you not have asked whether it was considered acceptable in London?'

'Why would I do that?'

'To save yourself some embarrassment.'

She looked unconvinced. 'I do not care a fig for what others think.'

He was both shocked and in awe of her unusual spirit. And therein lay the danger. He feared that he had inherited his father's lack of judgement when it came to lovely wilful women.

'You should care.' He sounded stiff and disapproving when he had wanted to sound wise.

'Why?'

'Because being considered beyond the pale is a lonely place when it costs so little to conform to accepted mores.'

'Do you always conform?' she asked, and there was an irritating hint of derision in her voice.

'I adhere to sensible rules, but I do not follow fashion, Society follows me in that regard.'

She glanced around. People were watching them and smiling at them benignly.

Her expression changed. She looked quite put out. 'Do you mean that now my choice to paint my toenails is considered acceptable simply because you asked me to dance?'

'I also mentioned to someone that it was a Parisienne fashion that I found quite charming when I was there.'

She showed not the slightest pleasure in his words. 'I see.'

What an infuriating, paradoxical woman to be sure.

Somehow, he had to make her understand that London Society was quite different than that of Paris or other European courts. It was his duty as a gentleman, if nothing else.

The music ended and he walked her back to her aunt, where there was more than one gentleman waiting to ask her to dance.

There would be no chance to say more, and neither was this the place to have a serious discussion.

'I will take you driving in the park tomorrow afternoon,' he said. It was the perfect solution.

'I beg your pardon.'

'No need,' he said. 'I will call for you at four.'

'Oh, but—'

He bowed. 'Thank you for the dance, Countess.' He walked away before she could argue.

Not even the wayward Countess would refuse an invitation to drive with him during the fashionable hour. Not only would it be the perfect opportunity for her to be fully accepted by Society, but it would give him the privacy he needed to explain just why acceptance was important.

And then, having done his duty, he would not need to have any more to do with her.

Which was exactly what he wanted.

Barbara had thought about sending round a note to the Duke's residence to cancel their drive.

An invitation she had not actually accepted but that he, autocratically, had decided she would not refuse.

Upon reflection, she had decided that it might be the ideal opportunity to ask him to…mind his own business…to stay out of her affairs…to stop interfering and let her make her own mistakes.

However she phrased it in her mind, it sounded churlish.

Clearly her idea that she might use him to turn the *ton* against her was not working.

Perhaps it was time to come up with a new plan. And quickly, or her dear father would have her married in a trice the moment he arrived.

Running away was an option.

But as yet, she had not found a buyer for the jewels. Therefore she did not have any money.

She could not afford for anyone she knew to learn she was selling them in case Father found out. He would definitely try to stop her.

Nor did she want to let them go for a pittance. She needed someone with wealth who was not a member of the *ton*.

She could work in the interim, perhaps? There were not many options for a woman with few skills. Perhaps she could become a governess. Or a housemaid. But without references it would be difficult to find a decent employer.

Besides, running away felt like giving up. She wanted her independence, not to swap one unpleasant future for another.

There had to be a better way.

If only she could think of it.

Meanwhile, she had to go driving with the Duke.

She waited patiently while her maid gently eased her hatpin through her coiffure.

'Does it feel secure, my lady?' the young woman asked. 'I noticed that today it is rather breezy.'

Barbara gave her head an experimental shake. 'Perfectly secure, thank you.' She picked up her reticule and headed downstairs.

Her aunt looked up from her needlework and eyed her up and down. 'For once I cannot fault your style.'

She wasn't foolish enough to try a wardrobe malfunction a third time. 'Do you like it? I had it made in Paris.'

Her aunt smiled. 'It is elegant, perfect for someone of your height.'

Hmm. Everyone always mentioned her height. At five feet seven inches, she was as tall if not taller than many Englishmen. Not the Duke though. He was delightfully tall.

She cut off the stray thought.

While many men did not like a woman who towered over them, it was not enough to scare them off should they be attracted by her fortune in jewels.

A knock sounded at the front door. She kissed her aunt and headed down the stairs to where the butler already had the front door open.

His Grace stood upon the step looking magnificent

in his redingote of navy blue and silver buttons and his shiny top hat.

He bowed. 'Good afternoon, Countess. For once, the weather is cooperating. If you are in need of a blanket to cover your legs, please do not hesitate to let me know.'

Always the gentleman, this duke. Did he ever lose his implacable calm? Was it all an act, this chilly exterior? A way of hiding his true feelings? She had an irrational urge to find out.

Irrational and foolhardy.

He escorted her to the open carriage of forest green waiting at the curb and handed her up.

The groom holding the horses' heads stepped back as soon as His Grace picked up the reins, and they moved out into the late-afternoon traffic.

He was an excellent whip. His driving seemed effortless and yet the traffic was busy, and a lesser man might have struggled to control his horses.

'I was of a mind to cancel our engagement,' she said after a few minutes. 'After all, you did not give me the opportunity to refuse or accept, but simply issued your invitation like an order.' And she wasn't going to let him get away with it.

'Then why didn't you?'

'Because I wanted to know what it was that you had to say to me that required us to be alone. Or alone as we can be with a groom behind us.'

He gave a grim smile. 'You are not one to mince words, are you, my lady?'

'Why should I be? I've told you before, I believe in calling a shovel a shovel.'

'How enchanting,' he said with obvious sarcasm. 'Briggs, I shall not need you any more today. I will see you back at the stables.' The groom touched his hat and jumped down, his expression noncommittal.

'So I was right.'

'About what?' said the Duke.

'About you wanting to say something of a personal nature.'

A small smile touched his lips. 'Yes, you are right.'

That smile did something to his face. While he was definitely handsome, when he smiled, he became more…human, less remote. That smile did something to her insides, made them flutter strangely. She did not like it at all. At least, she did not want to like it.

'Well?' she asked.

He did not answer, apparently busy guiding his horses around a brewer's dray, where the unloading of casks was causing a good deal of commotion.

'Why on earth are so many people gathered here?' she asked, surprised by the crowd of unkempt folks on the pavement and dodging in front of the traffic.

He cast her a sardonic glance. 'They are hoping a barrel will split and they can snatch up the dregs.'

They were past now and she looked back. Indeed, some of those gathered were holding pewter mugs and other containers, while the carter yelled at them to keep back if they didn't want their toes crushed.

'How awful that people feel the need to scoop beer

from the ground.' Cobblestones smeared with mud and dung and… She shuddered.

He did not answer, but his mouth set in a firm line as if he too were horrified by the idea.

They turned into Mayfair, and it was not long before they arrived at Hyde Park.

The fine weather had brought out the park saunterers and other open carriages. As they moved along the row, the Duke acknowledged acquaintances with a casual wave or a bow.

'Well, Duke, what was it that you felt the need to say to me?'

His expression remained grim. 'Since you seem to value the worth of direct speech, I will not mince words.'

He sounded almost…angry.

'Please, feel free to unbridle your tongue.'

'Very well.' He paused for a second or two as if organising his thoughts. 'I understand that living in Europe for the past many years means that you have not been exposed to the ways of English Society. From the first, you have been oblivious to the niceties of the good conduct expected of a well-brought-up young lady.'

She could not help it. Her jaw dropped and she gasped.

He cast her a look of irritation. 'You said I should speak my mind.'

She got herself under control. After all, he was telling the truth. 'Pray, continue.'

'You see, while I do not know what standard of manners pertain to young ladies on the Continent, if you continue on as you are, you will find yourself cast out of any decent Society here. Surely that is not what you want?'

The mere fact that he was questioning her on that score gave her pause. This Duke was not a stupid man.

'What have I done, that is so dreadful that Society would cast me out? As you put it.'

'Has your aunt told you nothing of Society's ways?'

She did not want to get Aunt Lenore in trouble. The poor dear was terrified Papa would cut off the allowance he was providing for Barbara's care. 'My aunt is a dear and I will not have her pilloried for my mistakes.'

He sighed. 'I am glad to hear you say it, but I suppose you have her wrapped around your little finger.'

'She keeps telling me that things are against the rules for those new upon the town, but she forgets I am not some ingenue up from the country. I have been married twice. Those rules do not apply to such as I. And besides, I do not see what business it is of yours.'

There, that ought to put an end to his sermonising.

She folded her hands in her lap.

Xavier did not know what business it was of his either. Even as he had spoken, he had felt the awkwardness of his position.

He had set out with good intentions, it was true, but who was he to give this woman a bear garden jaw? A cousin might take it upon himself, a brother perhaps or her father, but he was…a friend? Perhaps not even that. Merely an acquaintance.

Looking at her, with the first blush of womanhood—and perhaps a bit of anger—upon her cheek, it was hard to imagine that she could have been married twice.

'I speak only as someone who has your best interests at heart,' he said.

'Pompous ass,' she responded under her breath.

He decided to ignore her words. He doubted she knew she had spoken them out loud.

A woman passing in a barouche bowed in their direction.

Gloria Lang. Now Lord Glover's mistress, she had thrown her lures at Xavier when he was first upon the town. He had succumbed to her charms briefly and ended by paying her handsomely to extricate himself, having discovered she was a money-hungry woman with the morals of an alley cat.

Xavier ignored her greeting.

'Who was that?'

'Who are you talking about?'

'The lady who greeted you and you did not acknowledge.'

'I saw no lady.'

'Aha. I see.'

He glanced down. Her dark eyes glittered with anger. Fascinating. It was the first time he had been able to read the expression in those mysterious depths.

'What do you see?'

'You consider her beneath your lofty notice. What

did she do? Shop in Bond Street in the afternoon? Waltz three times with the same gentleman?'

He raised a brow at the litany of crimes she considered serious enough to warrant a cut direct. 'You see, I was right. You have not the slightest town bronze. I fear you will fall afoul of the gossips before many more days are out. But since you do not appreciate my advice, I shall say nothing more.'

Her dark eyebrows drew together and she looked thoughtful. And enchanting. And quite beautiful.

'I apologise,' she said. 'I was wrong to dismiss your concerns. Perhaps they had some merit. Aunt Lenore has been away from London Society for a long time and she has forgotten the most serious solecisms a lady might commit. If she ever knew them. I believe I might need someone to advise me. I would not like to be ignored in the manner you ignored that poor woman. She looked crushed.'

Astonished by the complete turnabout in her manner, by her small voice and obvious anxiety, he stared at her.

And 'crushed' was not the word he would have used to describe Gloria's reaction. 'Gnashing her teeth' or 'furious' would be a better choice of words.

'I think if the examples of dire social solecisms your aunt gave you are those you mentioned, she is indeed somewhat out of touch.'

'Well, she did tell me not to wear red to Almack's,' the Countess said. 'But honestly, I felt like that was more of a challenge than a rule. And I was careful to pick a colour which my dressmaker called geranium, since it had an orange hue rather that the blood red of Burgundy. I really cannot wear the virginal white that is expected of a debutante. That would be doing it too brown.'

'You might have worn green, or yellow or...'

'Ugh. With my skin tone all of those colours make me look insipid.'

She certainly had not looked insipid at Almack's.

'Well, you suffered no ill consequences from it, so it is of no matter.'

'I suffered no ill consequences because you danced with me.'

Frank to a fault. He could not help it—he cracked a laugh.

She grinned back, a saucy, delighted grin that made him want to smile like a fool.

He lowered his brows in a frown.

'And,' she continued, 'if I am not mistaken, while I assured everyone that my painted nails were all the go in Paris, it was not until you confirmed my words that people stopped turning their noses up.'

'Quite possibly.'

'Why?'

'Why what?'

'Why do people accept your word as if it is gospel? Because you are a Duke?'

'Partially, I expect. But also, I have shown myself to be a man of exemplary character, though I only say so because of the nature of our conversation. They trust I would not lie to them.'

She gave a little shiver. 'Is that true? You would never lie?'

He thought for a moment. 'I would not lie in order to cause someone harm or to give myself advantage over others.'

'Oh, my.'

'You find this remarkable?'

'No, no,' she said hastily. 'Most admirable, I am sure.'

He had the feeling she was mocking him. He did not care. These were the mores he had been taught by his great-uncle after his parents died. All his life they had stood him in good stead.

They reached the end of the row and he turned the carriage around.

There were a great many more people in the park. Sooner or later, they would be forced to a stop by the slowing traffic, which would mean there would be no further opportunity for meaningful conversation.

She touched his arm in an impulsive movement. Tingles radiated from where her fingers gripped his sleeve.

Only by force of will did he prevent his arm from jerking away. Not because he did not like her touch. He did. Very much. But because the sensation of being touched so intimately was both delightful and shocking.

'I know,' she said, a smile breaking out on her face as she gazed up at him. He had the dreadful urge to kiss the corner of those upturned lips. 'I have the perfect answer.'

Perfect answer for him kissing her mouth?

'I—'

'My aunt made a list of the rules I should follow. Why don't you make a list of the things that I absolutely must not do? Things that would be absolutely terrible, even for a widow. Then I will know exactly what I must avoid.'

Xavier stared at her, wanting to kiss her so very badly.

Kissing her would be a terrible thing to do. It would ruin her completely in the eyes of Society.

And yet he was so tempted.

Devil take it, the girl was a witch if she could make him forget himself so completely. He had almost decided Miss Simon was the one. He couldn't go around kissing other women in public.

'Kissing in public would be top of the list,' he bit out.

'Right,' she said. She scrabbled in her reticule.

'What are you doing?'

'Looking for my notebook. I need to write these things down. I don't want to forget any.'

He spotted Julian approaching them on foot with the clear intention of greeting them.

'We do not have time for this now. I will call on you later in the week, and that will give me time to prepare a list.'

She looked disappointed but shrugged. 'Very well.'

'I am sure you can manage to keep out of trouble until then,' he said.

'I can try.'

'No. You will do so.'

'Well, I won't kiss anyone in public,' she said, suddenly cheerful.

Lord help him. He needed a change of topic.

'Let me introduce you to my friend Pettigrew. We went to school together. I think you will like him.'

Everyone liked Julian. He was such an easy-going fellow compared to Xavier. Easy-going and in need of a rich wife. But Xavier doubted his friend could handle such a strong-willed female as the Countess had turned out to be.

Damn it, why would he even think that? If Julian wanted to marry the Countess, why shouldn't he?

Chapter Seven

Never in Barbara's wildest imaginings could this drive have turned out so perfectly.

The Duke was going to provide her with a list of the things that would get her into hot water.

She was very tempted to kiss him then and there.

She almost giggled at the wayward thought.

'Countess, may I present my friend Julian Pettigrew? Julian, this is the Countess of Lipsweiger and Upsal.'

Pettigrew, who was a nice-looking, fair-haired man of around the same age as Derbridge, took off his hat and swept an elegant bow. 'Countess, welcome to London. If you want to meet London at the fashionable hour, Derbridge is certainly your man.'

His cheerful demeanour, so unlike that of his friend, was thoroughly engaging. She smiled at him. 'We haven't actually met anyone at all, until now,' she said.

'What? Are you so top lofty, Derbridge? Where are your manners?'

'The Countess and I have been enjoying the fresh air and the fact that the carriages were actually moving for a change. Besides, we haven't met anyone worth an introduction.'

Pettigrew clutched at his heart in mock pain.

'Except you, Julian,' the Duke amended hastily and with mock sorrow.

'So I should think,' Pettigrew said.

'Well, you would be, if it wasn't for that terrible waistcoat,' the Duke said.

The waistcoat in question, peeking out from Pettigrew's coat, was a peacock blue colour with bright yellow flowers embroidered on it.

'Nonsense,' Pettigrew said. 'My tailor assured me this was a perfect waistcoat for spring.'

Barbara was enjoying the interaction between the two men. Derbridge seemed much more at ease with his friend, almost human.

It showed a softer side she hadn't known existed.

'I will recommend you to *my* tailor,' the Duke said dryly.

Pettigrew chuckled. 'At last. I've been asking you to do so for weeks. I thought this might tip the balance.'

The Duke laughed.

A deep, rich, genuine laugh. It made her smile.

'*Touché,*' the Duke said. 'Very well, you shall have it.'

This playful side charmed her down to her toes. How unexpected! Clearly, these two were good friends.

Knowing that the Duke had a good friend made him seem more approachable. On the other hand, she did not want to like him too much. She needed him to despise her.

'Will you be attending the Rankins' ball later this week?' Pettigrew asked her. 'If so, may I beg a waltz?'

'Of course.'

He touched his hat. 'I bid you good day, then, Derbridge.' He sauntered off.

'Do not be taken in by Pettigrew's nonsense,' Derbridge said.

He was frowning after his friend as he set his horses in motion.

'You have known him a long time, I think,' she said.

'Since I was seven, actually, when I started school.'

'How fortunate for you to have such a friend.'

'You do not?'

'No. I went to several schools when I was younger and never had the chance to form any close attachments.'

'Oh, really? Why so?'

'Father's work, I suppose.' She certainly wasn't going to mention that half the time he'd *forgotten* to pay the fees and she'd been asked to depart after a term or two.

The Duke regarded her silently for a moment, as if he suspected that she wasn't being forthcoming.

'He travelled a great deal,' she added. 'Diplomatic corps.'

'I can see how that would make for an unsettled life.'

'I suppose you have a great many friends like Mr Pettigrew, having attended the same school for years.'

'I have a great many acquaintances,' he said, 'but very few friends like Pettigrew.'

She felt him stiffen slightly and followed the direction of his gaze to where a group of young people accompanied by a couple of maids, or perhaps governesses, were walking alongside the gravel road. They seemed to be having an enjoyable time. The young men, or boys really, were jostling elbows with each other, no doubt trying to get the older girls' attention.

'Why, that is Miss Simon, is it not? The young woman I saw you dancing with last night.' The only other woman he had danced with, if she recalled correctly. The woman it was rumoured he thought to make an offer of marriage.

She looked very pretty in a sprigged muslin gown and a lilac Spencer.

'It is, indeed.' He bowed, and the young woman raised a tentative hand in greeting.

He drew the carriage to a halt and, after a glance at those around her and possibly an admonition to keep their distance, she approached.

She glanced up shyly from beneath her flower-decorated bonnet and dipped a curtsey. 'Your Grace.'

'Miss Simon. Good afternoon. Do you know the Countess of Lipsweiger and Upsal?'

'We have not met,' Barbara said when the girl just stared at her. 'It is a pleasure to meet you, Miss Simon.'

'Likewise,' Miss Simon murmured, looking at the ground.

How awkward. 'Perhaps I should alight and allow Miss Simon to take my place,' Barbara said.

Miss Simon cheeks turned scarlet, and she glanced back at her group. 'Oh, I wouldn't dream of it.'

One of the young men who was with the group drew closer. 'I say, sir, that is a bang-up rig.' His eyes were shining as he inspected the equipage. 'And those bays are matched to a T.'

The Duke looked bemused. 'Thank you.'

'Adam, this is His Grace, Duke of Derbridge, of whom I spoke.' Miss Simon said.

The young man flushed. 'Adam Stallton, Your Grace.' He bowed.

The Duke acknowledged this courtesy with a nod.

'Please excuse Adam, Your Grace. He is new in town and he is in alt about everything he sees.'

'Whereas you, Miss Simon, find it all a great bore,' the Duke said in an amused tone.

'Naturally,' Miss Simon said, wide-eyed. 'One does.'

The Duke's expression changed to coolness.

Barbara wanted to shake the foolish girl. Couldn't she see he was teasing and respond in kind? The Duke was going to be bored in her company in less than five minutes if she continued in that manner.

Someone ought to take her in hand and help her see that if she wanted to win the Duke's affection, she needed to have a little more spirit.

The Duke and Miss Simon gazed at each other as if searching for something to say.

Gah. 'You chose a pleasant afternoon for a stroll, Miss Simon,' Barbara said. 'I think spring is finally upon us.'

'Yes, I think so,' Miss Simon agreed.

'And I see you have other members of your family with you.'

'Yes. My mother and I are staying with my aunt. These are my cousins and their friends. Both my cousins are still in the schoolroom so not yet out, but we thought it was such a fine afternoon we would go for a walk.'

'How lucky for us that we should meet.'

Again her face turned pink. No doubt she had been sent out to see if the Duke might be driving out at the fashionable hour.

Too bad he had not been alone.

'If you would like to walk with Miss Simon, Your Grace,' Adam Stallton said, 'I would be happy to drive your carriage.'

'Adam, please,' Miss Simon said sharply, clearly mortified.

Barbara stifled the urge to laugh. While the Duke had perfect control of his horses, they were a spirited pair and would tax the abilities of the best of whips. She could just see the Duke allowing this young man to take the reins. Not.

'I thank you for your kind offer, Mr Stallton, but I believe I will have to forego the pleasure of Miss Simon's company, since the Countess is due home shortly. Perhaps I may call on you tomorrow, Miss Simon?'

'If you wish, Your Grace, only I thought we were to see you at our at home the day after tomorrow?' She could not have sounded less welcoming. What was the matter with the girl?

***

Two mornings later, Xavier stared at the list he had written. Ridiculous. Most of it was common sense. Don't kiss a gentleman in public. Don't visit a bachelor's quarters. Don't wave to a male acquaintance standing in the window of a gentleman's club. Don't attend a boxing match. Don't be seen in a gambling hell. Don't run off with a married man. Don't be taken up for stealing, or any other criminal activity.

What decently brought-up woman would do any of those things?

Not even Gloria, who he considered barely decent, would do such things.

He was tempted to tear the damn list up.

Better the Countess stick to those innocuous little faux pas she had quoted in his carriage a couple of days before.

He certainly did not want to put ideas into her head.

He stilled, recalling all of the things she had been accused of doing since she had arrived in London a few weeks ago.

All the things a debutante would be warned not to do.

Could she have been deliberately flouting the rules? If so, why?

He shook his head. It was beyond belief. No. He had met her aunt, the woman was as totty-headed as anyone he had ever come across.

The mistakes the Countess had made were things that anyone new to London might do without proper guidance.

Look at that young chap with Miss Simon, suggesting he drive Xavier's carriage. No one with a smidgeon of understanding of the rules and protocols would have dared make such an offer.

No. The Countess was being poorly advised by her aunt. And he could hardly blame her for her aunt's failures.

Except maybe with regard to the dress she wore to Almack's. She had admitted to being instructed not to wear red.

Geranium, indeed.

Still, she had looked stunning.

He opened his desk drawer and tucked the list inside. This list idea had been a bad one, no matter what the reason behind her request.

It was best forgotten.

He glanced at the clock on the mantel. Four already? Dash it. Why was he sitting here daydreaming, when he had promised to attend Mrs Simon's at home this afternoon? Fortunately, it was a short walk and not raining, though it was overcast.

He gathered his hat and coat and gave orders for his carriage to pick him up in Mount Street in one hour so he could drive to his club afterward. Fifteen minutes later, he was ushered into Mrs Simon's drawing room.

Surprisingly, the drawing room was crowded.

Mrs Simon hurried to greet him when the butler announced him.

'Your Grace.' She dipped a curtsey. 'How kind of you to attend our small affair.'

Xavier glanced around. Half of London seemed to be there. Miss Simon was surrounded by a group of young people, including the Stallton fellow he had met in the park. Today she wore a pale pink muslin gown with lace at the neck and hem. Ringlets of light blond surrounded her heart-shaped face. She looked sweet. One of the other girls whispered something in her ear and she put her hand over her mouth, clearly hiding a giggle.

He felt a tug of irritation.

He had expected to find very little company given that the Simons were newcomers to town and hardly member of the *haute ton*. He had hoped to have some quiet conversation with Miss Simon. She seemed nervous around him, and he wanted to try to make her comfortable.

Clearly not today.

And the thought of joining the giggling group of adolescents set his teeth on edge.

Perhaps he was mistaken in thinking Miss Simon the perfect bride.

She was very young.

She must have felt his gaze, because she glanced up. And blushed wildly.

'Dowager Countess of Lipsweiger and Upsal, and Miss Lowell,' the butler announced.

Without thinking, Xavier turned from his potential bride to be to take in the Countess as she breezed into the drawing room in a vibrant blue gown with her aunt in tow.

There was a flash of amusement in her dark eyes,

beneath the dramatic cast of her dark eyebrows, and the jaunty small hat on her dark curls.

It was like staring at the sun after looking at the moon.

He stopped himself from crossing the room to greet her. Instead, he forced himself to approach Miss Simon.

As he drew near, the group around her seemed to melt away. Even the brash Mr Stallton took himself off.

It was all a little too obvious to Xavier's taste. Mrs Simon must have had something to do with it. Damn it, he hadn't made any sort of declaration, and he didn't like the idea that he was being jockeyed into position.

Miss Simon gave him a scared glance and he realised he was frowning. Or scowling, as Julian would have it.

'Good afternoon, Miss Simon.'

'Your Grace.' She dipped a low curtsey.

'I hope you find yourself well?' he asked.

'Yes. Oh, yes. Very well. And you?'

'I am well also.'

She sent him a hesitant smile.

Whereas she had seemed at ease with the young people before he arrived, now she looked like a nervous cat, ready to run up the nearest set of curtains if he so much as breathed wrong.

She waved her fan vigorously. 'It is very warm in here, isn't it?'

'I suppose it is.' He had not noticed it as being particularly warm.

'Would you like to take a turn about the garden?' she

said breathlessly. 'The spring bulbs are at their most beautiful at the moment.'

She sounded as if she were repeating a lesson.

A warning prickled across his skin. He glanced casually around the room and saw that her mother was watching them intently.

And Miss Simon was looking anxious.

'Why don't I open a window instead?'

'Oh,' Miss Simon said faintly. 'I do not think Mama would like that.'

'Nonsense. If you are hot, a little bit of air will help enormously.'

'But surely a walk in the garden—'

He strode to the nearest window and pushed up the sash. Not much more than a crack, but enough to let in a bit of a breeze. The curtains wafted gently into the room.

'That is better, isn't it?'

Miss Simon gazed at him for a moment and then her expression changed to relief and she smiled. 'Much better.'

She looked lovely. Happy. As if—

Right then, the Countess joined them. 'Miss Simon. I have you to thank for my presence here today. Your mother said you most particularly asked that she send me an invitation.'

Miss Simon's smile once more became nervous. 'Mother said it was too short notice, but I am very glad you decided to come.' She glanced from Xavier to the Countess and then down at her toes, apparently at a loss for further words. Then said in a rush, 'I was going to show His Grace the garden. All the spring flowers are in bloom. It is quite lovely. Perhaps you would like to see it?'

The Countess looked surprised. 'I am sure I do not wish to intrude upon your tête-à-tête.'

'No, no. His Grace does not wish to see the gardens, do you?'

It seemed Miss Simon was now hoping to speak to the Countess alone. What was the minx playing at?

But she was right, he did not wish to be alone with Miss Simon. He had absolutely no intention of proposing to her today. It was far too early in their acquaintance, and he certainly wasn't going to allow his hand to be forced.

'Miss Simon is right. I have no interest in flowers.'

'I for one adore spring flowers,' the Countess declared. 'It is such a delight to see colour after the drab of winter.'

It was a delight to see her after the drab of debutantes.

Xavier clamped his jaw shut before he said something stupid.

When they stepped through the French doors from the drawing room along a path and into a small walled garden, Barbara gasped at the dazzling array of colour.

Spring bulbs of every variety and hue met her gaze in every direction.

'How beautiful.'

'My uncle loves Holland bulbs. For years, he even tried to grow a black tulip,' Miss Simon said. 'He thought he could make a fortune.'

'I think the Duke will be sorry to have missed this.'

'Well, to be frank, I am glad he did not join us, My Lady. He scares me to death.'

'My dear Miss Simon, the Duke is a gentleman. Nothing to be scared of, I am sure.'

'You seem so at ease in his company, I thought perhaps you might be able to offer me some advice. All Mama says is "be your sweet self."'

'I think your mama is probably right.'

'Countess, I c-can't be myself when he frowns at me so.'

'Please, call me Barbara, if we are to be friends.'

The child looked up at her. 'I am Isabelle.'

'Isabelle, you must be doing something right, because he definitely seems interested in you.'

Isabelle's eyes sheened with unshed tears. 'All I can think is, why me? I always thought Adam and I... We are neighbours, you know, and dreamed of— But now all Mama can think about is being the mother-in-law of a duke and the advantages it will bring to my younger sisters.'

Saddened, Barbara plopped down on the nearby bench. Had not she herself gone through something very similar? Commanded to wed where she had no interest?

Isabelle sat beside her and dabbed at her eyes with her handkerchief, sniffled then blew her nose. 'At first,

I was flattered. I mean, he is a Duke and he is not terrible looking, I suppose.'

Barbara couldn't quite believe her ears. Not terrible looking? In Barbara's eyes, the Duke was one of the most handsome men she had ever met. Compared to the manly and darkly handsome Duke, the Stallton lad, for example, was a weedy, spotty youth. Well, there was no accounting for taste. Poor Derbridge. Poor Isabelle.

'Perhaps if you let him know your heart is engaged elsewhere...'

Isabelle shuddered. 'I couldn't. Mama will murder me. And besides,' she said in awed tones, 'it would not be so bad being a duchess. I mean, to be so rich... If only he would stop frowning at me. I feel as if I am doing something wrong all the time.'

Once again, Barbara felt a stab of pity for Derbridge. And a touch of annoyance at Isabelle too. On the other hand, she could understand why his wealth and position might attract the young and impressionable girl. Not to mention that she had seen no sign from Derbridge that he was looking for a love match.

But if Miss Simon truly cared for someone else, wouldn't that make life unbearable to both of them as time went on? Or perhaps once wed they would simply ignore each other for the most part, once duty was done.

Her heart ached for both of them. She knew what it was like to be pressured by family into doing the 'right thing' to suit others. She also knew how it felt to be stuck in a loveless marriage.

Not that her father loved her more because she had obeyed his wishes.

She took a deep breath. 'I really do not think I am the right person to offer advice. I barely know the Duke.'

Isabelle sighed. 'Mother says this Season is my one chance to make a good match and help my sisters. And that if I don't, I will be left on the shelf like my Aunt Bertha.'

Aunt Lenore had also been left on the shelf, but Barbara had no idea if it was by choice or because no opportunity had presented itself.

'I see. My advice is to give yourself time to get to know the Duke better. Do not be rushed into anything before you are sure.' It was the best she could offer, without seeming to interfere in something that was not her business.

'C-could you mention to him what I said?'

'About the frowning.'

She winced. 'Well, that and well, about you know—my preference for another.'

Her stomach sank. It all sounded a bit melodramatic. 'I do not know. If the opportunity arises, perhaps.'

Miss Simon beamed. 'Oh, thank you. I knew you would help me.'

'I—'

'There you are!' The plump figure of Mrs Simon came through the gate.

'I have been searching everywhere for you. Isabelle.'

'I was about to return to the house,' Isabelle said quickly, jumping up.

Her mother nodded briskly. 'People are leaving. You need to come and bid them farewell.'

'Yes, Mama.' The pair hurried off.

Barbara sauntered along the path between the tulip beds, yellow on one side and pink on the other, trying to imagine telling the Duke not to frown at his intended.

'Countess.'

Startled, she turned.

Derbridge? Here? After he had already refused a walk in the garden with Miss Simon?

The sunlight that made the flower colours so vivid made his hair gleam with hidden gold highlights and made him look taller and more substantial than ever.

'Your aunt asked me to seek you out. She is waiting to leave.'

Barbara gritted her teeth at her aunt's obvious ploy to throw her and the Duke together. Not only was it unconscionable, given his interest in Miss Simon, it was absurd. The Duke barely tolerated her for the most part.

'I was admiring the flowers. They are beautiful, are they not?'

He opened his mouth then closed it again.

How odd when he usually said whatever was on his mind. 'You do not agree?'

A wry smile twisted his lips. 'I was going to say they are not nigh as beautiful as you, but then I prefer hearty roses to these pallid, short-lived *monocotyledons*.'

The breath left her body in a rush. Her mind whirled, leaving her speechless. 'I cannot tell if that is a compliment or not,' she said, finally, laughing lightly.

He gave her a quizzical look. 'I believe I was stating a fact.'

Her heart gave an odd little tumble, which was not what she wanted. The man was practically engaged. 'Well, it seems I must leave beauty behind and return to my aunt.'

'About this list we discussed.'

'Ah, yes.' Her ticket to freedom. 'Do you have it?'

'I have decided against the wisdom of providing such a list.'

'Why?'

'Because upon reflection, anyone with a smidgeon of common sense would not commit the sort of social solecism that would be on such a list, and I do not think you are a lackwit.'

She raised an eyebrow. 'Another compliment? You are overflowing with them today.'

A brief smile touched his lips. How could Isabelle think him only tolerably handsome when faced with such a boyishly charming smile, however fleeting? 'I cannot imagine you intend to turn to a life of crime, or to start practising blood sports in public, or to commit adultery with a married man.'

'Unlikely.' She huffed out a breath at his examples. 'No, those are not things I might mistakenly do.'

'You see?'

'Well, it seems I am safe, then. I shall enjoy all that London has to offer with impunity.'

His famous frowned returned. She found it intriguing rather than frightening. She wanted to know what he was thinking. Had he realised he had just given her a carte blanche that was not at all a good idea?

On the other hand, he had no idea why she had requested the list in the first place. And since speaking with him about it, she had discovered one or two very wicked things a lady might do to ruin her reputation, which happily did not involve the ruin of anyone else.

He pursed his lips. 'I wanted to discuss this further, but unfortunately I have another of these dashed affairs to attend.'

'Two in one afternoon. Your secretary is keeping you busy.'

'Unfortunately, he had accepted the other before I received the invitation to this one.'

They walked along the path to the gate.

'You could have cancelled the first one, I assume?'

'It was from an old friend of my mother's. She is bringing her daughter out this Season and I had promised I would attend.'

How interesting to learn know he would not break a promise for convenience's sake.

He really was a stickler for the rules and, annoyingly, she thought better of him because of it.

They parted at the French doors into the house and he went to take his leave of his hostess.

Barbara found her aunt in conversation with a couple of her friends in an antechamber adjoining the drawing room.

'Are you ready to depart, dear?' her aunt asked.

'I am.'

They searched out their hostess and Isabelle.

Isabelle gave her a speaking look and leaned forward. 'If you ask him, will you let me know what he says?'

Inwardly, Barbara groaned. How on earth would she broach such a topic as that with the Duke?

Chapter Eight

Xavier perused the note from the tenant who had rented the small cottage in Chelsea that he and Perry had discussed. She thanked him for his kindnesses over the years and regretted that she could not renew her lease, but she intended to move in with family. She had been a nice old dear and he had often called in on her on his way to town to drop off the odd basket of apples or potatoes.

It was a shame she had left. It was difficult to find good tenants. With a sigh, he added the matter to the list of things to discuss with his man of business.

His butler scratched at the door and entered with a letter on a silver tray. 'Hand delivered, Your Grace. The footman said it was urgent.'

It was from Mrs Simon, cancelling his engagement to drive Miss Simon in the park the next day. Apparently, Miss Simon had contracted measles from her younger brother, who had visited them the previous week. The family would be retiring to their home in Derbyshire until Miss Simon was well again. Mrs Simon hoped the

Duke would not contract the disease and looked forward to renewing their acquaintance later in the Season.

Measles.

Had he had them?

He was pretty sure he recalled having spots at some point or other. Yes. He was positive, now he thought about it. He had measles when he was eight.

Poor Miss Simon. And now it seemed any prospect of an engagement, should that be his decision, would of necessity be delayed.

A feeling of lightness buoyed his spirits. As if some burden had been lifted from his shoulders. A sense of reprieve.

A disturbing response to a postponement of his plans.

He straightened his shoulders. He had decided it was time he settled down and he could procrastinate no longer. And so it would be. Miss Simon would return in two or three weeks and things would move forward.

Swiftly, he crafted a note to Mrs Simon expressing his regret and hoping for a speedy recovery for her daughter.

In the absence of Perry, who had gone on leave to visit his family, he would have to visit the florist himself to arrange for a bouquet of flowers to be sent to the afflicted damsel.

What of the Countess? Had she been informed? She had been in pretty close quarters with the young woman at the Simons' open house the other day.

Mrs Simon's note gave no indication that she had informed anyone else.

He penned a second note advising the Countess of Miss Simon's illness. It looked impersonal, clinical, without emotion and rather officious.

Perhaps it would be preferable to deliver the information in person, during a casual conversation. He glanced at the clock. Far too early for morning calls.

He would go to his club and visit the Countess a little later, before she had a chance to set out on morning calls of her own, but not so early as to signal over-eagerness on his part.

Or perhaps he should simply assume Mrs Simon would have communicated with the Countess.

Damnation! He was dithering like a schoolboy hoping to catch a glimpse of the Latin master's wife.

He called for his coat and hat. He needed some sensible male conversation about politics or farming or... anything.

On his way, he dropped in at the nearest florist, picked out a variety of hothouse flowers, wrote a suitable card to Miss Simon and stepped out into the street.

The day was cooler than it should be for this time of year, and black clouds threatened yet another downpour. The wind tugged at his hat forcing him to keep a hand on it as he strode down St James's Street.

For a moment, he refused to believe what his eyes told him was true. A woman he recognised instantly as the Countess, standing in front of Boodle's, waving. Did she not realise where she was?

He hurried to her side. 'My Lady.' He sounded breathless.

She turned gazed at him with an expression of surprise. 'Your Grace. Imagine meeting you here.'

He stepped between her and the view from Boodle's windows. 'Imagine,' he said dryly. 'I am on my way to my club. More to the point, what are you doing? This is St James's. You ought not to be here.'

'My brother-in-law, Charles, is in there. I need to speak with him urgently and the porter refused to take a message. What else was I to do?'

He gazed at her in astonishment. 'Ladies do not visit gentlemen's clubs.' He could not help sounding scandalised.

'This is an emergency. I went to his lodgings first, but they said he had come here.'

She went to a bachelor's lodgings? Here? In St James's? If she had been seen…her reputation would never recover.

A vision of her calling at his house flashed across his mind. He imagined himself pulling her inside his front door and…kissing her. Hard.

His body heated at the thought. Damn it all. What was he thinking? Furious with his own lack of control, he glared at her. 'Great heavens, woman, do you have no sense? Do you not care about your reputation?'

Her gaze widened in astonishment, but somehow, he had the sense of amusement lurking in the depths of her eyes. 'Of course I do.'

'It doesn't seem like it.'

'Can you give a message to the Count for me?'

'First let us leave here. Then we will discuss next steps.'

He took her by the arm and drew her back the way he had come.

She tugged her arm free. 'You cannot tell me what to do.'

'For goodness' sake, don't be a little fool.' He caught her arm again. 'Walk with me.' This time she did not pull away. 'It wouldn't be so bad if you had brought a maid or a footman. Let us hope no one saw you.'

'Someone did,' she said cheerfully. 'A man waved back. I was hoping he would come outside to ask me what I wanted.'

Devil take it. 'Didn't your aunt tell you that St James's is out of bounds for any woman of good breeding?'

They turned onto Piccadilly. A man with a tray of pies balanced on his head dodged around them.

'I really do not see why you are so annoyed,' she said, waving off a lass selling lavender. 'I simply needed to speak to my relative. And besides, you said that as long as I did not commit a crime or run off with a married man, I need not worry.'

He held on to his temper. 'Clearly, I was wrong to think you had a smidgeon of common sense. If you were recognised, you might as well leave town right now. Any woman sighted on St James's will be seen as beyond the pale of good Society. No hostess will accept your presence.'

An odd expression he could not read passed across her face. 'Are you sure?'

'Positive. As a chaperone, your aunt is worse than useless.'

'Do not say such things.' For once she sounded truly concerned. 'You must not blame Aunt Lenore. I will not have it. I am at fault for my own mistakes.'

He glanced around. What the devil was he to do? 'Walk with me in the park where we can speak freely.'

'Do you think you should? Won't talking to me tarnish your reputation also?' She threw the words at him like a challenge.

He grimaced. 'Unlikely.'

'Because you are a duke.'

He nodded. It wasn't fair, but there it was.

They strolled along the Queen's Walk in Green Park. He looked about him for somewhere they could talk without the chance of being overheard. He guided her across the lawn to a large oak tree with branches that dipped low, providing a bit of a screen. It wasn't ideal and they could not stay here long.

'I think you are making a great fuss about nothing,' she said dismissively, gazing up into the branches above her head.

His ire rose once more. 'Listen to me, you little fool, you are one whisper away from ruin. Do you not understand this?'

She backed up until the trunk halted her progress, clearly surprised by his anger.

She frowned at him. 'What does it matter to you?'

What indeed? It shouldn't matter at all, but for some

reason it did. 'You asked me for advice. Now I am giving it.'

'Then what are you suggesting?'

'It all depends on whether or not you were recognised.' He removed his hat and ran a hand through his hair. 'Why the devil would anyone think going to a gentleman's club would not be a problem?'

Defiance filled her gaze. A dare. A challenge. 'In Paris a lady is welcome everywhere.'

He stepped closer, forcing her to raise her gaze to his face, reminding her that for all that she was tall, he was taller. Larger.

Her soft lips parted on a breath. Her eyelids dropped a fraction. Her chest rose and fell with short sharp breaths.

His heart pounded in his chest. His blood, a moment before warm with anger, now ran like fire through his veins. Desire.

Only by ironclad will did he restrain from unbearable temptation.

'I—'

She raised her palm, face out as if holding him at bay. He took a breath.

Her hand pressed against his chest, then slid upwards, around his nape, and she went up on tiptoes and pressed her mouth to his.

Luscious, soft lips moving slowly.

He pulled her close, responding to her touch in a blinding instant, ravishing her mouth, stroking her back, pulling her close and hard against his body.

For a moment his mind was blank, but his body was alive as it had never been before. Out of control.

He pulled back.

Gasping, they stared at each other.

Her fingertips touch her full soft lips. 'Oh,' she whispered. 'My word.'

Ashamed, that he had let his desire control him, he glanced down at his hat lying on the grass at his feet. He must have dropped it.

Barbara's heart pounded so hard she could scarcely breathe. She wanted to twirl, to laugh, to skip. All she could actually manage, given the trembling in her legs, was to brace herself against the rough bark of the tree trunk behind her.

She had never felt quite so giddy.

The Duke, on the other hand, looked positively appalled.

Shocked from his head to his toes.

But he had kissed her back. Most definitely he had, and with unmistakable ardour.

He bent and picked up his hat.

When he straightened, he stared at it as if he had never seen it before, turning it by the brim. Finally, he looked at her with a shamefaced expression. 'I beg your pardon.'

Not what she had expected.

She wasn't sure what she had expected him to say, but it was not that. After all, she had kissed him.

Much to his dismay, apparently. Well, if he didn't

like it, it was his own fault. He should not keep interfering in her plans.

Perhaps now he would stay out of her business.

She lifted her chin, under that steady and uncomfortable stare. 'I still need to get word to my brother-in-law, you know.'

He grimaced. 'I will escort you home and then seek him out to give him your message. I will also do my best to scotch any rumours about your presence outside Boodle's, should anyone mention it. I do wish, however, that you had brought your maid or a footman.'

She stifled the urge to smile. 'I shall do so next time.'

'There will not be a next time,' he said repressively. 'It might be possible to plead innocence the first time, but not a second time.'

Clearly, he was prepared to give her the benefit of the doubt, this time, but hopefully his forbearance would not last very long. 'Very well.' She tried to look meek and accepting.

His glare said she had not succeeded.

He held out his arm and walked her back to her residence.

It was odd how easily they walked side by side, their steps in perfect harmony. Odd how neither of them felt the need for polite conversation.

Odd how delicious the kiss had been.

Oh, she had not intended to think about their kiss. That had been a moment of madness. And he had clearly disapproved of her forwardness.

Her heart contracted, as if squeezed. An unpleasant, painful feeling.

Why on earth would she care if he found her improper? Indeed, that would suit her purpose very well. Would it not?

A man of his stature only had to give her the cut direct and she would be ruined. *Persona non grata.* Beyond the pale for ever. Let Father try to marry her off then.

Now was not the time to let her attraction to a man interfere with her plans to avoid being forced into yet another unpleasant marriage.

Indeed, the Duke would be the perfect foil for those plans, if he wasn't about to become engaged to Miss Simons.

She recalled her promise to her friend.

How would one approach such a delicate matter? Not on the street, that was certain. Nor in any public place. After all, the information would come as a shock. Who knew how he might react.

Anger. Disappointment. Heartbreak?

Was it possible that his heart was engaged? It did not seem so, when seeing them together. He seemed more like an uncle than a besotted suitor.

Perhaps that was because he was good at hiding his true feelings.

'Do you think love is important in a marriage?' she asked. Shocked at the baldness of her question, she stumbled slightly.

Catching her up, he glanced down at her with his

usual frown. 'I think there should be mutual liking, certainly.' His mouth tightened. 'I am not sure love enters into it. One's duty to one's family must come first.'

'At the expense of one's heart?'

'Romantic love is highly overrated. It leads to all kinds of erratic behaviour. Take Caro Lamb, for example. A disaster. All brought about by overheated imagination and nonsense.'

Anger was a hard lump in her throat. 'You assume one's family has one's best interests at heart.'

'I would assume they have the family's best interests at heart.'

'And the individual's best interests mean nothing?'

'In time, no doubt the family's interests and the individual's will coincide.'

The few warm feelings she had felt towards him dissipated. He understood nothing about the misery an arranged marriage could impose on a woman. Why would he? He was a man.

And he did not deserve such a sweet young woman as Miss Simon. She certainly did not deserve to be married to a man who did not have a heart.

'What if...what if one of the pair has fallen in love with someone else? Would the marriage not be untenable for both?'

'Are you saying you have fallen in love with someone unsuitable?'

Ugh. How obtuse. But then she was rather beating about the bush. 'I am not talking about me, but rather about a friend.'

'A friend. I see.' He sounded as if he did not believe her. 'While I do not think love is a prerequisite for a good marriage, I do believe a man has a right to expect fidelity in his wife.'

But a woman had no right to expect the same in a husband. No doubt as soon as *he* was wed, he would be off seeking a mistress, just like Helmut.

'I am sure Miss Simon will do her best to meet your exacting standards. Perhaps if you did not frown at her quite so much, she might be a bit more comfortable.'

He stopped and turned to face her. 'Are you saying Miss Simon is in love with someone else?'

He'd honed in on the real import of her words without difficulty. She hesitated. This really was not for her to say, but—'I think she believes her heart is engaged elsewhere, though it is quite possibly only puppy love and could easily be overcome. Her family considers you the better match.'

'They would.' His tone was dry. 'In any case, I have made no commitments to Miss Simon, so she is free to do as she pleases.'

The chill in his voice sent a shiver down her spine. Surely he could not be hurt by her revelation?

'I am sorry to be the bearer of bad news.'

'Did she ask you to reveal this piece of information?'

'She asked for my help. But she is terrified of upsetting her family.'

He sighed. 'Then I see I shall have to carefully withdraw from the lists. I would prefer you to say nothing to her about our conversation today. I think perhaps she does not have the wit to carry off such a delicate matter.'

Surprised, she stared at him. She had half expected him to be angry and dismissive of the idea of a rival. Perhaps even hurt or...affected somehow.

The man really did not have a heart. Or if he did, it was frozen beneath the weight of honour and duty.

The thought caused her an unexpected pain in the region of her heart.

They arrived at her front door. 'I will keep my counsel,' she said, though Miss Simon must surely guess Barbara had spoken with him. 'And thank you for your assistance this morning. I do hope you can get my message to the Count.'

He blinked, clearly noticing the change in her demeanour.

'I will do my best.'

'Shall I see you at the Andersons' drum in Chelsea tomorrow?'

'Chelsea?' He frowned. 'I do not recall if I received an invitation, but if I accepted, I shall attend.'

Always so dutiful. She felt a surge of pity. The poor man needed to have some fun. The question was, could he be lured out of his armour for long enough to enjoy himself?

And might she be the woman to help him do so? Their kiss hinted that she might very well be and if so, now he would no longer be pursuing Miss Simon, it would help her own plans along very nicely.

Having seen her to the door, the Duke bowed and strolled off down the street.

Inside, Barbara handed her outer raiment to the footman who opened the door and found her aunt in the drawing room embroidery hoop in hand.

'Who was that with you?' her aunt asked, trying to look as if she hadn't picked up her embroidery a second before Barbara arrived.

'You saw it was the Duke.'

Her aunt cast the embroidery aside. 'Where did you meet him? What did he say?'

'Um... He walked me home from Green Park.'

Her aunt's eyes grew round. 'How very kind of him.'

'Supremely.'

'Did you tell him about Miss Simon's illness?'

'He already knew. Her mother wrote to him before she left London.'

'Oh.' Lenore picked up the fabric she'd been working on and put it down again. 'Was he terribly upset?'

'Not particularly. He did send her flowers, I gather.'

'Oh.'

'What are you thinking, Aunt?'

'It occurs to me that some men do not like a woman who is ill all the time.'

'Are you saying I should use the opportunity to engage his attention?'

'Well, when you put it like that, you make it sound rather scheming, which I cannot like, but something of the sort.' She patted at her perfectly coifed hair. 'I heard from your father this morning.' She was trying to sound casual and failing. 'He will be with us in two weeks' time.'

Two weeks? That was not a great deal of time in which to get herself banished from Society. 'I wonder why he did not write to me?'

'He said he was in a hurry, on urgent business, but would write more later.'

He was always on urgent business, and Barbara wasn't going to hold her breath waiting for a letter that would never come.

'I shall look forward to it. By the way, the Count of Lipsweiger and Upsal will probably call on us later today. I wish to speak with him.'

Her aunt gave her a sharp look. 'There is something I do not like about that young gentleman.'

'Really?'

'There is something calculating in his eyes.'

Her aunt was such a bad judge of character. She thought the cold-hearted Duke was wonderful and took exception to a man who had always been kind to Barbara. 'Nonsense. He is a good friend as well as my brother-in-law, and I hope you will treat him as such.'

'I am not so rag-mannered as to treat him any other way, my dear.' She popped to her feet. 'I shall ring for tea and you will tell me all about your conversation with Derbridge.'

Not a chance. Or about her plans for the cold-hearted Duke.

A scandalous liaison revealed at some important public event, preferably with a member of the royal family present, the recently married Princess Charlotte for example, would suit her purposes very nicely.

Or since the newlyweds were rarely in town, perhaps an event attended by the Prince Regent. There was bound to be something on the royal calendar.

Xavier strolled around the vacant cottage. It had been rented out furnished to his last tenant and, as he had expected, everything was in order. It could be rented out again immediately.

Hopefully the next tenant would be as satisfactory as the last.

Normally his man of business would have inspected the place before advertising it for lease, but Xavier had decided to visit it on the way to the Anderson event, since the cottage lay nearby their house.

When he'd checked his diary, it was clear he had not accepted the Anderson's invitation, but in the absence of his secretary, nor had he declined.

While they would not be expecting him, he doubted they would turn him away even though he knew them only vaguely. As he recalled, they fancied themselves to be intellectuals, friends to artists and so forth. Their circle consisted of a lot of painters, sculptors, writers of bad poetry and the like. People whose morals, in his view, left much to be desired, if only half of the rumours about them were true.

The sort of people Great-Uncle Tom would mutter about as *not good ton.*

He locked up the cottage and returned to his phaeton. The night was unusually warm given how bad the weather had been this summer and, since the moon was full, he had decided to drive himself.

At the point where the lane joined the main road, he hesitated. Did he really want to go to this party? Was he really unable to resist the lure of this woman?

Devil take it. He had already made this decision. He was going.

He turned left, passing through the village of Chelsea and turning into the drive of the Anderson mansion.

The windows at the front of the house were ablaze with the light of candles, and several carriages were parked along the edge of the driveway.

He could hear the sounds of music and chatter as he pulled up. It seemed the ball was not inside the house but outdoors.

After leaving his equipage with a groom, he walked around the side of the house rather than entering by way of the front door. The terrace and the garden beyond were lit by lanterns hanging from trees and posts. Couples were waltzing on the flagstones to the music of an orchestra who were inside the house beyond the open French windows, while groups of people chatted and mingled on the lawn.

It reminded him of Vauxhall without all the hoopla.

A waiter approached him with a tray and he helped himself to a flute of champagne. Very good champagne.

'Your Grace?' A stout balding gentleman approached him, beaming. 'Anderson, at your service.' He bowed deeply. 'How good of you to come. My wife will be delighted.'

No doubt. 'Thank you for your invitation. I regret I did not reply. My secretary is away on family business at the moment.'

'Oh, no need to worry about that, Your Grace. You are always welcome.'

Xavier stifled a yawn. It would be more interesting if just once someone told him to leave. 'Thank you.'

'Let me introduce you to some of our guests. Some are inside dancing, but most are out here in the garden where it is cooler.'

Xavier glanced around. 'No need. I believe I know most people here.'

'Well. I do not believe you have met my wife.' Anderson led him to a dark-haired woman as thin as Anderson was corpulent. 'My dear, His Grace the Duke of Derbridge is here.'

The woman spun around. She curtseyed deeply, clearly trying to hide her surprise. 'Your Grace. What an honour.'

'You have a fine night for a party,' he said.

Her face lit up. 'To be honest, we did not plan to be outdoors. It was only at the last minute this afternoon, when I realised how warm it was, that I asked our butler to see if he could put up some lights. He has worked wonders, I must say.'

'Indeed he has.'

Xavier could not stop himself from looking around.

Trying to see if the woman he had been thinking of all day was here.

'He will be delighted by your compliment, Your Grace.'

What? Who? Oh, yes. The butler. 'Good.' He heard a distant splash. 'Your property runs down to the river?'

'It does. Some of the young people are punting. I am a little concerned about how safe it is in the dark, but you know young people. I should introduce you to our daughter. She can take you down there if you wish.' She scanned the lawn. 'Now where has she gone? She was here a moment ago. I will find her for you.'

Exactly what he needed. An introduction to another young female in search of a titled husband.

'Do not trouble yourself. I will find my own way.' He bowed and wandered off, aware that Mrs Anderson would no doubt scurry off to find the missing daughter to announce the news of his miraculous appearance.

He should not have come.

That was the trouble with those who lived at the edge of the *ton*. They didn't understand that a Duke was not a prize stallion waiting to be put to the stud at their convenience.

Which was maybe what made the Countess so interesting. She made no effort to attract his attention. In fact, quite the opposite.

The idea was refreshing.

As he walked down the slope towards where he assumed he would find the river, the number of lanterns decreased until only one small string hanging from posts lit the way. He could see nothing either side of the path except a cluster of lights in the direction of the river.

As he drew closer, he could see the shape of the boat house, a few people sitting on benches on a dock, or milling about, and a couple of rowboats on the water near the dock.

No sign of the Countess, but something inside him said he would find her here, where people were doing risky things, like taking a boat out on the water with only the moon to light their way.

'Good Lord, Derbridge. I didn't expect to see you here.'

'Julian, old fellow. Nor I you.'

They shook hands.

Julian introduced him to the people on the dock, none of whom he recognised, except the Countess's brother-in-law.

'I did not see you as someone who would enjoy this sort of romp,' the Count of Lipsweiger and Upsal said. His teeth flashed white in the lantern light.

'Nor I,' Julian murmured.

Xavier shrugged. 'I like to surprise. Is that your sister-in-law on the boat?' he asked.

The Count peered out into the darkness of the river. 'No. She was dancing the last time I saw her.' He leaned closer to Xavier, lowering his voice. 'May I offer a word of advice?'

'About what?'

The Count glanced at Julian who took the hint and turned away to speak to one of the women.

The Count pursed his lips. 'It is not my place, of course.'

The back of Xavier's neck prickled strangely. There was something in the man's tone that spoke of secrets. Xavier gave him a hard stare but saw only a blandness in his expression. 'Speak up. I don't bite.'

'I suggest you beware of the Countess, that is all.'

'Because?' Xavier said.

The Count put up a hand. 'Well, two husbands, two deaths... Enough to make any man wary, surely. But no doubt all a terrible coincidence.'

What the devil! Was he implying there was some truth to the Countess's black widow title?

'Ah, excuse me. Here are my friends. They will drown if they are not careful.' He laughed lightly and moved off to assist a couple trying to alight from a skiff.

Frowning, Xavier gazed after him. He had no need of anyone's advice. He was nothing if he was not careful. But the warning seemed strange coming from a relative the Countess seemed to like and trust. Perhaps the man desired her for himself.

An odd pang twisted in his chest. Jealousy? When did he ever have cause to be jealous of any man?

'All is well?' Julian asked, joining him again, also watching the Count steady the skiff.

'Of course,' Xavier said. 'Why would it not be?'

'You have a rather martial light in your eye, that is all. As if you want to give someone a good drubbing.'

Xavier shook off his dark thoughts. And clapped his friend on the shoulder with a chuckle. 'Nonsense.'

He didn't give a fig what the Count thought. He was perfectly capable of looking after himself.

A breathless young woman joined them on the dock. 'Papa is going to unveil the sculpture for the bidding. He wants everyone to return to the ball room.'

Xavier sighed. It was only when he had read the invitation that he had realised that the main purpose for the gathering was to auction off a sculpture in support of a new art gallery.

No doubt it would be the work of some unknown artist. And no doubt he would be expected to win the bidding.

He really did not like these sorts of public displays of giving. He preferred private donations to causes he deemed worthy.

Nevertheless he trailed the group making its way back to the house.

A shadow caught his attention. A person off to the side of the path, at the edge of the light.

His throat dried in an instant. He had no trouble recognising the woman. By her shape? By her scent? He wasn't sure.

He moved to confront her. 'Good evening, Countess.'

'Duke. I heard you had arrived and had made your way down here.'

She had intentionally come to find him? His heart picked up speed. 'I gather our host requests our presence in the ballroom.'

'You go. It is too hot in there. I want to look at the stars and cool off.'

Did she never do anything in a normal civilised way?

'Please go,' she said. 'I am perfectly content by myself.'

He wasn't perfectly content to leave her alone in the dark.

'I will walk with you.'

'If you must.'

Hardly welcoming. He took her arm and walked her down the slope.

The little boats that had been out on the water were now tied neatly to the empty dock.

The Thames drifted by slowly on its way to the city, gently lapping against the bank.

She sat on one of the benches and looked up at the sky. 'Too many trees to see the stars,' she said.

He sat beside her and looked up. Only the moon was visible between the branches. 'You would likely get a better view out on the river.'

She glanced at the boats. 'Yes. You are right. If I knew how to row…'

'Would you like to…'

They spoke at the same time. They laughed. It sounded awkward.

'I can be your oarsman,' he said. 'If you wish.'

Like some sort of eager youth, he held his breath.

Chapter Nine

When someone mentioned that the Duke had been seen arriving at the party, a little spurt of excitement had left Barbara feeling breathless.

There was no doubt about the attraction between them. Their kiss beneath the tree in the park had been ample proof. But he was so controlled, so aloof, she wasn't sure he wanted to acknowledge it.

There was only one way to find out.

So she had followed the path down to the water.

And now he was offering to take her for a boat ride.

The river reflected the moon as a silver stripe across the sluggish flow. Why not?

She rose from the bench. 'Indeed, let us look at the stars.' Each of the boats had been furnished with cushions and he selected one. He held her hand as she stepped aboard. She arranged herself in the bow, resting her back against the pillows. It was surprisingly comfortable.

He unhooked the rope from its fastening and lithely stepped over the gunnel. He made it look easy. He picked up the pole and set them in motion moving into the middle of the river.

'You have done this before,' she said, trailing a hand over the side. The water was chilly. One would not wish to fall in.

'I used to row when I was at university.'

'Oxford or Cambridge?'

'Oxford.' For some reason he sounded surprised that she did not know. No doubt all the ladies of his acquaintance studied Debrett's and knew everything about him. 'All the Melville men attend Oxford.'

'What about the women? Where do they go?'

The boat wobbled a fraction. 'I have no idea. I presume they have a governess.'

Typical male. No interest in the education of the females of his family. 'I see.'

'There have only been sons for the past two generations.' The defensive note in his voice was surprising.

She lay back on her cushion and gazed upwards. 'I can see the plough perfectly, and Ursa Major.'

'You know your stars. Are you some sort of bluestocking?'

She chuckled, an intentionally low and throaty noise. 'Do I seem like a bluestocking?'

'Pettigrew says bluestockings are women who wear unattractive clothes and spectacles and quote Mary Wollstonecraft every five minutes. He advised me to avoid them like the plague. So no. You do not seem like a bluestocking.'

'If you think so little of women who have brains, it is

no wonder—' Insulting him was not what she wanted to do.

'No wonder what?'

'It doesn't matter. Come, sit beside me.' She slid over a few inches. 'The evening is clear and the stars particularly fine.'

He hesitated. He must have guessed she had been about to say something derogatory. Blast.

She heard him sigh. Then he set down his pole, eased in beside her and lay back.

'That wasn't very kind of me, was it?' he said. 'To repeat such nonsense about bluestockings.'

Surprised, she pushed up on one elbow and looked down on him. 'No. Not very kind. And also patently false. While I do not count myself as a bluestocking, I do count myself as reasonably intelligent and well-educated. I cannot see why men only want empty-headed widgeons for wives.'

He reached up and tucked a strand of hair that had fallen forward behind her ear. 'You are certainly not that, Countess.'

'But that is what the male half of society wants me to be, so they can decide my future.' Her father did. Both of her husbands had. How many times had she been told not to worry her pretty little head about something that had concerned her? Something important. Something for which she had a solution. But would they listen to her ideas? Certainly not.

'What sort of future is it that you would like?' he

asked. No one had ever asked her such a question before.

Surprised and pleased, she sank back down into the cushions. 'Freedom to choose.'

'To choose what?'

He sounded so puzzled. He simply had no idea.

'Everything.'

'No one has freedom in everything.'

'Men have the freedom. They just do not use it.'

'No. You are wrong. If people went about willy nilly doing whatever they pleased there would be chaos.'

'Why?'

'Because—'

'You do not believe people would choose to do the right thing?'

'I know they wouldn't.' He rolled over on his side and gazed down into her face, blotting out her view of the stars.

His face was shadowed and she could not see his expression. She could feel the warmth of his body along her side and the heat of his breath on her face, her lips, her... She reached up and pulled his head down. Their lips touched lightly, then fiercely.

His kiss was heavenly.

His arm went around her back, his knee pressed between her thighs.

She groaned and kissed him back with ferocity.

On a gasp, he pulled away. 'Do you see?' he said hoarsely. 'People left to their own devices do not do the right thing.'

'This is not the right thing?'

'What? Of course not. A gentleman is not supposed to take advantage of a lady, no matter the circumstances.'

'Pish posh. Are you telling me you are not enjoying this?'

'Enjoyment does not make it right,' he said stiffly, pulling away.

'It doesn't necessarily make it wrong. Do you never do anything for the pleasure of it?'

He sat up with a jerk. The boat rocked wildly.

'Madam, were I to do what I badly want to do for the pleasure of it right now, I would be bedding you in the bottom of a very unstable craft.'

'Then why don't you?'

She couldn't put it any clearer than that, could she?

'If you think to trap me into a marriage—'

She laughed out loud. 'I wouldn't marry you if you were the last man on earth. I have no wish to marry anyone. But that does not mean I do not want to have the pleasure of a man in my bed from time to time.'

'I think your family might have to say something about that.' He sounded utterly shocked.

'My family might try. But no one can force me or you to marry if we do not wish it. Can they?'

'By law they cannot. But Society—'

'Society always blames the woman in such matters. So why would you care?'

'I am not a blackguard, madam.'

'I think you do protest too much.'

'I think you are far too bold to be considered a lady and certainly not proper wife material for a man in my position.'

Startled by his brusque honesty, she stared at him speechless and wide-eyed.

He grimaced. 'Yet I find myself deeply attracted to you. I desire you more than I have ever desired any other woman. I—' He took a deep breath. 'I beg your pardon. That was wholly uncalled for.'

Hardly. Not after the way she had goaded him. And his admission pleased her far more than she had expected. 'At least you are being honest for a change. I desire you too. Unfortunately, this little boat is far too small for us to see our desires to fruition. Perhaps I should pop round to your townhouse tomorrow afternoon?'

'Are you really so shameless?'

This was uphill work. Given his ardour a moment ago, if he was not tempted now, he never would be. He was as passionless as a potato, or a lump of coal, or a dead stick.

Perhaps she needed to look elsewhere to make a scandalous liaison.

He leaned over, nothing more than a large shadow, blotting out the moon and the stars. Then his mouth found hers and he kissed her.

Hard.

Passionately.

Feverishly.

She flung her arms around his neck and pulled him

close, wanting to feel the weight of him on her body. Delving into the recesses of his mouth with her tongue.

Inviting him to do the same to her. He tasted her lips, stroked her tongue with his. Delicious.

She arched into him.

He groaned and eased his body over hers, pressing one knee between her thighs. Her skirts hampered his intent and he reached down and—

The boat bumped something and rocked madly.

He cursed and sat up.

'What is it?' she asked.

He chuckled ruefully. 'We hit the bank.'

She could see now they were back beneath the trees.

She let go a sigh. Such an amazing kiss. She had never experienced anything like it.

She reached up for him.

He caught her hand in his. 'Someone might see us.'

'I don't care.' She was missing the feel of him against her body too much to give a damn. Her blood was racing hot through her veins.

'I do,' he murmured softly, leaning down and touching his lips briefly to hers.

'Ugh, always caring about what others think.' She sat up.

'Hush. I have an idea.'

He rose and picked up the pole and pushed them off.

At first, she assumed he was heading back to the dock, but as the lamplights receded she realised they were heading downstream.

'Where are we going?' she whispered.
'You will see.'

Xavier pushed hard on the pole. The little boat surged along on the current. He could not believe he was actually doing this.

How could she be so relaxed? His blood ran hot and his body hardened once more at the sight of the sensual woman sprawled on the cushions in front of him.

'I hope you know where you are going, Your Grace,' she said with a mischievous laugh that tugged at something inside him. Like a call to some wildness.

Recklessness struggling to be free.

'Xavier, please, Countess,' he said.

'Then you may call me Barbara,' she said softly.

'I know exactly where I am going, Barbara.' At least he was pretty sure he would recognise the little landing stage at the bottom of the garden of the cottage he had visited earlier.

There could not be too many places along the bank with a willow tree hanging over the water and with a *to let* sign nailed to it.

If he recalled correctly, there were about eight houses along the river between the cottage and the Andersons' house.

The moon picked up a willow trailing fronds into the water. He pushed the boat towards it and was pleased to see the sign he had nailed up barely an hour or so previously.

'Here we are.' He tied up to the little platform.

'Where is "here"?' she asked, taking his hand and coming easily to her feet despite the rocking of the boat.

He helped her up onto the rather decrepit landing stage. He wished now he had organised its repair, but his previous tenant had not been interested in boating.

'A cottage I own.'

'Oh? Who lives here?'

He pointed to the sign. 'No one. It is vacant.'

Would she balk at this bold move? He was beginning to think he had lost his mind.

'How lovely.' She threw her arms around his neck. 'What a clever duke you are.'

The rickety platform shifted beneath their feet.

'Oops,' she said, clutching at him and laughing.

He laughed too, like an idiot boy on an adventure. An illicit adventure.

He helped her up the bank. It was damnably dark in this garden. Fortunately, the cottage was a good deal closer to the river than the Anderson mansion. He held her hand and they followed the pale moonlit shapes of the flagstone path leading to the terrace.

'Wait here,' he whispered. Why he was whispering he wasn't sure, but it felt as if speaking too loudly might break the spell.

Swiftly, he made his way around to the front of the house by way of the side alley.

He banged his knee against some sort of structure.

Right. The back gate. He swallowed a curse and slowed down. She wasn't going anywhere.

He felt his way along the wall to the front door and opened it.

The entrance hall was pitch-black, but he had no trouble locating the lamp he'd snuffed out earlier and relighting it.

Now able to see his way clearly, he soon had the French doors unlocked and left the lamp on a table while he went outside.

She was standing at the edge of the terrace, looking down to the water reflecting the pale silver of the moon. Moonlight glinted in her hair and made the skin of her bare arms look translucent, like a painting of a Roman goddess.

'What a pretty view,' she said, glancing at him as he came up beside her.

He put his arms around her from behind and with his chin on her shoulder looked out at the view. He had no words to describe how he felt at that moment.

Happy?

Excited?

Nervous?

What a fool he was allowing this woman tempt him into doing something so outlandish.

He rubbed his cheek against hers. He should put a stop to this right now.

She turned within his arms, her arms slid around his waist and leaned into him.

Something inside him seemed to snap. A sort of breaking sensation in his chest. Painfully sweet.

He stiffened, disliking the feeling. 'This is madness.'

He realised he had spoken out loud.

'Totally mad,' she agreed. 'And we really must not be away too long or we will be missed.'

He lifted her hand from his shoulder, kissed the back, the palm, and her wrist.

What had made him do such a strange thing? The feel of that delicate palm against his mouth had been and incredibly tender experience.

His body had tightened yet he felt almost weak.

She shivered.

'Are you cold? Let us go indoors.'

Inside, with the lamplight glowing on her face, her lips were curved in the most tempting smile he had ever seen.

Desire choked him.

He could not speak.

He kissed those smiling lips and lost himself in the pleasure of her response. The urge to throw her down on the nearest rug and plunder and pillage was nigh overwhelming.

He broke the kiss. 'Barbara.'

She swept a lock of hair back from his face.

'Xavier,' she murmured softly.

He loved the sound of his name on her lips. So few people ever used his first name.

His father had.

He presumed his mother had.

His stepmother had always used the title he had inherited at birth. Lavrock. Viscount of. His stepmother was all about titles, so Great-Uncle Thomas said.

He shuddered.

'What is it?' she whispered, gazing at him intently.

'Nothing. An old memory.'

'Not a pleasant one, I'm thinking. A past lover?'

'Of course not.'

She looked doubtful.

'How could I be thinking of another woman when I have you in my arms?' It wasn't a lie. He had not been thinking of a woman of the sort she supposed.

He bent his head and kissed her.

She stroked his back as if offering comfort as well at the pleasure of her body aligned so perfectly with his.

And he once more lost himself in the headiness of her mouth and tongue duelling with his and the heated blood of lust rushing thought his veins.

He walked her backwards to the sofa and began to ease her down onto it.

She broke the kiss.

Disappointment filled him. Was this all a tease?

'Isn't there a bed?' she murmured. 'That sofa looks much too small for a man of your size.'

His cock hardened to granite.

Barbara saw a flash of surprise in Xavier's expression. Had she gone too far? Been too bold?

Did he expect her to behave with more decorum? Surely not?

'There is a bed,' he said, his voice gravelly. He picked up the lamp and took her hand.

She loved the way his warm palm enclosed hers. He made her feel feminine. Protected.

A pang of guilt tightened her chest. He was the one who needed protection. From her.

But he was a man and a duke. He would easily weather any storm.

Unlike herself. Once news of their entanglement got out, and it would as soon as she could manage it, her reputation would be ruined.

'Through here,' he said.

He opened a door off the hall.

The bedroom was almost entirely filled with a four-poster bed with cream silk hangings embroidered with flowers and birds.

'How pretty,' she said.

'I'm glad you approve. The last tenant was a single lady. I brought the furnishings over from Woodburn.'

So matter-of-fact. The closeness she had experienced on the terrace, seemed to have faded.

Once more he had withdrawn into himself.

Was he worried about something? Her intentions, perhaps? She hopped up on the bed and lounged back on the pillows, looking at him from beneath her lashes.

'Do you keep a mistress?' she asked and rolled over onto her side.

His eyebrows shot up. His eyes widened. 'What? No. I mean, not recently.'

'Don't sound so defensive. I only ask because I would

not like to think I was treading upon another lady's toes. Or poaching.'

He perched on the edge of the bed and his hand closed warm and possessive around her ankle. 'I am not defensive. But I am surprised that you think I would attempt a seduction if I already had a lover.'

'Is that what you are doing? Seducing me?'

A wry smile touched his lips. 'I think the seduction is mutual.' His hand slid up her calf, stroking gently.

A very delicious sensation.

'Mmm…' she said, reaching out to stroke his cheek and gazing into his eyes. 'Definitely mutual. As long as you understand there is nothing more in it than pleasure.'

There, she had said it, and was that relief she saw in his gaze?

And why would she be disappointed. Wasn't that her whole purpose?

'A fling, then?' he murmured, leaning forward. He pressed a brief kiss to her cheek.

'An interlude,' she said softly, turning her head to catch his hovering mouth with her lips.

He stretched out beside her and deepened the kiss, expertly teasing her lips and tongue with his, until she could scarcely remember her own name.

One large hand moved over her body, gently exploring her shape, the curves of her breasts the dip of her waist, the swell of her hip.

She curled her hand around the strong column of his

neck, and turned towards him, arching into him, aching to feel his body against hers.

He slid an arm beneath her, holding her close while his other hand swept the skirt of her gown upwards and stroked her thigh.

Heavenly.

They slowly drew apart. The heat in his gaze sent fire running along her veins.

'I want you naked,' he said. 'And your hair down. But we have to return to the party.'

'I know. I want you naked also.'

She reached down and unbuttoned his falls and pulled his shirt free. 'But this time, we will have to make do with... Oh...' He was huge and hot and so very ready. She caressed him, feeling the weight of his balls, the hardness of his shaft.

She glanced down but the lamp cast shadows and his shirt got in the way.

She shifted down the bed to see him better. He really was a big man. She curled her hand around his shaft and moved with long slow strokes.

He gasped and caught her hand, stilling it. 'Making do is not really my style.' His voice was hoarse. 'But I will make an exception, since we have so little time.'

He pressed her back against the pillows and came up on his knees astride her hips and caressed her breasts through her gown with one hand, while the fingers of his other hand played among the curls of her quim. He found the centre of her pleasure with his thumb and pressed and flicked and…

She fell apart.

Even as she felt the rush of bliss, he thrust into her and passion began to rise all over again.

She captured the cheeks of his bum in her hand and felt the muscles contract beneath her fingers as he stroked her insides with his hard length.

His pace increased, hard and fast and he reached between them to…

'Yes,' she said as her body tightened unbearably at his firm touch.

'Yes. There.'

He groaned, pressing harder and faster, in time to his thrusts.

She tipped over the edge from excitement to release. And he came with her, moving aside at the last moment to spill his seed into the tails of his shirt.

He collapsed heavily onto the pillows, one arm lax across her chest, and they lay panting in harmony.

'My goodness,' she whispered. 'Twice.'

He groaned softly. 'Nearly didn't. Was hard to wait. Too many days of wanting you. Too damn hot.'

She giggled.

'It isn't funny.'

Such a serious man. Even in this. 'No, it is hilarious.'

'Oh, God,' he said, and chuckled.

She laughed.

They both dissolved into laughter, holding each other.

Gradually their laughter subsided.

For a moment she thought he had fallen asleep.

'We must go,' he said.

'Yes.'

'Would you—?'

As strange sort of joy filled her. 'Yes.'

'I mean, would you meet me here again? I need to make this right.'

'I said yes, did I not?'

'Oh. When?'

'One afternoon next week. I will let you know which day.'

'I do not know if I want to wait a whole week.'

Nor did she. She hadn't known that such pleasure existed. Her first husband had been a disaster in bed. Too old. Too sick. Her second had certainly enjoyed himself, and she had wanted to please him. At first. But now she realised how selfish he'd been.

If only she had met Xavier first.

She sighed.

'Having regrets?' he asked, frowning.

'Yes. I'm regretting we have to hurry back.'

'But we must.'

He was his usual stern self, already standing up, tucking in his shirt and buttoning his falls.

He reached over and helped her off the bed.

She glanced in the mirror to pin up some stray tendrils of hair. Her lips were rosy from his kisses. Her gown a little crumpled. She smoothed the creases and turned to face him.

'Ready?' he asked.

'Yes.'

The sooner they left, the sooner they could return here.

'I will remove the *to let* sign first thing in the morning,' he said.

'Perfect.'

Chapter Ten

The next day, Xavier took a last look around the cottage where he had spent such pleasurable moments the previous evening. He was sure he had forgotten nothing. As he had promised, he had removed the *to let* signs from the front and back of the cottage as well as mentioned to his man of business that he would not be leasing the cottage in the near future.

He had also brought in some provisions. Some bread, butter and cheese for the pantry. A few bottles of champagne. Tea and biscuits. Comestibles he imagined one might need for an afternoon dalliance.

He had purchased them at a grocer in town, where he was not known.

Last but not least, he had hired a woman to come in every morning to clean, do laundry and any other required tasks. She was to be gone by noon.

He had done everything possible to ensure to keep his and Barbara's liaison private.

Now he had to wait until Wednesday afternoon to see her again.

He did not like waiting.

He locked the front door and drove home to receive the news from his butler that his secretary had returned from his leave.

He ought to be pleased, but now that meant there was another person to keep in the dark about his whereabouts.

He strode now the corridor to the back of the house.

Perry rose from his desk outside Xavier's office. 'Good afternoon, Your Grace.'

'Perry.' He shook hands with the young man. 'How is your family?'

'Well, sir.'

'And the wedding went off all right?'

'It did, Your Grace.'

'Good.'

'My brother-in-law sends his thanks for your most generous gift.' Perry handed over a note.

'Thank you.' Xavier read the note and set it aside.

Perry gestured to the pile of mail. 'Shall I begin with this?'

'Please. I have missed you, as you can see.' He hesitated. 'Please do not make any arrangements for me on Wednesday afternoons. I wish to keep those free for the time being.'

Perry's eyebrows rose, but he simply nodded.

Xavier had never made that sort of request before.

Damn. He hated this hole-and-corner stuff.

This was what came of getting involved with a reckless woman like the Countess. One lost all sense of propriety.

He should have given her the cut direct the moment she started her nonsense. Instead, he'd picked up the gauntlet she'd tossed at his feet.

It wasn't too late to end it.

No one had looked at them askance when they had returned to Anderson's party. The guests had been too busy gawping at what had to be the worst bronze sculpture he had ever seen in his life, and fawning over the artist who'd created it.

Of course they had entered the house separately. Not even Julian had commented when he'd joined him in viewing the sculpture.

The only person who had indicated that he might have noticed something was Barbara's brother-in-law. There had been a slightly quizzical expression on the man's face when their gazes had met shortly after he entered the ballroom. But perhaps he also had been puzzled by the statue.

'There is a letter here from the Simons,' Perry said. 'It arrived yesterday.'

Xavier drew in a quick breath. Was Mrs Simon announcing her daughter's return to London? And if so, how was he to answer? After Barbara's revelation that the girl's heart was engaged elsewhere, he certainly had no intention of continuing his suit.

Thank God, he hadn't spoken of his intentions to anyone, even though people had guessed he was thinking of making her an offer. And if Mrs Simon had got her hopes up? That was not his fault.

He broke the seal on the missive. It was an apology.

Because her daughter had gone behind her parents' back and become engaged to the Stallton fellow.

It wasn't difficult to see the mortification in the woman's words. Or the disappointment.

Xavier, on the other hand, wanted to shout *Huzzah!*

'It seems Miss Simon will not be returning to town this Season,' he said, and tossed the note onto Perry's desk. 'Please send a note of congratulations upon her daughter's engagement.'

Perry was staring at him as if trying to understand his reaction. Perry of course knew that she was one of those he was looking at as a prospective bride.

'It is fine,' Xavier said. 'Truly.'

Perry nodded. 'Very well, Your Grace.'

It was fine. More than fine. Xavier felt as if a great weight had been lifted from his shoulders. Now he was free to pursue his interest in the Countess without one iota of guilt.

A dalliance.

Hopefully, he would get Barbara out of his system and be able to return to his normal, peaceful way of life.

And start looking for a bride once more.

That thought caused an odd sinking sensation in his stomach which he decided to ignore.

'The Count of Lipsweiger and Upsal.'

Barbara looked up at the butler's announcement and set her embroidery aside.

'Charles.' She held out her hand in greeting. 'How

good of you to call. Steadman, will you please send up the tea tray?'

The butler bowed and left.

Charles bowed over her hand. 'You are looking beautiful, my dear,' he said. 'More radiant than ever. England agrees with you.'

There was something probing in his tone. It was more an enquiry than a statement.

But then Charles had always been one to care about her, when her husband hadn't given a damn, so she could not fault him for that. Not that she was going to reveal her secrets to him. At least, not yet. Not until it was to her advantage.

'Thank you. Yes, I am beginning to find my way I think.' *In more ways than one.*

'I understand you wished to speak with me in private. I had a message at my club, another at my lodgings and yet another from the Duke. What is it that is so urgent, and why not speak of it last night when we were at the Andersons'?'

'It is no longer urgent,' she said, surprised at his accusatory tone. 'I wanted to advise you that Miss Simon had contracted the measles.'

He looked puzzled. 'What is it, the measles?'

'Oh. Hmm… I have forgotten the word for it in German, but it is when a child gets a great many spots along with a fever.'

'*Masern*, you mean?'

'That is it. Masern. Dreadful infection. And you were

with Miss Simon right before she came down with it. Have you had it?'

'Yes, as a child. I got it from Helmut, as a matter of fact.' He looked sad.

'You still miss him, do you not?'

'I do. Sometimes. He was not the best of men, we both know this, but he was still my brother.'

He had been a horrible man, in Barbara's opinion. But like a fool she had not seen past the charming facade. Well, she would not make that mistake again.

The Duke might be handsome and a fabulous lover, if their first encounter was anything to go on, but she had no doubt as to his intentions.

Thank goodness.

And soon she would be free of all this need to pretend to be the dutiful daughter.

'I appreciate you caring enough to warn me,' he said. At her invitation, he sat beside her.

At that moment, the butler entered with tea.

They sat in silence while the butler attended to his duties. They had always done that when he had come to call on her the few times she was in residence at his brother's house, after Charles had warned her that his brother's servants would report all her conversations back to him.

Alone again, he smiled at her as she handed him a cup of tea.

'You remember exactly how I like it.'

'Of course. It is not so long ago that I last poured tea for you.'

'Your aunt tells me your father is arriving soon.'

She stared at him, surprised. 'Yes. Sometime in the next two weeks, I gather.'

'You will be happy to see him.'

'Not especially so.'

'No?' He sounded surprised.

'No. Father wants me to marry again.'

'You do not wish it?'

'No.'

'Are you sure? You do not want a family, children, of your own?'

She shuddered. 'Not in the least.'

'Was my brother aware of this?'

'I think your brother convinced me of this.'

He sighed. 'Ah. But not all men are like my brother.'

'No. You are not. You have been a good friend to me.'

'More than a friend, I hope.' The look in his eyes was warmer than she expected.

Her heart sank. 'Charles. Please. I—'

He put up a hand. 'No, no.' He laughed, his teeth flashing white in his beard. 'You misunderstand. I mean that we are brother and sister still.'

She let go a breath of relief. For a moment… 'Yes, brother and sister.'

'Then you will take the advice of your brother. Give it some time before you discount marriage altogether.' He put down his cup and patted her hand. 'You know…' His eyes twinkled. 'Do they not say better the devil you know? Sometimes friendship is better than so-called love in a marriage.'

Her jaw dropped. 'You are confusing me.'

'I am merely offering to you some advice, but be assured, whatever you decide, you will have my full support.'

He pulled out his watch and flipped open the lid. 'Oh, my goodness. I will be late for an appointment if I do not hurry.'

He got to his feet and kissed her hand.

'Please call again,' she said, shaking a finger at him. 'When you have more time. I want to hear news from home. How things are now the war is over.'

'Yes. Of course. You will be interested in all I have to tell. I will be sure to call when we can have a long chat. In the meantime, if there is anything I can do for you, anything at all, please do not hesitate to let me know.'

'I will. I certainly cannot think of anything at the moment.'

He clicked his heels, bowed and left.

Barbara took a deep breath. The feeling of disquiet in her breast did not go away.

She poured another cup of tea and leaned back.

Was he offering friendship, or something more like marriage?

Why on earth would he want to marry his dead brother's wife? It must be a misunderstanding on her part. Something lost in his mental translation of German to English.

Not once since they had met had he seemed romantically interested in her. Nor she him.

They were friends, who were related by marriage, nothing more.

She rang the bell to have the tea tray removed.

Tomorrow she was to meet Xavier. Her heart picked up speed. Perhaps Charles could be useful with regard to her plan after all. Not now. But in the near future.

She would need to think about it carefully.

Nothing must go wrong when she let herself be caught in a sordid affair in as public a way as possible.

Xavier paced the small living room. 'Paced' was too strong a word. He walked from the French doors to the sofa and back.

What he really wanted to do was stand at the gate and watch for her carriage to arrive.

He compared his watch to the clock on the mantel. They both said the same thing. Half past two. She was late.

Perhaps she was not coming after all.

Something could have prevented her leaving given the clandestine nature of their meeting.

He would give her another half an hour and then he would leave.

The minutes ticked by slowly.

At ten to three, he flung himself down on the sofa. The tension inside his chest was a dull ache. She wasn't coming.

He'd made a fool of himself. For the first time in his life, he had somehow let a woman get under his skin.

Luckily no damage was done. He leaned back and

gazed at the ceiling. Why on earth would he care? She was a heartless, reckless woman just like his stepmother, and so what if he was as horny as hell? There were plenty of other women who...

The front door opened. 'Hello?'

He leaped to his feet and went to greet her.

She was breathless, laughing and talking at the same time. She looked adorably flustered. 'Oh, you *are* still here. I was quite certain you would have given up on me by now. Aunt Lenore insisted I drop her off at her friend's house on my way, and then the friend came out to say hello and I simply had a terrible time getting away.' She removed her hat and hung it on the hook by the door.

He looked outside. 'Where is your carriage?'

'I had the coachman drop me off outside the Andersons'. He will return for me at six.'

Four hours. It wasn't as much time as he would have liked.

'Won't Mrs Anderson deny seeing you, should anyone ask?' It was her excuse for going out without her aunt.

'Why would anyone ask? And besides she is holding one of her ghastly *musicale* afternoons, budding artists playing their hearts out all over the house and gardens. It would be quite easy for a person to be missed in the crowd of hoi polloi in attendance.'

He could not keep from laughing. 'Those "hoi polloi" consider themselves very well-educated connoisseurs of the art world.'

'Pretentious blowhards. If they had actually met a *real* artist or musician, they would be a great deal humbler. And knowledgeable.'

'As you have?'

'Naturally. In Vienna, some of the finest composers and artists abounded. One could hardly move without falling over a Gerard or a Lawrence or a Beethoven.'

The names of the masters tripped off her tongue like a shopping list.

'It does make the Andersons' gathering, as you describe it, seem a little pedestrian. Come, let me offer you some refreshment. Tea? Or something more fortifying?'

'Tea will be perfect.' She frowned. 'You have hired a cook?'

'No. I can make tea. And buttered toast if you would care for some.'

'Oh, my. What a surprise.'

'Not really. All boys learn the art of survival at boarding school, be he earl or duke or common old mister.'

He went to the kitchen and put the kettle on the hob. She stood in the doorway watching him.

'I would have thought a duke would have had tutors at home, rather than go to boarding school.'

'I had those in the summer months. Mostly to keep me out of mischief. I think my great-uncle found me a bit of a handful.'

'You spent summers with an elderly uncle?'

'There wasn't much choice. My mother died when I was five. And my father when I was twelve.'

'Oh, poor you. My mother died when I was born, but Father is still going strong.'

He gave her a sharp look. 'You sound as if you wish he wasn't.'

Her eyes widened. 'Did I? Oh, goodness. Of course I do not mean that. Not at all. I just wish he wasn't quite so…taken up with his work.'

'You miss him?'

'No. I refuse to miss a man who doesn't miss me.' She waved a hand. 'Enough of Father. I would think only of you.'

He would like to have delved further into her relationship with her father but she clearly did not want to talk about it. And it really was none of his business.

He poured the boiling water into the pot and added some shortbread to a plate on the tray holding the cups and saucers that he had readied earlier. How had he guessed she would prefer tea to wine?

'I will bring this through to the sitting room.'

She went ahead of him and he could not help but notice the way her gown clung to her figure, outlining the rounded shape of her bum that he had caressed almost a week ago.

And had been longing to see in all its naked glory.

He swallowed. He was not a beast. He was a man. He would give his lady tea before falling on her like a plundering pirate.

But fall on her he would.

She sat on the sofa and patted the seat beside her. 'Shall I pour?'

'Please.' He leaned back, forcing himself to relax.

Her movements were graceful and sure. The turn of her wrist elegant. Her dark eyes expressive when she held up a lump of sugar.

'One lump,' he said, proud of how calm his voice sounded when his heart was beating a steady tattoo in his chest.

He loved watching her move.

He took his cup and they sipped quietly for a moment.

'So where did you spend the summers with your uncle? At the family seat in Dorset? St Baldwin's, isn't it?'

His throat constricted. He never went to Dorset. He never discussed his life there. It always made him feel too uncomfortable. Sad. Angry. Out of sorts.

He forced his voice to be calm, distant. 'I see you have been looking me up in Debrett's, after all.' He didn't mean it to sound like an accusation, but it was one of a sort.

'That is why it is printed, is it not?'

He hated how people thought they knew all about him because of what they read. And then assumed it gave them some sort of access to him as a person. As if he had no private life at all.

But Barbara was not simply a stranger met at a party. Surely he could not blame her for being curious.

Indeed, perhaps he should be pleased that she cared enough to look.

'I spent my summers at Woodburn. Its proximity to London made it more convenient for Great-Uncle Thomas.'

'I see.'

'And I preferred it to St Baldwin's.'

The chill he always felt when talking about St Baldwin's, settled around his heart. He opened his mouth to explain.

Good Lord, was he going to pour his heart out to this woman and ruin the day? Certainly not.

'It's a big draughty old pile that was once a monastery right on the cliff tops.'

'It sounds like the sort of place a boy would love to run free.'

He bit back a harsh retort. He was not going to discuss his feelings about St Baldwin's.

'What about you?' he asked. Debrett's hadn't listed anything about her family except that her father was a diplomat, which he had already known. 'Where did you grow up?'

'In boarding schools.'

Likely why she was so well-educated. As well as her life experiences, of course.

'And your summers?'

'Mostly at boarding school. Once I was invited to go to visit a friend for two weeks and another summer I spent with my Aunt Lenore, but the poor dear found me far too exhausting.'

'Summers at boarding school? But surely everyone is gone in the summer?'

She turned her gaze on him and took a thoughtful sip of her tea. He had the feeling she was playing for time. Getting her emotions under control.

For some strange reason he wanted her to reveal her true feelings. It didn't make any sense. There was nothing worse than listening to people complain about their circumstances.

She smiled briefly. 'There was usually someone there. The housekeeper. Footmen. The gardener.'

Was that hurt he saw in her eyes? He could imagine his own feelings of sadness if he hadn't been able to go to Woodburn in the summer holidays. He tried to keep the astonishment out of his voice. 'You could not join your father?'

'I did,' she said matter-of-factly. 'When I was old enough to be of use.' She put down her cup and turned towards him. 'But enough of these childhood memories. Perhaps you will show me around the cottage. I saw very little of it when we were here the other evening.'

Chapter Eleven

Barbara had seen something like sympathy in Xavier's piercing blue eyes. Had she somehow let her disappointment at her father's abandonment for so many summers show in her voice?

The last thing she wanted was his pity.

She wanted him intrigued and enchanted, not pitying.

'Show me the garden. Last time, I had an impression of lawn and trees lit by the moon, but very little else.'

His beautiful smile warmed her insides. 'Certainly.' He took her hand and brought her to her feet.

'It is a very small property. I hope you will not be disappointed.'

He opened the French doors and they stepped outside.

'As you see, it is quite secluded.'

It was indeed. Tall bushes and hedges obscured the view on both sides. Flower beds, with roses bushes not yet in bloom along with other plants, hugged each side of the lawn in front of the hedges.

Grass, recently mowed, swept down to the river, which was partially hidden by an enormous willow tree whose twisted branches dangled long pale green fronds into the water.

He linked his fingers with hers and they walked down the flagstone path to the edge of the water.

A small and ancient wooden platform jutted a couple of feet out from the bank. 'No wonder our landing the other night was so unsteady,' she said.

'I know. I should never have attempted landing there in the dark. It could have ended in disaster.'

'It was fun.'

His frown deepened. 'It was reckless.'

She laughed. 'Stop worrying so much.' She turned to look at the cottage from this angle. 'What a pretty place it is to be sure.'

They walked back up the gentle rise.

'I think you have seen most of the inside,' he said, ushering her in. 'There is another bedroom at the front, which the last tenant used for a work room.' He opened the door to a chamber that looked out onto the street.

The room was bare except for a large table and curtains at the window.

'And next door here,' he opened a door, 'is a room for bathing.'

There was a large bath, a commode and a fireplace.

'That bath is huge,' she said.

'I gather the previous owner was a large man who enjoyed bathing every day. He had this installed. I saw no point in changing it when I bought the house. But my tenant said it took far too much water to fill it and did not use it.'

'So this house has not been in your family for generations.'

'No. It is a recent acquisition. My tenant was the wife of an old family retainer. When he died she had nowhere to live, so I offered her this place.'

'That was very kind of you.'

'I saw it more as a duty than a kindness.' He shut the door.

He did not like being accused of softer emotions, Barbara decided. Why would that be?

Perhaps it wasn't ducal or something?

'And here we are back at the bedroom.' His voice deepened. Her blood hummed along her veins and the sensual note in his voice.

'It looks just as charming in daylight as it did by candlelight,' she said, trying not to sound breathless.

'As do you.'

Warmth enveloped her. Pleasure at his compliment. She turned to face him.

He held his arms and she moved into his embrace.

'You are a flatterer, Your Grace,' she said, rising up on her toes to kiss his cheek.

He turned his head and his lips found her mouth instead.

They fit together so well, she thought vaguely. He was tall and broad of shoulder, yet their bodies aligned beautifully as he bent his head to kiss her deeply, his arms pulling her tight against him. She combed her fingers through the hair at his nape, caressed his shoulders, his back.

So lovely.

He made her feel slight and feminine instead of tall and gawky.

Both of her husbands had been on the short side and embraces had been uncomfortable.

He broke their kiss and gazed down at her. 'Thank you for coming today. I wasn't sure you would.'

Overcome by his obvious happiness, and unused to anyone really caring if she was present or not, she was about to make some flippant remark about who could refuse a duke, when she stopped herself.

He was, she was certain, being sincere. She had the feeling that to brush aside his appreciation would be hurtful.

'I promised I would,' she said. 'And I would not go back on my word for all the world.'

His Adam's apple in his strong column of throat moved as he swallowed.

His gaze travelled from her face and down her length. 'You are so damned beautiful,' he murmured. 'I desire you more than I have desired any other woman.'

'Good,' she said, once more overwhelmed by the directness of his words.

His smile broadened. 'Good? Is that all you have to say?'

'What more is there to say?' She leaned into him and rested her cheek on his chest, not wanting him to see her expression, lest he see the longing that had risen up inside her. The yearning to be truly loved.

It was an impossible dream.

'Oh, I desire you also, Your Dukeness. And yet here we are shilly-shallying around having conversation.'

This time a little flippancy was needed. She'd learned how to do that early in her life. To guard her heart from pain.

'Your Dukeness?' He laughed, a low rumble in his chest against her ear. 'What am I to do with such a saucy wench?'

She tilted her head and smiled up at him. 'Your wish is my pleasure.'

He hissed out a breath. 'Do you have any idea what those words do to me?'

She smiled innocently. 'Naturally, I do.'

He groaned. 'Then my wish is to see your hair down around your naked shoulders—as a start.'

She pulled the single pin strategically placed to hold the coiled locks in a bun at her nape.

Tenderly, he ran his fingers through her hair and brought it forward over her shoulders.

He nodded. 'Lovelier than I had imagined.' He lifted a brow. 'But that is only the first part of my wish. Next…'

As if some mischievous deity peeped in through the window and approved of the unfolding scene, a beam of sunlight pierced the window and fell on Barbara's face.

Xavier caught his breath at the gleam of gold on her skin. Like fairy dust. For a moment he was dumbstruck.

Inwardly, he shook his head at the fanciful notion.

He forced himself to speak, yet words did not seem to express the feelings inside him.

Perhaps it was just as well.

'I love how your hair waves at the ends.'

'It is a terrible bother,' she said, picking up a strand from her shoulder and looking at it with a frown. 'I have sometimes thought about cutting it.'

'Never,' he said, horrified by the idea.

'It is just hair. It takes ages to dry when I wash it. And ages to get the tangles out. You have no idea.'

He wanted to sit and brush the tangles out for her. To help her dry it before the fire.

He blinked. Never in his life had he felt such a peculiar longing. 'I think you would be sorry if you cut it.'

'No. I think you would be.' She laughed and pressed her forehead to his. 'Is this why we are here, to discuss my hair?'

He closed his eyes briefly. 'No.' He kissed her deeply and lost himself in the taste of her sweet mouth, the feel of her lips on his, the touch of their tongues, the feel of her back beneath his hands and the sensation of hers around his waist.

He wanted to be closer. Her narrow skirts impeded his desire. He reached behind her waist and tugged at the end of her gown's laces.

He could not hold back his huff of impatience. 'Why does ladies' attire have to be so damnably complicated?'

She turned her back to him. 'You will find it easier if you can see what you are doing. I assume you know how it works?'

Slightly affronted by her question, he quickly pulled free the ties, eased the gown off her shoulders and let it fall to the floor.

She stepped out of the puddle of cotton at her feet.

He frowned. There were no ties for her stays.

She spun around and he saw the fastenings were at the front between the rise of her full breasts. She undid them before his brain had a chance to direct his fingers to the task.

She cast them aside in a swift, practised movement.

He bent and kissed the rise of each breast where it rose above the sheer fabric of a chemise that left little to the imagination.

Her breasts were gorgeous. A lovely handful of ripe womanly flesh with rose pink peaks furled into tight buds.

He tested the weight of one in his hand and felt the hard little nub against his palm.

His cock, already hard, pressed unbearably against the fabric of his trousers.

He reached down and caught the hem of her chemise. Obligingly she lifted her arms in a sinuous motion, and he pulled the garment up and off over her head.

Her hair fell about her shoulders, the heavy locks falling over her breasts, hard nipples peeking between the river of chestnut strands.

Her waist was narrow, her stomach flat, with a tiny dimple hiding her belly button. Beautifully flared hips and a dark triangle of tight curls at the apex of her thighs almost brought him to his knees.

'You are quite the loveliest—'

'Do you always talk so much?' she whispered, reaching out to untie his cravat.

He glanced at her face, her eyelids were heavy, her breathing rapid.

And suddenly he could wait no longer. He had to have her. Now.

He tore off his coats, pulled free his cravat. Pulled his shirt over his head.

All the while she watched him with that heavy-lidded gaze wandering down his body to his groin. Taking him in with and expression that said she might want to swallow him whole.

Naked but for shoes and hose, he picked her up and deposited her on the bed. He toed off his shoes, tore off his stockings and joined her. Kneeling by her side, he looked down at the glorious length of her, sprawled upon the pillows.

She liked to sprawl, limbs lax and open. She had done the same thing on the little barge the other night.

She knew what that did to him, for her gaze was fixed on the evidence.

He lay down beside her, and she turned towards him, arching into him, skin to skin, her breasts flattening against his chest, her head tilting up, her lips searching for his mouth.

He pressed her back and came over her.

His mind told him to slow, but his body urged him to press home into her hot depths.

With a groan he reached between them, entering her

body with his fingers, feeling the wet and heat, using his thumb to strum that little bud that had brought her apart so swiftly before.

She was so ready.

Little moans and cries of need filled his ears. He drove into her. So good.

He was going to—

He held still, waited for that terrible want to ease.

Once more in control, he moved gently but surely inside her. He raised up on his hands and gazed down into her face. Her eyes were closed, her face softened by desire, her lips parted on shuddering breaths.

He kissed her lips, her chin, the rise of her breast. Her nipple.

He gently drew it into his mouth and suckled.

Her hips rose. She made a high keening sound. And fell apart.

Too fast. Not yet—

All thoughts broke in a paroxysm of pleasure.

Only a panicked instinct had him leaving the sweet channel of her body the instant before he came undone. He spilled on the sheets.

They lay panting side by side.

Blackness enveloped him, no matter how hard he tried to remain conscious.

Barbara could not move. She could only breathe. Floating on warm bliss, she wanted to turn her head, to look at Xavier. Darkness descended...

How? she thought as consciousness seeped in. How

could it be? So fast. So overwhelming. As if he had some power over her.

Nothing in her experience had prepared her for this.

The other night, she assumed she had drunk too much, been mistaken in what she felt had happened.

No mistake.

Her heart seemed to grow large in her chest.

A feeling of tenderness wrapped in longing overcame her.

A tear leaked at the corner of her eye.

Why?

What had this man done to cause her to feel such a mix of emotions? Happiness. Sadness. Longing for...

She dashed away the tear and gained enough strength to roll over on her side. Gazing at his face. At the haze of stubble already shadowing his square lean jaw, at the length of his lashes curved above his prominent cheekbone. The jut of his nose. The heavy eyebrows without their habitual frown for once.

He looked younger. Almost boyish.

She brushed the lock of hair back from his broad forehead.

And resisted the urge to kiss his full lips.

They were lovers, nothing more. He was her path to freedom from the need for another husband, though he did not know it.

In exchange, she was providing him with a little fun that some instinct told her he needed. Badly.

His eyes opened, bright blue and fully alert.

'Did I wake you?' she whispered.

'I wasn't asleep.'

'Ooh. You will be punished for telling fibs.'

He chuckled and with a small groan rolled onto his back. 'You sound like my governess.'

'Did you like your governess?'

She'd heard tales of privileged young men and their sisters' governesses.

'Good Lord, no. She was ancient. And had a mole on her chin which grew thick black hairs. She scared the hell out of me.'

'Oh. Do I scare you?'

He pulled her close and tucked her into the crook of her arm as if she weighed no more than a feather. 'Yes.'

Ouch. She had not expected that. It hurt.

He put a finger under her chin, raising her face. He pressed a swift kiss to her lips. 'Never have I met a woman who caused me to lose control the way you do.'

'Control?'

He frowned at her. 'You know. Too soon.'

She recalled Helmut and how he'd pounded into her over and over and never had she felt the bliss she had with Xavier. 'I like it fast.'

'Hmm,' he said, sounding unconvinced. 'Next time, I will do better.'

She must have made a sound of concern, because he chuckled.

'Don't worry. You will like it just as well, if not better.'

She did not see how on earth it could be better. Indeed, if it replicated her experience with Helmut, she would be severely disappointed. But she had not lured him into her bed for pleasure. He was going to rescue her from a fate worse than death.

Even if he never knew it.

The likelihood of him ever speaking to her again after she exposed their affair to the world was exceedingly slight, especially when he realised she was the source.

And she would endure whatever was needed in the meantime, the way she had always endured.

Sadness filled her. Loneliness.

Up until these last few minutes this visit with Xavier had been so...lovely. More than lovely. Amazing. Wondrous. Blissful...

There was no sense in her wishing for what could not be. She had made up her mind.

They lay side by side in silence for a while. She knew he wasn't sleeping because his hand stroked her hip and his breathing, while even, was not the deep breaths of sleep.

But the silence was companionable. Comfortable. Calming.

Meanwhile the room slowly darkened.

'What is the time?' she asked.

He turned his head to look at the window. 'It must be after four.'

'I needs must leave soon.'

'Yes. We should not tarry longer.' He arose, keeping his back to her, and pulled his shirt over his head, hiding her view of all his lovely, muscled flesh. When he turned back, his shirt tented very obviously at his groin. He desired to make love again.

A breath caught in her throat. Her heart picked up speed. She wanted the same.

She almost said something provocative. But no. She really must leave.

'Up you get,' he said, holding out his hand.

He helped her down from the bed and assisted her with her clothing.

Finally, he lifted the heavy weight of her hair with a frown. 'I don't think there is much I can do with this.'

She picked up the brush on the dressing table. It was clean. No sign of the previous owner's hair.

'It is new,' he said as if guessing at her thoughts.

She began pulling the brush through her hair.

He took it from her and began teasing out the tangles.

His face in the mirror was intent, his touch gentle.

A spark of something sour rose in her breast. 'You have done this before.'

Jealousy. Surely not?

'I believe I have.' His voice was distant. His expression remote.

'You believe?' The edge of her annoyance sharpened.

His gaze focussed. He looked at her in the mirror.

'It isn't important.'

'I am sure it isn't.' Mistresses were ten a penny no doubt, and likely he'd had a score of them.

He put the brush down.

She gathered her hair in one hand and deftly twisted it into a bun at her nape. She pinned it firmly.

'Amazing,' he said.

Not so amazing when you were left on your own for weeks on end to tend to yourself.

'I am ready,' she said.

'Wait. I will escort you.' He sat and pulled on his pantaloons.

'I don't think that would be a good idea,' she said and went into the living room to fetch her hat and her reticule.

He stood in the doorway of the bedroom watching.

'When shall I see you again?' he asked.

The thought of seeing him again made her foolish heart tumble over.

No. No. It was not that she wanted to see him. She had to see him. And at some point be seen.

'Same time next week?'

'But you will come to the theatre with me in the meantime. I have a box at Covent Garden. I will send a message.'

'Go with you alone?' she said, startled and intrigued. Perhaps this would be her opportunity.

'Certainly not. I will invite a group of friends. Julian. A couple of others that you know.'

Something she could use to her advantage? She would have to think about it.

'I will invite your aunt also, of course.'

Bother. She hated the idea of embarrassing Aunt Lenore. 'I am not some debutante in need of a chaperone, you know.'

He frowned.

She did not want to arouse any suspicions in his mind. She waved an airy hand. 'It is your party. You must do as you wish.'

When she stepped out onto the front step, he remained in the shadows of the small hallway. The door closed with a sharp click.

A feeling of joy filled her. Joy and wonder and happiness. She almost skipped up the front path. Why? Because of the way he made her feel? Surely not. No. It was because everything was going according to plan.

A twinge of regret touched her heart. It was a shame that this delightful interlude would be so short-lived. Perhaps she could wait a few more weeks before—

No. Father would arrive soon. He always did when she wanted him least.

She could not afford to delay.

Chapter Twelve

One did not invite a mistress to attend the theatre with one's friends.

Xavier stared into the fire opposite his study desk. The afternoon had turned cool, and flames danced yellow and red among the coals. Almost the red of the gown he had seen her in first.

Geranium.

Such a reckless woman.

Nor did a gentleman invite a single lady to his box, even if she was a widow, unless his intentions were honourable. He would not, for example, have invited Miss Simon and her mother, unless he was on the verge of making her an offer.

He could just imagine the triumph on Mrs Simon's face were she to receive such an invitation. Or indeed on the face of any of the mothers of debutantes who had been thrown at his feet this Season. What of Miss Lowell, Barbara's aunt? Would she have *expectations*?

Indeed, what would the *ton* make of such an invitation to the Countess? The betting books at White's would go wild.

What on earth had he been thinking? He had not been thinking with his brain, that was certain. His small head had been in control.

Lust made a man stupid.

It had certainly made his father stupid enough to risk his life. And he had suffered the consequences.

Xavier had no intention of following in his father's footsteps. He had not made a point of circumspection all these many years just to fall prey to the first temptress to cross his path.

Xavier ran the pen's feather through his fingers, tapped it against his cheek, a soft irritating tickle of sensation.

Damn it! What did he care what the *ton* thought? He had issued the invitation and he would not back out.

But nor would he be trapped by a scheming woman.

He would invite Lady Cowper to bring along the other two young ladies she had recommended, and their mothers. After all, Barbara had been on Emily's list.

Yes. That would work. Problem solved. Nothing particular about such an invitation at all.

Barbara might not be best pleased with the arrangement, but he had informed her others would be invited.

It would do.

He cast his pen aside.

He would have Perry send out the invitations first thing in the morning.

His butler scratched on the door and entered.

'The carriage is waiting, Your Grace.'

'Still raining, then?'

'I am afraid so, Your Grace. Pouring, in fact.'

'Very well. Thank you.' He had intended to walk to the gymnasium, but since he had several places he intended to go afterwards, he ordered the carriage put to.

He was glad of it too when he made the dash from the carriage into the gymnasium on Old Bond Street.

The burly old porter greeted him with a cheerful grin. 'You are in luck today, Your Grace. His nibs is in a feisty mood.'

'Good.'

While some gentlemen preferred to get their exercise practising with a button-tipped rapier at Angelo's next door, Xavier preferred the physicality of boxing.

There was an element of risk. A fellow could actually get hurt if he didn't concentrate. A bloody nose or a black eye soon woke a chap up. And Xavier was known for doing a bit of damage of his own.

He always came away from a session at the gymnasium feeling calmer, more in control.

Lately he'd been feeling as if he was headed down a slippery slope and losing his grip.

The hall was crowded at this time of day, gentlemen intently watching those fighting on stages either from the ground or from the overlooking balcony. Arguments regarding form. Shouts of encouragement lingering with the smell of stale sweat and tobacco smoke. An all-male preserve.

He stripped down and sat on a bench to await the

next available sparring partner, watching a couple of likely lads flourish and weave and bob.

Someone sat beside him. 'Your Grace.' His accent was light but recognisable.

The Count of Lipsweiger and Upsal. Was he to meet the fellow everywhere?

'Count,' Xavier said, not taking his gaze from the battle in the ring.

'Please, call me Charles.'

'Xavier,' he said, still focussed on the match.

Charles held out his hand and Xavier shook it.

The smaller man sparring looked outmatched, being light and with shorter reach, but he was fast. He ducked beneath the other fellow's arm and hit him flush in the face.

'Good hit,' Xavier muttered.

'Very good,' Charles agreed. 'You are an aficionado of this sport? You will box?'

'I find it good exercise,' Xavier answered as he always did.

But it was more. It helped him remain in command of emotions that sometime grew too big for him to contain. Emotions that might lead to doing things he would regret later.

A few solid punches to his jaw or chest, or gut, seemed to set him back on the right track.

Master of his thoughts and actions.

No reckless, thoughtless, ill-considered acts. Like becoming to enamoured of a certain Countess.

'Do you box?' he asked Charles.

The young man shook his head. 'I like to watch, and wager. But no.' He gave a charming grin. 'My face is my fortune. I like the ladies too well to ruin it.'

Cheeky sod. Xavier grinned and clapped him on the back. 'The ladies like a man who can stand up for himself.'

'Ladies like my sister-in-law, included.' Charles laughed lightly. 'I think you don't take my advice to be wary.'

Xavier gave him a sharp look. Had Barbara been confiding in her brother-in-law?

He had no time to enquire further as Jackson ducked under the ropes and gestured to Xavier to join him.

'Good luck, my friend,' Charles said.

Xavier narrowed his eyes. Were they friends? He did not feel any great warmth from the fellow. 'It is not a matter of luck. It is a matter of skill.'

He joined Jackson and his sparring partner in the ring. When he glanced back, the Count had left.

Xavier frowned. At some point he and the Count—Charles, he corrected himself—were going to have a long conversation.

He balanced on the balls of his feet and feinted, before landing a blow to the other boxer's shoulder.

'Oh-ho,' said Jackson, 'One of those days, is it?'

His hand flashed out and hit Xavier on his bicep, numbing his fingers.

Yes. This was what he wanted. He circled to the left and watched for an opening.

* * *

When Barbara saw the other occupants of the theatre box, she kept her smile fixed firmly in place, but it was hard not to feel let down.

Why on earth would Xavier have invited two other ladies and their duennas, in addition to his friend Pettigrew and another gentleman she did not know?

Or perhaps they were just visiting the box before the performance started?

But no, there were nine chairs in the box in three rows. Was he trying to tell her she was of such little importance to him that— Well, it certainly scotched any idea of using this event to reveal their affair.

Suddenly irritated, she turned to leave.

Aunt Lenore grabbed her arm. 'Where are you going?' she whispered forcefully.

'Somewhere less crowded,' she said.

'You cannot leave,' Aunt Lenore said. 'That would be rude.'

Xavier turned from speaking to one of the other ladies. 'Countess. Miss Lowell. Welcome.'

She peered at him. Was that a bruise on his cheekbone? The light was not good, too many shadows cast by the oil lamps... But surely that was a cut on his lip too?

'Were you attacked by highwaymen?' she asked.

Aunt Lenore nudged her with an elbow.

Was it impolite to notice that a man looked as if he had been in the wars?

Xavier touched his bottom lip. She had the urge to touch it too. And taste it and—

She squeezed her thighs together and relished the tingle between her legs. Their next assignation could not come soon enough.

Who would have imagined such pleasure while accomplishing one's ruin? Perhaps she wasn't so disappointed that it would not end tonight.

'A sporting accident,' he said smiling. 'Your seats are in the front row with the other ladies and the gentlemen will sit behind. May I introduce you to Miss Redhill and Miss Graves?'

The two young ladies and their companions curtsied, giggled and tried to look interesting.

'What a crush,' Barbara said under her breath.

'I thought you might like to meet some of your peers,' Xavier said, obviously hearing her words, 'since I have noticed you do not know very many people in town as yet.'

By design.

She intended to be in London no longer than a few weeks.

'How kind of you to think of me.'

'I am always thinking of you.' He hissed in a breath and glanced around.

Clearly, he had not intended to say that out loud.

Interesting. And exciting. And wonderful. She tried to quell the rapid beating of her heart with deep, slow breaths.

But why had he invited all these other people, giving her no opportunity to fully enjoy his company?

Did he intend to hide his interest from the *ton* and protect her reputation?

Hmm. It seemed they might be working at cross purposes.

The orchestra struck some chords and the audience and the guests in his box settled into their seats.

Xavier took the chair behind hers. She knew it was him, she could smell the woody depths of his cologne and feel his presence like the slide of his hand on her breast. Her nipples tightened.

Never had she experienced such a visceral reaction to the mere presence of a man.

Was she too attracted to this man? It would not do to become enamoured. She shifted uncomfortably.

Someone waved from a box on the other side of the theatre. Charles? She borrowed Aunt Lenore's opera glasses. It was indeed Charles.

She waved back.

He was seated beside a young woman she did not recognise.

Aunt Lenore took possession of her glasses and also trained them on Charles. 'Ah,' she said in a low voice. 'As I suspected. Your brother-in-law is looking for a rich wife.'

'Why would you say so?'

'The young lady beside him is the heiress to a great fortune.' She gave a snort of distaste. 'A mill owner's daughter. They have been seeking a title for the last two years. I wonder at the Count, stooping so low.'

'She looks like a perfectly pleasant young woman.

No doubt if Father could have come up with a mill owner's son for me, he would have. Provided he was rich.' After all, he had married her off to a man old enough to be her grandfather to further his ambitions.

'Never!' Aunt Lenore declared. 'It would ruin the family name and you know how important that is to your father.'

'Too bad Father didn't have a son. The family name dies with him.'

'Not for the want of trying,' Aunt Lenore said.

No indeed. Barbara had never been enough for him. He'd kept trying until her mother had died in childbirth. What she did not understand was why he never married again.

Still, he had lots of time to father an heir; after all, he was only sixty. Far younger than the man he had first married her off to.

The theatre lights dimmed.

In the dark, Barbara became doubly aware of Xavier at her back.

She felt as if his gaze rested upon her and not the stage.

She did her best to resist the urge to look at him, but it was no use.

She glanced over her shoulder.

Their gazes met.

Heat zipped along her veins. She could feel the echo of his hands on her skin, his lips on hers. Desire rose.

She cast him a provocative smile intended to acknowledge the sensations she was feeling as well as tease him with the promise of the future.

His indrawn breath, a light hiss of sound that no one else would notice, was a joy to her ears.

His response stirred excitement low in her belly, and a whisper of something painful in her heart.

There was no reason not to be pleased at his reaction. She wanted to storm his defences, make him forget he was a gentleman.

But she did not want to lose control of her own emotions. She had fallen hard for Helmut, against her better judgement, and look how well that turned out.

Never again would she trust a man to have her best interests at heart. Her father had not. Helmut had not, and certainly there was no reason to think Derbridge would be different.

Barbara focussed on the play. Some sort of farce. Aunt Lenore seemed utterly engrossed, as did the other two ladies, laughing at the antics of the actors, but all Barbara could think about was Xavier sitting behind her. The scent of his cologne filled her nostrils, the warmth of his large body seemed to permeate through her gown and heat her back, his breath surely brushed her cheek.

Again, against her will, she glanced over her shoulder. As she did so, a large warm hand rested lightly on her waist.

'Are you in need of something?' he asked.

You. It was a shocking admission, even if it was only to herself. 'No thank you.'

He leaned back, the flimsy chair creaking beneath his weight. Such a large man.

And the loss of his hand's warmth made her shiver. How ridiculous.

She had been attracted to him from the very first moment she saw him. Was she become a moth to his flame instead of the other way around? Her breathing shortened.

Perhaps, after all, he was the wrong man to use for her purpose.

Xavier knew he was behaving badly, despite the presence of others in his box.

All of them would have realised by now where his interest lay.

He took a deep breath and sat back in his seat.

What was it about this woman that made him forget all of his good resolutions?

He had thought the trading of a few hearty blows yesterday at the gymnasium would have tired him out and cooled any trace of recklessness.

Apparently not, since he wished like hell that he was alone with Barbara, instead of hosting a bunch of other people in whom he had no interest at all.

Well, except for Julian. Maybe.

Barbara wasn't exactly helping matters. The brief but all too provocative glances she sent his way were enough to drive a man to insanity. With just a look, she could remind him of the way she had felt beneath him in that little bed in the cottage. The way he had felt coming apart while he was inside her. The heat of their mutual bliss.

The peace of the aftermath, where he had no thoughts but an incredible sense of well-being.

He had thought that by bedding her, he would bring this unnatural fascination in her to an end. Instead, it had only increased his desire to bed her again.

But not just that. He enjoyed her company. She amused him.

She also made him wish things were different. Wish that he wasn't bound to his duty and his title. Wish that he was free to please himself.

He clenched his fists at his sides. These were not the thoughts of a rational man.

He wasn't a schoolboy fantasising about the headmaster's wife or the cheeky upstairs maid. He was a duke, with responsibilities and the family honour to uphold. He had a duty to the title to find a suitable wife and ensure the future generations of Melvilles.

And the Countess, a widow and a woman who seemingly did not give a fig for her reputation, was not the wife he sought.

Thank God she did not seem to be interested in marriage. Marrying a woman who caused him to lose any semblance of control would be a disaster.

Was this what had happened to his father? Had he too been so entranced by his second wife as to lose all reason?

If Xavier allowed himself to think about those days,

he certainly recalled his father being happy to the point of joyful.

And Xavier felt an odd twinge of envy.

The curtain went down and the liveried staff of the theatre entered to turn up the lights in the box.

Xavier rose and moved among his guests, offering refreshment. 'How did you enjoy the farce?' he asked Miss Graves, after she had indicated her wishes to the footman.

The young woman smiled brightly. 'It made me laugh. I especially liked the horse. He was funny.'

There had been a horse?

Oh, right. Two men in a horse costume. He'd seen it, but it simply had not registered.

'Indeed. Very amusing.'

From the corner of his eye he noticed Barbara slipping out of her chair and making for the exit.

He caught her before she opened the door. 'May I be of assistance?'

Her eyes widened and he found himself being drawn into their velvety depths.

He blinked.

She had said... Oh, yes. The withdrawing room.

'Miss Lowell should accompany you,' he said, looking around for the older woman.

'Oh,' Miss Redhill said, 'I need to freshen up. May I accompany you, Countess?'

Xavier stepped back and watched the two ladies join the throng in the hallway outside the box. They seemed to know where they were going.

'What game are you playing?' Julian said, joining him at the door.

He glanced down at his friend. 'What do you mean?'

'First, you cannot take your eyes off the Countess, and second, you look as if someone took a log to your head. I have never seen you so bruised. What did you do? Forget to duck?'

In truth, he'd been horribly distracted thinking about Barbara when he should have been focussing on his opponent. He wasn't going to say that to Julian.

He touched his lip. 'It's nothing. A lucky shot.'

'More than one, by the look of it.'

He certainly wasn't going to tell his friend about the fine set of bruises on his ribs. 'So?'

Julian shook his head. 'And the Countess?'

'You know very well I do not favour one woman over another. All the ladies here are my guests this evening.'

'And you haven't given the other two more than a perfunctory glance.'

'You are imagining things.'

His friend shrugged. 'As you wish.'

Xavier forced himself to leave the door and return with Julian to the rest of his guests, who were sipping champagne and discussing the play. He took a glass from the tray the footman offered him and joined Miss Lowell. The older woman gave him what he could only describe as a predatory smile.

'So kind of you to invite us, Your Grace. Such an honour.' She twitched at her shawl and patted her grey curls.

'It is my pleasure,' he said, wishing her and the rest of them to the devil.

What had made him think this was such a good idea?

A footman touched him on the elbow and handed him a card. 'A gentleman at the door, Your Grace.'

He glanced at the card. Ah, yes. His new friend Charles. 'Have him come in.'

Charles strode in, clearly looking around for the Countess.

Xavier shook his hand and the footman offered him a glass of champagne.

'Good to see you again,' Xavier said, trying to sound welcoming. 'Your sister-in-law will be back in a moment or two.'

'I hope she did not set out in the direction of my box,' Charles said with his so charming smile.

Xavier tamped down his irritation. 'She went with another lady to the withdrawing room.'

'Ah, I see. Well, while we are waiting, I want to ask you about a horse that is running at Newmarket. I understand you are the expert.'

'Well—'

'He is,' Julian said. 'Which horse is it?'

'It is one from his stable, actually. I was wondering if the Duke thought of him—Lucky Chance out of Lady Luck.'

Good God. Xavier had forgotten that the horse was running on the morrow. He'd been so busy making arrangements with regards to Barbara it had gone out of his mind. Never had that happened before.

He frowned. 'I don't give advice regarding entries from my stables,' he said coolly. 'The horse is fine. But there are several other good horses entered in that race.'

'His Grace is modest,' Julian said. 'The horse is more than fine. I have money on it.'

Charles nodded at Julian. 'Then I shall take your advice, my lord.'

'And it is Julian you will blame if you lose your money,' Xavier said a little more harshly than he intended. What was it about this fellow that rubbed him the wrong way? Not his relationship to Barbara, surely?

'Charles!' Barbara said, looking delighted. 'How lovely to see you.'

Xavier gritted his teeth and smiled at the pair of them as if he was happy to see them reunited.

'May I say how beautiful you look this evening,' Charles said. His gaze focussed on her necklace and he seemed to tear his eyes away with difficulty to make his bow.

Too low a bow in Xavier's opinion, and his smile far too charming. Fawning, he would call it, or ingratiating. Grovelling.

Hard to believe they were genuine after his *warnings*.

The Countess clearly welcomed his attention.

In Xavier's opinion, he was someone Barbara should be wary of. Should he warn her? Or would she think he was interfering where he had no right? Worse yet, would she think he was jealous of the fellow?

Perhaps it was all in his imagination.

Chapter Thirteen

'How are you enjoying London?' Barbara asked Charles. 'Are your business affairs going well?'

His brown eyes sharpened. 'Not as well as I had hoped.'

'Oh, dear.'

A look of distaste crossed his face. He turned his back to the guests in the box and lowered his voice. 'Given that the estate owes a great deal of money, I have been unable to raise a mortgage.'

'I am sorry to hear it. You do not deserve to be left with his debts.'

'My brother was a fool when it came to money.'

'Not a complete fool. He did have his claim to his estates upheld and a bit more besides.' Her father had seen to it as part of the marriage settlement.

'As was right and just,' Charles said with a little more acid in his voice than gratitude.

She stared at him in surprise. 'I gather it was no easy matter.'

He smiled. 'Naturally the family is grateful for your father's assistance in *that* regard.'

His gaze rested on her necklace for a moment then flickered away, but there had been a possessive look in his eye that made her want to hide it from his view.

'What are you two in a huddle about?' Pettigrew asked, joining them. 'Countess, if he is asking you to wager against Lucky Chance at Newmarket tomorrow, do not do it.'

Charles laughed. It sounded a little forced to Barbara's ears. 'Would I do such a thing? The horse is the favourite to win.'

'One of the Duke's horses? If it is anything like Lucky Lady, it will be as fast as the wind. I would certainly not bet against it.'

'You have seen Lucky Lady?' Charles asked.

'Yes. I visited the Duke's stables. They are not far from town.'

Charles was looking at her curiously. 'I did not know you were interested in racing?'

'I am not. Not really. But I like to ride.' She grinned at him. 'I had never ridden a racehorse before.'

'You minx,' Charles said, grinning back. 'Why am I not surprised?'

Julian stared at her. 'Xavier let you ride Lucky Lady? How extraordinary.'

Was he giving her the lie? 'I assure you he did. Why don't you ask him?'

Julian shook his head. 'Oh, I believe you, Countess.' But there was an odd expression on his face.

She had no time to question him further as the next play was about to begin.

Charles surreptitiously squeezed her hand and whispered as he bowed. 'I will call on you tomorrow.' In a louder voice he said, 'I must return to my box or my friends will think I have deserted them.'

She glanced over at the box where she had seen him earlier. The young woman had her opera glasses trained on him. 'That would be rude, indeed.'

And it seemed that her aunt was correct. Charles needed a rich wife.

What a shame that Helmut had been so feckless.

She returned to her seat. Derbridge did not return to his. It seemed he had exchanged seats with his friend Pettigrew. He was now seated between the other two ladies, leaning forward, whispering in their ears, eliciting giggles.

She wished him well of the gigglers.

No. That was beneath her. He was simply doing his duty as a good host. Wasn't he?

And why would she care? Their relationship was nothing but a fling. After all, the man still had to find a suitable bride.

A strange hollowness filled her chest. A painful ache. A wish that she had met him when she had been young and innocent.

Good heavens! Next she'd be wishing to marry the man. And as she knew to her cost, once a woman married, she became the property of her husband. She was never going to let that happen again.

While they waited for the curtain to rise, she turned to Pettigrew with a smile.

'You and His Grace are old friends, I think? How long have you known him?'

'Since we were lads barely breeched. We were at Eton together, then university.'

'A longstanding friendship, then.'

'Indeed. There is no one more loyal to his friends than Derbridge.'

'Yet he rarely smiles.'

Pettigrew pressed his lips together in a small grimace. 'There is no denying he is a serious fellow.'

'Has he always been so?'

Why was she asking all these questions? Because something inside her wanted to know more about the Duke than he was prepared to tell her himself. Even though every instinct told her it was a mistake.

Learning more about him might make it harder to part from him.

And that she must do. Eventually. What? Was she thinking she could delay?

'He used to be more light-hearted,' Pettigrew admitted in a low voice. 'Though I hope you won't tell him I said so. He changed when the responsibilities of the dukedom were landed on him. After his father's death he was all work and no play. His great-uncle saw to it.'

'How old was he when he inherited?'

'About twelve, I think.'

So young. She knew what it was like to be alone at

such a young age. Her heart contracted in sympathy for the small boy set so large a task.

'He was lucky to have you as a friend during such an awful time.'

Pettigrew shook his head. 'I wish I had been a better friend. I didn't see him for three years. When he returned to school, he had changed. I do my best to cheer him up, but that's when he took up boxing and got the sobriquet the dour duke.'

The Derbridge she knew was far from dour. At least, he was when they were alone.

'Boxing?'

'Didn't you see the bruises?'

Men and their sports.

'I suppose he spars for exercise.'

'Hardly. If he wasn't a duke, he'd probably be a champion. I was surprised to see that someone had actually managed to land a punch.'

Pugilism. She shuddered. She had not expected him to have such a violent streak.

'This is a regular pastime, then?'

'Everyone knows if you want to find Derbridge, go to the gymnasium first thing in the morning, unless he is out of town.'

The dour duke who boxed for pleasure.

She had thought she was beginning to understand her lover—now she had her doubts.

The curtain slowly rose.

Something across the theatre attracted her attention. A movement. A stir in the audience.

'Well, well,' Pettigrew said. 'Someone has arrived in the Royal Box.'

Barbara strained to see who it was and then she knew.

Her stomach dropped.

Father.

With a woman she did not recognise. He wasn't supposed to be arriving for another two weeks. Why on earth had he not let her know he was in town?

Why could she not learn that he didn't give a fig for her?

The play began.

Heart racing, she tried her hardest to take in the events on stage, but all she could see was her father across the theatre while she felt the bars of filial duty closing in around her.

Xavier frowned at the dismay on Barbara's face at the moment the curtain went up.

He sensed it had nothing to do with the play and everything to do with those who had entered the Royal Box.

He cast a glance over the occupants. None of whom he recognised. He did however recognise the Order of St Michael and St George on the chest of an older gentleman. A portly, balding man seated with a woman alongside another middle-aged couple. That man was a diplomat.

And therefore... He glanced over at Barbara. She was staring at the box. At her...father?

Her expression said she was not at all happy.

She turned her head to look at Xavier, as if aware of his perusal. Their gazes met. He raised an eyebrow in question.

She gave a little shake of her head, which he could not interpret, and then studiously directed her attention to the stage.

After a moment or two, he leaned towards Julian seated beside him. He indicated the Royal Box with a jerk of his chin. 'Who is that woman?' he asked softly. Somehow, Julian seemed to know everyone.

Julian gazed across the theatre for a moment. 'Why, it's Maria Wells, if I'm not mistaken. Widow of a baron who lost his money in some investment scheme.'

'And the gentleman with her?' he whispered. 'The one wearing Orders.'

Julian's eyes widened. He darted a glance at Barbara. 'Ambassador March. What—?'

Xavier put up a hand, forestalling his friend's curiosity. 'I thought so.'

His stomach sank.

What had he been thinking?

She was the daughter of a man who was clearly a friend of the King, or his son the Prince, or he would not be in that box. And he'd seduced her.

Against his better judgement.

Oh, he could tell himself that she had seduced him, pretend he was not to blame, but that would be utterly dishonourable. And inaccurate. He had wanted her.

And had used all the means in his power to accomplish his ends.

A cold chill settled in his chest. If he was anything close to honourable, he would make her an offer of marriage.

He really was his father all over again.

Marrying an outrageous woman because she was beautiful and intriguing and all the things he did not desire in a wife, because his lust for her was out of control.

He sank back in his chair.

If Great-Uncle Thomas was looking down from the heavens he would be shaking his head.

You are too much like your father to make a good duke.

All these years he had set out to prove Uncle Thomas wrong, to make his uncle proud, to restore the honour to his family name, and what had he done?

He'd let his lust for the so-called black widow divert him from his path. Was that part of her attraction? The idea that she was dangerous.

And if word of their dalliance became known, there would be nothing for it but marriage.

Damn it all, why did that make him feel…hopeful? Was he really so besotted he hoped for an excuse to ask her to wed?

He must have lost his mind.

Not entirely, he hadn't. After all, she was from a good family, she was beautiful and if she wanted to save her reputation by becoming a duchess, she would need toe the line of propriety from thenceforth.

As her husband, he would make sure of it.

He was not like his father.

It was strange that Barbara had not mentioned her father's arrival in London. Although, as he thought about it, about her reaction, it seemed she had been surprised to see him.

While the play on stage elicited gasps and laughter from the audience, Xavier was too busy with his own thoughts to pay much attention until the curtain fell for the next intermission.

As he rose to see to the comfort of his guests, he saw Barbara already on her feet and standing with her Aunt at the back of the box. He manoeuvred his way to her side.

'Thank you for a wonderful evening, Duke,' she said with a bright smile that he found rather brittle.

'Leaving already? The play is but half over.'

Miss Lowell looked disgruntled and twitched at her shawl. 'Our apologies, Duke. My niece has a headache. The smoke from the lamps perhaps.'

Or the sight of her father in the Royal Box? Why would that be?

'I am sorry to hear you are not well.' He gestured to one of the footmen who had entered to offer refreshments. 'Please arrange for Miss Lowell's carriage to be brought around.'

The man hurried off to do his bidding.

'Allow me to escort you down to the street.'

'We mustn't take you away from your other guests,' Barbara said.

'Most kind,' her aunt said at the same moment.

'I insist,' Xavier said. 'Covent Garden at this time of night is no place for ladies to be waiting alone.' He caught Julian's eye. 'I will be back momentarily,' he said to his friend.

Never one to be slow on the uptake, Julian nodded.

He would look after Xavier's guests until he returned.

Xavier glanced over at the Royal Box. Several people had arrived over there, and one of them was the Count of Upsal and Lipsweiger. Strangely, he and Barbara's father were in the back corner of the box and engaged in an intense discussion.

He ushered Barbara and Miss Lowell out of the box and down the stairs to the foyer.

'What a pleasant evening, Duke,' Miss Lowell said, opening and closing her fan with a snap. 'A very fine performance. I shall be sorry to miss the end, but...'

'You may stay if you wish, Aunt,' Barbara said, her voice chilly.

'No, no. If you are not well, I must make sure you are looked after. Your father would expect it.'

'Father has a great many expectations.' This time her voice was like ice.

The footman he had sent in search of their carriage strode into the lobby. He touched his hat.

'The carriage is waiting, Your Grace.'

Xavier escorted the ladies outside and down the steps. He handed Miss Lowell in first and then Barbara.

He held her hand a little longer than was needed and she glanced up. The anxiety in her eyes took him aback.

He wanted to offer her some sort of assurance. 'I am sure you will feel more yourself in the morning.'

She shook her head slightly as if to indicate his words were no help at all.

He released her hand, closed the door and watched their carriage move off.

He needed to get to the bottom of what was wrong between Barbara and her father.

'I expected a warmer welcome, daughter,' the Ambassador said, the morning after Barbara had attended the theatre with Xavier.

Barbara lifted her chin. He must think she would feel blessed to have him call.

When she was a child, she would have done anything to gain his attention. And he hadn't taken the slightest bit of notice. Until he'd realised she could be of use.

At first, she had basked in his warmth towards her, until she'd realised he cared nothing for her, and only cared about the advantage she brought to further his ambition.

He had done well out of her marriages. He was now not just a minor diplomat but an ambassador to Portugal with a medal to prove his worth to the crown.

'How good of you to call, Father,' she said coolly. 'It would have been nice to have been forewarned of your presence in London.'

'Barbara,' Aunt Lenore said, fussing with her lace collar. 'Your papa is a busy man. You cannot expect—'

'But I do expect,' she interrupted. 'I expect him to show common courtesy and inform me of his intended arrival.'

'Nonsense, child.' Her father flicked dismissive fingers. 'When the King commands my presence, I cannot be dawdling about writing letters. I come post-haste.'

'I doubt the King knows you exist.' The King didn't know anyone existed if what Barbara heard was true. The King was completely mad.

Her father glared at her. 'What has you out of sorts? Your aunt tells me you left the play early last night because of a headache. I hope it is not measles. I gather it is going about.'

'If you knew anything about me, Father, you would know I had measles when I was six. But, of course, you would not recall. I was at school at the time.' At school all alone and terrified she was going to die. The nurse had been horrible to her, because father had *forgotten* to pay the school fees for more than one term.

Truth to tell, he'd probably forgotten he had a daughter.

'Tsk-tsk. Barbara. Do not speak to your father with such disrespect,' Aunt Lenore said.

She would sooner not speak to him at all.

'Why are you here, Father?'

'Cannot a father visit his own daughter?'

He could. But he rarely wanted to. 'How very paternal of you.'

'I was pleased to see you wearing the Lipsweiger

parure last night, my dear. It becomes you. You should wear it as often as possible.'

Suspicion writhed in her stomach. Father never asked her to do anything unless there was a purpose behind it. 'Why would you care?'

He shrugged. 'It adds to your consequence. I hear you have been making a bit of a stir. Only the wealthiest can get away with that sort of thing. Might also attract an advantageous offer.'

Her stomach dipped. 'I am not looking to attract any sort of offer.' She should not wear the jewels ever again.

'Listen to your father, dear,' Aunt Lenore said. 'He understands these things.'

He might. But then again, he might not.

'It is also important to your claim that you wear them,' Father said. 'In public. Where they can be seen. Evidence of legitimate ownership.'

She needed evidence? 'Are you saying there is a question of my legitimate ownership?'

Her father puffed out his chest. He always did that when he wanted to appear more important than he was.

'Certainly not. But it wouldn't do to let people think there was.'

Father and his plots. She would never understand what was going through his devious mind.

He gave her a considering look. 'I hear you and the new Count are as thick as thieves.'

She stiffened. 'What do you mean? We are friends, that is all.'

Her father pulled at his bottom lip, the way he did when he was plotting some scheme to his advantage. 'He's looking for a wife.'

Her breath caught in her throat. 'Marry Charles? Are you mad?'

He shrugged. 'I wouldn't have to provide a dowry. He would get what he sees as his family's jewels. And your future would be assured. I know you like the fellow. You spent enough time in his company.'

Her future would be assured the moment she reached twenty-five years—or managed to sell the jewels that were rightfully hers. Yes, she liked Charles. Yes, she had spent a great deal of time in his company, because he was the only one who ever showed her any sympathy after she discovered her husband was a despicable philanderer who had only married her to ensure her father would help him gain his lands back after the war ended.

Now father wanted her to marry his brother?

'I have no intention of marrying again. Ever.'

'Child, you are being ridiculous.'

'I am not a child.'

'You are certainly behaving like one.'

Aunt Lenore wrung her hands together. 'Barbara, you are young. And you do like him. I know you do. Such a charming man. If only such a man had offered for me.'

She liked Charles as a brother-in-law. But not as a husband. She shook her head. 'No.'

Her father shot her a quick glance. 'There is another way.'

Barbara held her breath. Would he finally agree to let her go her own way?

'You could marry this duke of yours. If he will have you.'

'The Duke?' she said faintly. She turned to her aunt. 'What on earth have you been saying?'

'I only said he seemed interested.'

'And when did you say this?'

'When I wrote to your father, of course.'

She needed to nip this in the bud. 'The Duke has no interest in marrying me, and even if he did, I have no interest in marrying him.'

'His Grace the Duke of Derbridge,' the butler announced.

Barbara wanted the floor to open and swallow her whole. The Duke must have heard her words; she had spoken loudly and with vehemence.

Even so, her heart leaped at the sight of his handsome face. The bruises had faded as to be almost imperceptible, unless you knew where to look for them. And the cut on his lip was little more than a tiny mark.

He looked absolutely gorgeous.

If he had heard what she'd said, he showed no sign of it. He smiled pleasantly as he entered the room. 'I beg your pardon, Miss Lowell,' he said. 'Your man did not tell me you had visitors.'

Father looked like a fox who had just been granted access to a hen house. He stepped forward, hand outstretched, lips in a wide smile. 'A pleasure indeed, Your Grace. March at your service.'

Xavier shook his hand. 'Lord March. I have heard of your work at the Congress.'

Everyone had heard of it. Father had made sure of it. No doubt Xavier thought her father the best of men. Bitterness swept through her.

Chapter Fourteen

As usual, Xavier hid his distaste for the man who gripped his hand a little too long and smiled a little too much.

All his life he had been subject to the sort of ingratiating bonhomie displayed by Lord March.

It was why he limited his circle of friends to those who were not impressed by his wealth and his title.

Like Barbara, apparently.

The words he heard her speak before he entered the room had given him pause.

It was with reluctance that he had come here this morning to tell of her of his plans to speak with her father about making her an offer. Reluctant because she was not at all the sort of woman he had intended to wed. A woman who made him feel more alive than he had for years. Alive to the point of recklessness. Though he was sure he could control it better than his father had.

Certainly, if he had to marry someone, why not Barbara? She had more of a brain than most of the other young ladies he had met, and she made him laugh. Not to mention her other attributes.

Xavier, however, unlike his father, would not be led by the nose, or any other part of his anatomy.

After much thought in the dark reaches of the night, though, he had conceded that perhaps, as long as she was prepared to behave as a proper duchess should, they could make it work. After all, he was a man as well as a duke, and there was much he enjoyed in their relationship.

Now, hearing her adamant declaration that she did not want to wed anyone had made him think again. He wasn't so sure he had come to the right decision.

He hadn't given any thought to her family connections either. March was a man who would do anything to advance his career. Xavier knew this about him from his conversations with Castlereagh after his return to England. The foreign secretary had disdained the career diplomat. But March wasn't the only one Castlereagh had complained about, and Xavier hadn't taken a great deal of notice, glad only that peace was being actively discussed.

At the time, Castlereagh had not mentioned March had a daughter.

'Oh, Vienna,' March said with patently false modesty. 'It was little enough I did. Though I must say a couple of the clauses in the agreement gave a great deal of trouble until I discovered the wording that saved the day.' He puffed out his chest, no doubt to draw attention to the Order he wore.

'Your country has shown its gratitude, I see.'

'Yes indeed. The King. Most gracious. And what of you, Your Grace? I hear your stables have been producing some of the finest racehorses in the country?'

He made the difference between them sound stark. One man serving his country and the other indulging in fast horses and gambling.

'We do our best,' Xavier said.

'I am a good judge of horseflesh. If you wish for advice, I would be happy to give it.'

Xavier almost laughed out loud. He raised an eyebrow instead. Never before had anyone had the nerve to offer him advice on his racehorses.

Barbara gave her father a glare of such loathing, it took Xavier aback.

She turned got up and went to the bell. 'Shall I ring for tea, Aunt?'

'Oh, yes. Yes, please do, dear.'

When Barbara turned back the expression was gone, replaced by a smile of amusement.

Perhaps that look had been imagined. Certainly neither March nor Miss Lowell indicated that they saw anything amiss.

The butler came and took the request for tea.

'Do you plan to remain long in London, March?' Xavier asked, filling a pause that seemed rather longer than usual.

'I return to Lisbon in a week or so. I have reports to make, meetings to attend with the Cabinet.' He gave

Xavier a sort of knowing smile. 'And other more personal business.'

The butler arrived with tea and Miss Lowell hovered over the tray, pouring from the teapot and passing the cups around.

'You must have been disappointed to leave Paris, Father,' Barbara said and sipped at her tea. 'Such a beautiful city, and of such importance.'

'Hah. Paris! A political hotbed. Wellington is welcome to it.' There was a touch of venom in his voice and a touch of triumph in Barbara's eyes at his response.

'I visited the Embassy in Paris not long ago,' Xavier said smoothly. 'The Embassy was most impressive. An hotel *extraordinaire*. Wellington is a lucky man.'

'It is magnificent,' Barbara said. 'Father and I stayed there briefly, before I came to London and he went to Portugal. How do you find Lisbon society, Father? Equal to Paris? Are there a great many beautiful ladies anxious for your return?'

'Do not talk nonsense,' March said. 'Lisbon is an important ally.'

'Albeit a very small one,' Barbara said. 'Well, I am sure you find plenty to do there.'

The Ambassador's neck turned red and the colour flushed upward into his face. 'I do my duty, daughter, as should we all.'

Barbara gave him a blank stare accompanied by a small smile, as if she had no idea what he was talking about.

March put down his cup and pulled out his pocket

watch. 'Oh, my word. Is that the time? I will be late for my meeting if I do not hurry.' He got to his feet. 'Perhaps you would care to walk with me to Whitehall, Duke? There are a couple of matters on which I would like to seek your advice.'

'I am sure His Grace has better things to do than advise you on which horse will win at Newmarket,' Barbara said. 'Indeed, I can tell you that if you would like a sure thing, you should simply make a wager on *his* horse.'

'Nonsense, Barbara. It has nothing at all to do with horses. Excuse my daughter, Your Grace. She has nothing in her head except foolish nonsense.'

It looked like a family squabble was about to break out. And for all that Xavier wanted to speak to Barbara alone, clearly now was not the time.

It would be better to wait for their assignation on Wednesday. 'I shall be delighted to accompany you, Lord March,' he said calmly. 'If I can be of assistance, it will be my pleasure.'

Miss Lowell got up and rang the bell. 'The gentlemen are leaving,' she told the butler, and he escorted them downstairs and let them out of the front door.

'Well!' Aunt Lenore said the moment the gentlemen left the room. 'What on earth were you about, Barbara? Such disrespect to your father. And in front of the Duke. What must he think?'

'I do not give a fig for what either of them thinks.'

Not true. Barbara had realised when she'd got home

from the theatre the real reason why she had not used the perfect opportunity to reveal their affair to all and sundry. True, the box had been crowded, and there had been no member of the royal family present, but many members of the *ton* had been there, as well as her father. It would have been so easy to create a scandal.

She just hadn't wanted to put Xavier to such embarrassment, when it was quite obvious, he had been doing his best to protect her reputation by inviting all those other people.

Though marriage was out of the question, she could not deny that she liked him too well to embroil him in a scandal, no matter how little damage it would cause him.

There was something else she really did give a fig about. Those hints dropped by her father just now. The fact that he thought her claim to the Lipsweiger jewels was tenuous made her stomach twist in knots.

Because the more she thought about it, the more she thought that was what he had actually been saying.

She went to the window and looked down into the street. Her father and the Duke were nowhere in sight. Two men disappearing together without a care in the world. Typical.

She would like to strangle her father. Now what was she to do?

She paced to the fireplace and back to the window.

'Stop,' Aunt Lenore said, covering her eyes with a trembling hand. 'You are making me dizzy.'

She opened her mouth to say something cutting and

closed it again. None of this was Aunt Lenore's fault. It was Father's.

She sat down on the sofa. 'He makes me so angry.'

'My dear girl. He is your father. He does the best he can for you.'

No. He did the best for himself. He always had. It had taken her years to admit it to herself, but now her eyes were fully open. There was no one to take care of her interests. Except herself.

And she was done letting Father walk roughshod over her life. Using her as a pawn to further his own ends.

And to have Xavier arrive right when they were talking about him. What a horrible coincidence. But at least he had heard the truth. When she brought their idyll to an end on Wednesday, it would not come as a surprise.

'I think it is time I left London,' she said.

Her aunt's mouth dropped open. 'In the middle of the Season? When you have such an opportunity to… I mean the Duke… The—'

'As I said, dearest Aunt, I have absolutely no intention of marrying him or anyone else. What I need to do is find a place to live where I can live out my days peacefully. Far away from London, from Society.' And from Father.

'And how will you accomplish this?' her aunt asked, with surprising force for one usually so vague. 'Who will keep you in the style you have so far enjoyed? It is no easy matter for a woman to depend on herself. I know this only too well. There are men who will take advantage of your lack of knowledge of the world. And what if you do not have sufficient income? Will you take in washing? Hire yourself out as a housemaid?'

Her aunt painted a very grim picture indeed. 'I will sell the jewels.'

'You know, living alone can be lonely when you are older. I think you should reconsider this aversion you have to marriage.'

'You seem to manage very well.'

'That does not mean I would not have preferred a husband and children. I was never asked.' She dabbed at her eyes with her handkerchief.

Barbara put an arm around her aunt's shoulders and gave her a quick squeeze. 'You can come and live with me.'

'That is very kind of you, Barbara. Indeed it is. But it is not at all what I would wish for you.'

She picked up her needlework from the workbox beside her chair. She stared at it, as if she had never seen it before.

She glanced warily over at Barbara. 'You know, marrying the Duke would solve all of these problems. Yours, since you would be well taken care of. Your Father's, because he would have all the influence he has ever desired as father-in-law to a duke.'

As her aunt spoke, Barbara felt the blood drain from her head. At first, she felt numb, then a cold chill coursed through her veins.

She clenched her hands in her lap. 'I see. Everyone's

well-being depends on me doing the right thing.' What about the right thing for her? Didn't anyone care?

'Even I would benefit,' Aunt Lenore continued dreamily, clearly not hearing Barbara's pain. 'No one would dare look down on me, were you a duchess. Not to mention, I would have been instrumental in making the match of the decade.'

It was like being caught in some sort of web, or a net, slowly closing around her. Logical words pressing in on her.

'It is a pipe dream, Aunt,' she said loudly enough to shake the elderly woman awake. 'The Duke is not about to marry a twice-widowed woman whose reputation hangs on a thread. He is seeking a woman who will be a proper wife and a proper duchess.'

Just saying it hurt. But it was true. She would be a terrible match for Xavier and he *must* know it.

Her aunt twisted her finger in one of the ringlets falling over her ears, then let it spring back into place.

'Perhaps you can somehow convince him you will change. It is clear that he likes you.'

She had absolutely no intention of doing anything of the sort.

Never again would she put her trust in a man. And that was what a wife must do, since once she was married she was no longer a person in her own right.

And as she had learned to her cost, she could not trust any man, even if she was drowning and he had a rope close to hand.

Oh, something inside her, the little girl who had sat

staring out of the dormitory window for the sight of her father, kept hoping Xavier might be different, but in her heart of hearts she knew it wasn't possible.

Father had never arrived to collect her in her hour of need.

Nor had Helmut for that matter. So why would Xavier be any different?

She would keep their assignation on Wednesday and bid him a fond farewell. And rather than drag his good name through the mire, seek a different way to bring about her ruin. That was the best she could do for him.

She ignored the twist of pain close to her heart.

Xavier mopped his face with the towel the trainer handed him.

'Are you mad?'

Xavier tossed the towel to one side and gave Julian a look of scorn. 'What are you talking about?'

'I saw you just now. That wasn't sparring, that was fighting. You are going to have a couple of lovely bruises tomorrow.'

New bruises to join the old ones.

'So will he.' He nodded towards his opponent. The man grinned.

He'd given as good as he'd got, and received a goodly sum for the privilege.

Julian shook his head. 'I haven't seen you in this sort of mood since your father died. What has happened?'

'I do not know what you mean.'

'Fighting like you wanted someone to hurt you.'

'It is exercise. Nothing more.' Trying to get the itch he had for the Countess out from under his skin, more like. He had come very close to making the worst mistake of his life.

Thank God her father had been present when he called or he would right now be receiving congratulations on his impending marriage.

Fortunately the time he'd had to reflect on the full import of his decision had stopped him from doing something so foolish.

Later today, when they met privately, he would tell her their affair was over.

Even if he had to beat himself to a pulp in the boxing ring to make himself do it.

She was not the sort of woman he wanted to wed. He should never have started an affair with her. He deserved a few bruises for being so stupid.

It had always worked when he was a lad at school. He rarely needed a real fight these days. A few rounds of sparring usually took the pepper out of his temper. Helped him regain control.

He took a deep breath. And put on his shirt. It seemed he definitely needed control when it came to dealing with the Countess.

And besides, she had made it very clear she had no interest in marrying him. He had, he realised later, been fortunate indeed to catch the tail end of her words. He could understand why she might not want to marry for a third time, even if he was a duke. He certainly did not wish her to be forced into it.

'Want to come to White's for luncheon?' Julian asked.

'I need to go home for a bath,' Xavier said. 'I have an appointment this afternoon.'

Julian looked disappointed but gave a shrug. 'Tomorrow, then.'

'Yes. Tomorrow.' By tomorrow, he and the Countess would have parted.

He just hoped she would not be too upset.

He did not like dealing with emotional women.

They reminded him too much of vague memories of his stepmother when her plans were thwarted.

Later that afternoon, walking down the path to the front door of Rose Tree Cottage, he was immediately aware that Barbara had arrived first.

He forced himself not to hurry. He had no wish to give any hint that he was anxious to see her again. To give her the wrong impression. To raise expectations.

He was merely looking forward to getting their farewell over and done.

He found her on the terrace looking out at the river.

She looked beautiful in a delicate muslin gown of pale blue. Calm. Stately. A wide-brimmed straw hat framed her lovely face, and a knowing smile curved her lips and lit her cat-like eyes as she turned to face him.

His heart seemed to jolt and then pick up speed. Hot blood coursed through his veins.

'Good afternoon,' he said, taking her hand, trying to ignore the rush of desire.

Yes, he would be well rid of this sort of emotional upheaval.

He kissed the back of her hand and turned it over, tracing the delicate blue line on her wrist with his gaze, feeling the pulse beat of her heart beneath his thumb.

He kissed her palm, inhaling the scent of her, wild, yet delicate and heady to his senses.

Her soft gasp made his body tighten.

'I wasn't sure you would come today,' she said in a soft murmur.

He gazed into her face. Her eyes were heavy-lidded and full of passion. Long lashes swept down and up, hiding her thoughts.

'Why would you think I would not?' he asked.

She reached up to cup his cheek in the palm he had kissed. 'After your encounter with my father, I thought you might be inclined to cut and run.'

He stiffened. 'I have never cut and run from anything in my life.' Inwardly, he shook his head at his words. Was not that what he intended? Was not severing their relationship cutting and running? But he wouldn't be doing so without letting her know. Not like some cowardly thief sneaking away in the dead of night.

She wound her arms around his neck and offered her lips to his.

He kissed her, hard, deeply, and let his body feel the pleasure of her softness melding against him.

She arched into him, sighing and moaning as their tongues tangled and nothing existing but the two of them.

When he broke the kiss, they were both breathing hard. She stared into his face, long and hard. Her thumbs ran along his cheekbones, and the faint twinge from an old bruise made him blink.

All his recent bruises were on his body.

'It is goodbye then?' she said softly.

What? How did she know? He had wanted to shield her from the pain of parting, somehow, and yet he could not. He must be honest.

'After today,' he agreed, trying to keep his voice gentle. He wanted to explain, but she touched his lips as if she did not want him to speak.

'Then today we will make memories.' Her eyes gleamed with wicked amusement.

He breathed an inward sigh of relief. She was not going to be upset, or angry, or throw things.

'Yes.' Memories. But memories were often painful things.

'I want to show you something,' she said. She took his hand and to his surprise lead him not into the house but into the garden.

Along the flagstones towards the river.

Her hand was so small, so delicate, so soft in his. And no gloves to spoil the sensation. He liked the way her fingers curled around his palm. He raised her hand and kissed the back of it. She looked up at him and laughter danced in her eyes.

But she did not stop.

Halfway down the garden she turned to pass through

a trellised arch with a bud covered rose bush clinging to it for support.

Beyond the arch was a hidden arbour surrounded by more roses twined around artfully placed trellises, and in the centre a seat, a statue and a small patch of sunlit grass on which someone had laid out a blanket and cushions.

'I forgot about this arbour,' he said.

'I had no idea it existed. Someone pruned the roses since last we were at the cottage, otherwise I would not have noticed it.'

'I have a gardener who looks after several of my properties.' He looked at the blankets. 'Are we having a picnic?'

She gave him a naughty sideways glance. 'I suppose you could call it that?'

His breath caught in his throat. She could not mean what he thought she meant.

Could she?

The high hedges meant they could not be seen by the occupants either side of the cottage, although perhaps they were overlooked from the windows high in the eaves. He glanced back and up.

Here amid the roses, they were completely hidden from view.

'You naughty minx!'

She sank onto the blanket cross-legged and leaned back on her hands, still laughing up at him.

He dropped to his knees facing her and, holding her face in his hands, kissed her lips briefly.

The brim of her bonnet got in his way. He untied the strings and cast it aside.

'That's better,' he said, leaning forward to devour her lovely, delicious mouth.

Slowly, she sank back on the cushions taking him down with her until they lay prone and entangled, her arms around him, his thigh between hers, her breast soft beneath his palm, with only the finest lawn between them.

No stays, he realised with a start, drawing back.

She pulled at his cravat, freeing the ends. 'Methinks you are wearing far too many clothes,' she murmured softly.

God help him. He was.

Chapter Fifteen

Barbara wanted this last assignation of theirs to be lovely, delicious and very, very naughty.

It was why she had arrived early. She'd eyed the sofa and the rug before the fire, but neither had seemed enough.

Only when she had wandered out into the garden and discovered this hidden gem of a garden had her imagination been fired.

Xavier was gazing at her in astonishment, and yes, delight.

He wasn't so stuffy as not to be able to see the possibilities. She flicked the ends of the cravat. 'Do you need help?'

Apparently jolted from his surprise, he sat up and divested himself of his coats and necktie, shoes, stockings and breeches, in pretty short order.

She lay on her side, one elbow, propping her head in her hand. What a pleasure it was to watch such a gorgeous man disrobe.

She reached out to help him with his shirt buttons.

He shook his head. 'Now you.'

Oh, she had planned this so well. She rose up on her knees. 'You need to undo the tapes at the back.'

He shifted so that he was behind her and did as she requested.

'No chemise?' he asked softly, running a finger down her naked spine between the edges of the gown.

She stood up and let the gown fall to the blanket. The sun on her skin was warm. The breeze a tantalising tickle.

'No stays. No chemise. Just me.'

He groaned softly, running his hands up and down her sides as if learning her shape with his fingers.

All she wore now were her sandals.

And kneeling as he was, he was perfectly placed to taste… She parted her thighs and put her hands on his shoulders.

He glanced up and must have read the invitation in her expression.

He grasped her hips in his hands and nuzzled at her quim.

She widened her stance.

A stroke of his tongue made her gasp. She reached down and guided his hand to her breast.

The nipple beaded and hardened at his touch.

Pleasure at his touch on her breast, and the slide of his tongue rippled through her. His hand left her breast and he leaned back on his heels, using his thumbs to part her nether lips.

He blew out a soft breath. The exquisite sensation on her feminine core weakened her knees.

She gasped, clinging on to his broad shoulders for dear life, and yet she did not fear falling—his firm grip around her hips held her effortlessly.

He inhaled deeply, then buried his face in her curls. Then he did something that made her cry out at the unbearable pleasure, so exquisite, so painfully sweet, the tension inside her snapped and she fell into hot bliss, like falling into a furnace full of sparks.

Heat suffused her body. A lovely relaxing warmth.

In the darkness that filled her mind, she felt him catch her and gently lower her to the blankets cradled in his arms.

It was a feeling of being protected and being desired and being loved. Longing to trust him with more than her body was nigh overwhelming. But if he let her down…

Moisture leaked from the corners of her eyes. Why did *he* have to make her feel these terrible, wonderful emotions?

He kissed her chin, the tip of her nose, her cheek. He must have tasted salt.

'Barbara?' he whispered. 'Love? What is it?'

Love. She could never be his love.

But he could be her lover. One last time.

She blinked away hope for something impossible and drew a fingertip down the side of his face.

'Come into me, sweet,' she said. 'I need you.'

He ripped his shirt off over his head and revealed his

erection, the hard shaft with the engorged head, showing he had seen to her needs before his own.

She cupped his balls in her hand, heavy and hot, and rough with crisp hair.

Brushing her hand away, he came over her and teased the entrance to her body with the head of his shaft.

Thought fractured and scattered.

Gripping his firm buttocks, she tried to draw him into her. He resisted easily though strain corded the tendons in his neck.

Lowering himself to rest on one elbow, he pressed little kisses to her lips, her chin, her jaw. He blew in her ear.

Tingles of pleasure ran down her spine to her core. She gasped.

He eased the head of his shaft a fraction deeper. Licked at her ear, then thrust his tongue deep inside.

She cried out at the myriad delightful sensations torturing her body. She felt boneless and tense and weak and alive and—

He gently cupped her breast, teasing the nipple until it furled into a hard tight bud.

And then he suckled.

She came apart.

He pushed into her, her inner muscles tightening around his shaft, every thrust pitching her upward again. 'I cannot,' she cried out.

'It's all right,' he said soothingly. 'Come with me, my sweet. Join me.'

The longing and sadness in his voice told her he knew this would be their last time together.

Disappointment and longing filled her. Longing and heartache. For her? For him? For them? She wasn't sure.

She arched into him, a counterpoint to each thrust, her legs coming up around his waist, opening herself to him, open and vulnerable, as she had been before.

He drove into her hard. Darkness and bliss beckoned and pulled at her. Her heart seemed to beat so hard she thought it might fly out of her chest. She clung to his shoulders, feeling the power and the strength of him in her fingertips and throughout her body.

The tension inside her snapped.

Pure white-hot bliss filled her. Her heart seemed to shatter at the same moment. A blinding pain that made her cry out.

He pulled away and spilled his seed on the grass, his chest heaving, his breathing rasping in his throat.

'I nearly...' He shook his head and collapsed beside her on the blanket.

She rolled into him, easing his head to rest on her shoulder, the heavy weight of his thigh across her legs a delicious heated reminder of what they had shared.

Delicious and heartbreaking.

Xavier came to with the sound of a bee buzzing somewhere close by and the scent of grass and roses and...woman.

Outdoors. He was lying in a tangle of nakedness with a light breeze cooling the sweat on his skin and grass tickling his leg. The blanket didn't do much to soften the ground beneath his hip.

He lifted his head to look at Barbara. She lay lax, naked and looking good enough to eat. He licked his lips, tasting the many flavours of this goddess of a woman who tempted him beyond his ability to resist.

How many times had she died in his arms. Three, he thought. It could have been more had he had enough control.

He had proved to himself he had little control where this woman was concerned. And he didn't actually care.

Some of the time.

He kissed the tip of her shoulder and lay back down.

She turned her head and those remarkable eyes regarded him from beneath heavy lids.

'Awake?' she murmured.

'Barely.'

Soft white skin, gilded by sunlight, she stretched lazily like a cat, arms above her head, her breasts rising to firm perky mounds, the muscles of her belly flattening above the delectable triangle of tight curls between her thighs, and yawned.

His mouth dried.

Desire stirred.

Faintly.

She rolled on her belly.

The shape, the curves and plane of her back like a voluptuous sculpture.

He stroked down her back and over the soft swell of her buttocks, his hand, the skin bronzed from the sun, the knuckles scarred from many battles in the ring, soothed by the billowy softness of her flesh.

Entranced by the vision and the sensual sensation, he continued to stroke, and she made a soft sound in her throat.

Like the purring of a cat.

'Like that, do you?' he muttered.

'Of course,' she murmured. Turning to face him, she parted her thighs and rose up.

And... God help him, he was ready.

Groaning at his own stupidity at letting her lead him by that male part of his anatomy that had no conscience while simultaneously revelling in the hunger for her that had lust gripping him by the balls, he knelt between her thighs, nudging her knees wider apart until his fitted between them, her quim open. He stroked along her slit and it was hot and slick and she pressed back into his hand with a soft sound of pleasure.

Control left him.

He guided his cock inside her and, gripping her shoulders, he took her hard and fast. His balls tightened. The sweet hot wetness tightened around his shaft, squeezing, flexing, and—

Bright light. Stark. White. Heat. The power of his orgasm shook him to the core. Struck him like lightening from a clear blue sky.

When he realised it was already upon him, he pulled clear.

Too late.

Too damn late.

His legs gave out. He sank to the ground. He felt her struggle weakly beneath him and somehow managed to move over enough to set her free.

Darkness swallowed him up in a void of hot bliss. His limbs were weighted by rocks, his chest heaving to draw breath.

Blackness swallowed him whole.

He felt her arms going around his torso, one arm burrowing beneath him. How long had he slept?

She buried her face in his neck. 'Oh, heavens,' she whispered between panting breaths. 'What on earth was that?'

Had she felt it too? The jolt of what felt like lightning. He had come so hard and fast his mind had completely blanked. He'd tried to wait. He had tried, he was sure.

He'd failed utterly.

'I don't know,' he said.

'It was...amazing,' she murmured.

Amazing and wild and glorious. Completely reckless. She could be expecting his child.

Barbara, carrying his child. The mental picture of her body swelling with his child was extraordinarily wonderful. Something sweetly painful pulled at his heart.

He groaned and threw an arm across his eyes to blot out the sun that had moved so it shone directly in his eyes, as well as to ward off the thoughts buzzing around in his head. They all ended up in one place.

They would have to wed.

'If you lie out here much longer you will burn,' he said. He could not let this happen again.

'I know,' she murmured softly.

She didn't move a muscle.

He needed to do something. To make her safe. To protect her from the sun right above them.

He could not move.

He must.

He forced himself up and grabbed one side of the blanket, covering her.

He sank down again.

'You?' she said.

'Shh. I'm fine.' He relaxed into the darkness.

It could not have been long before he awoke again.

The sunlight and shadows looked more or less the same. His skin was warm. Her breathing had slowed, and her eyelashes formed a shadowed crescent above her cheekbones. He leaned forward and kissed that delicate place, inhaling the lovely scent of a woman well-pleasured.

What would it be like to wake beside this woman every day? To know she would be at his dinner table every night. The thought pleased him more than it should if he were sensible.

Her eyelids fluttered, her lashes tickling his lips like a butterfly kiss.

'We should go indoors,' he said. 'We need to talk.'

One could not have a sensible conversation stark naked as they were. He was likely to get distracted again.

That might be fatal.

No. No sense fooling himself. What he had done

meant no going back. After everything he'd promised his uncle, and himself. He'd proved the apple didn't fall far from the tree.

He had always thought badly of his father for letting his lust control his decisions, but perhaps it wasn't only lust—there were other emotions, gentler, warmer feelings stirring deep within him, feelings that seemed to soften his resolve and make him want more than a suitable match. If he wasn't a duke and all that entailed...

What on earth was he thinking?

Great-Uncle Thomas would have been so disappointed in him.

Hell, he was disappointed in himself.

But, while he might have lost control, he still had his honour. He wasn't going to let her take that from him.

He helped her dress then pulled his shirt over his head and put on his breeches and shoes.

She watched him in silence as if she sensed something of his mood.

He went down on one knee to help her on with her sandals while she used his shoulder for balance.

The lightest touch. Fingertips only, but he felt it as if it was of momentous weight.

He fastened the buckle and guided her foot to the ground holding her ankle. Such a slender ankle. He had the urge to run his hand upward. They learned the curve of her calf. He glanced up.

She was watching him, her thoughts as mysterious as the small smile on her lips.

Kneeling before her this way, he could propose now.

He grimaced at the thought. There was nothing romantic about a marriage of convenience. It would be a matter of business. Terms. Conditions. Somehow, he had to make this right.

And there must be conditions.

He buckled the other shoe and stood up.

Barbara released Xavier's shoulder as he rose to his feet.

Such a tall man. And so handsome. She was tempted to kiss him.

Instead, she picked up the blanket and shook it out.

He took the other end and together they folded it in half lengthwise. Like a couple of laundry maids.

She chuckled.

He frowned. 'What do you find humorous?'

'Us. A duke folding the blanket like a domestic servant.'

He looked at her blankly.

It had sounded funnier in her mind than it did when spoken. 'Never mind.'

They came together and he took it from her and finished the job. She picked up the cushions and they walked up the path to the cottage.

'Where did you find this?' he asked, holding up the blanket.

She gestured to the bedroom.

While he put the blanket away, she tidied her hair and tied on her hat.

Could anyone tell from looking at her how she had

spent the afternoon? He came up behind her, looking at her in the glass. They smiled, the kind of smile only lovers could smile.

He picked a blade of dried grass from her hair, frowning at it, whether in annoyance or surprise, she wasn't sure, but then she really wasn't sure about anything with this man.

He took her hand and led her to sit on the sofa and sat down beside her. An expression of nervousness flickered across his face.

She removed her hand from his grip. 'What is it?'

'About what happened out there. My failure to… There could be a child.' He finished his words in a rush.

'Oh,' she said. Neither of her husbands had managed to give her a child. Of course, there hadn't been much of a chance with the first, and the second had been so busy spreading his seed around, begetting a child with her would have been luck indeed. His. Not hers. God, she would have been stuck there.

'While you are not the woman I envisaged as my duchess, I will marry you, of course.'

Anger stirred in her belly. She kept her expression and her voice carefully neutral. 'What sort of woman did you envisage?'

He wasn't looking at her. He was looking off into the distance as if recalling a memory. 'A more modest sort of woman, who would bring honour to the family name and take the duties of duchess seriously. Not the sort of woman who wears red to Almack's and has affairs.'

Hurt and insulted, even knowing that he was not

wrong, she lifted her chin and smiled sweetly. 'Well, you do not need to worry. I doubt there will be a child.'

'Are you saying you are barren?'

She straightened her back. 'Quite possibly.'

He shook his head. 'Unless you are certain, then I will not take the chance.'

'Well, that is very noble and honourable of you, Duke, but as you say, I am not at all the sort of woman you wished for a duchess, and you are certainly not the man for me.'

Shadows filled his expression. 'It will not do, Barbara. What is done is done. We will marry.'

Did he think to marry her against her will? She opened her mouth to speak but he did not pause to give her a chance.

'These are my terms. Abide by them and we shall get along.' He counted them off on his fingers as he spoke. 'There will be no affairs with other men while you are of child-bearing age. No gambling. No cause for gossip. You will always have the best for the welfare of our children in mind. You will attend functions of state by my side. Apart from the need to beget an heir, we need not see each other.'

She stared at him in disbelief and horror. Did he think so little of her as a person that she would either need or agree to such a list of conditions—or indeed, such a travesty of a marriage? Did he think he could ride roughshod over her with his terms without even giving her a say in the matter? 'Is that all?' she asked with deceptive mildness.

He frowned deeply. 'I believe so. I will inform you if I think of anything else.'

'No.'

He blinked. 'No what?'

'Thank you for your most flattering proposal, but no, I will not marry you.'

'Don't be foolish. Of course you will. You will never receive a better offer.'

She wanted to hit him over the head.

She stood up. 'You are certainly not the man I want for a husband.' She didn't want any man for a husband.

'I am sorry. I know you do not want a husband. I heard what you said, and I respect that you have your reasons, but we don't have a choice.'

'I don't care what you think or what you say. We are not getting married.'

'No child of mine will be brought up a bastard.'

The anger in his voice gave her pause. 'As far as we know, there is no child. So put it out of your mind.'

'If you do not care for your own reputation, then think about the child. Your family.'

Her heart picked up speed. She gripped her hands tightly. 'My father has nothing to do with this.'

He took a deep breath and regarded her coldly. 'Let us see how you feel after you have had some time to reflect, shall we? You are a sensible woman, and I am sure you will see that I am right.'

'Damn it, Xavier. You and your stupid honour. You have ruined everything.' She picked up her reticule and stormed out of the house.

She knew he would not follow, because he would not want to make a scene. Her carriage was waiting at the nearby inn not far from the Andersons' house as usual. John Coachman shot to his feet when he saw her entering the yard. With a last regretful glance at his mug of ale, he started shouting orders for the ostlers to put the carriage to.

Damn. Now what was she to do? Her father would be in alt at the thought of a duke for a son-in-law, if this somehow came to his ears. She would have to make sure it did not.

And heaven help her, Xavier's offer had been so very tempting.

Until he listed his demands. Another man who had no respect for women.

Not a chance.

Chapter Sixteen

Your Grace,

I am pleased to inform you that your concern about the arrival of additional responsibilities is unfounded.

You will be relieved to know that we have no reason for further conversation.

Sincerely,

B

Xavier had absolutely no doubt who the note was from, and the offhand tone of her words had left him fuming.

He clenched his fingers around the balled-up note in his pocket. It had been delivered right as he was leaving for a bout at Gentleman Jackson's. Of course he was relieved to learn she was not with child. Marrying in a hurry to disguise the arrival of a child never worked. People could count.

But that didn't mean they should not marry. They had been intimate. If news of their affair got out, she would be no less ruined. Why couldn't she see that it would be best to forestall any chance of that sort of rumour? His name would offer all the protection she needed.

Why did she have to be so damned headstrong when it could all be orderly and logical?

Xavier strode into Jackson's boxing saloon.

The owner took one look at him and shook his head. 'I think your temper has the better of you. No one here will fight you.'

Xavier glared at him. 'Since when does my temper have anything to do with it? My control—'

'Is not what it was.' The man shook his head. 'Recently.' He put a hand on Xavier's shoulder. 'You know it. Joe took almost a week to heal.'

Guilt filled him. He took a deep breath. 'You are right. I have let personal problems cloud my judgement.'

'Let me know when the problems are sorted out.'

'Are you not boxing today?' a familiar accented voice asked. 'How disappointing. I had hoped to watch today, after an appointment robbed me of the privilege last time.'

He turned to greet Charles. 'Apparently not.' He hoped he sounded calmer than he felt. 'There is no one available to spar.' Not exactly an untruth.

Charles raised an eyebrow. 'Shall we go to the club, then? Perhaps a brandy would not go amiss.'

What Xavier wanted to do was fight to exhaustion and calm. He still did not know how to deal with Barbara, or how he felt about her refusal. 'A brandy is a fine idea.'

With St James's Street only a few steps away, it was not long before they were seated in comfortable leather armchairs in a quiet corner of the reading room in White's and sipping in silence. At least, for a few minutes.

'What causes your frown?' Charles asked. 'I am guessing a woman. Am I right? Should I wager on it?'

Xavier felt his spine stiffen. Were his emotions really so obvious? He loathed the sort of gossip men liked to engage in. But devil take it, Charles wasn't wrong. 'The lady in question is being far from cooperative.'

'It is hard to imagine someone of your rank and wealth having difficulties with a female. But some can be unexpectedly spirited.'

Perhaps that was the problem. A rebellious female like Barbara would balk at any sort of restraint. Likely he had handled her badly.

'What is your advice for dealing with a wilful woman?'

Charles chuckled but there was an uncomfortable edge to it. 'Regarding my sister-in-law, you know my opinion.'

Xavier did not let his shock show on his face. At least, he thought he had not. 'Now, why would you think I was referring to the Countess?'

'I saw the warmth in your eyes at the theatre, my friend. And you have danced with her at every ball I have attended. I also see her expression when she regards you, when you are not looking her way. It is the way she looked at my brother before they wed.'

'Oh, and how is that?'

'Like the cat watching a bird.' He laughed. 'Ready to pull you down in her claws.'

'I thought you two were friends? She seems to think so. And yet...' He sipped his drink and waited.

Charles looked down at his hand on the table and spread his fingers. He looked up with a rueful smile. 'We are not enemies. Indeed, I did my best to, how do you say it, ease things between her and my brother. There were many arguments. It was not such a happy marriage. My brother was not as wealthy as she had expected.'

Xavier frowned. 'Are you saying she was disappointed because he wasn't rich? That she is a fortune hunter?'

Was she now trying to rectify the matter by trapping a duke? Except she wasn't, was she? She was refusing to marry him. Confusion filled him.

'I cannot blame her entirely for the unhappiness. My brother made promises he could not keep. She expressed her disapproval as only a wife can, if she wants to dishonour her husband, you understand?'

'You mean she took a lover?'

'And when my brother fought for his honour, her arrival at the duel... Well, it was a disaster.'

'Your brother died fighting over Barbara?'

'He lost concentration when he saw her walk on the field. It was the only time he ever lost a duel.'

What a strange way to put it. 'He had a habit of duelling?'

'It is common for all young men in Prussia to fight to the death. We do not box.'

There was a whisper of scorn in the other man's voice that set Xavier's back up. He took a deep breath. 'It was hardly her fault if he was killed in a duel.'

'True.' He shrugged. 'It seems she was unlucky. Twice.'

'And from there came the rumour she was a black widow.'

'Gossip travels fast.'

Making her the butt of jokes upon her arrival in England. Was it possible someone hoped to frighten off prospective bridegrooms?

Xavier finished his drink. He really did not like the way this supposed friend of Barbara's painted her character. It felt distasteful. 'I hope you will excuse me, I have business that requires my attention.'

He pushed to his feet and Charles rose with him.

They shook hands. 'Thank you for your company,' Charles said. 'I am glad you granted me this opportunity to get to know you better.'

'You are welcome,' Xavier responded, trying to make sense of his feelings about the things Charles had said.

'Please do not tell Barbara of this conversation,' Charles said. 'I only broached the matter because I do not want to see a man I admire follow in my brother's footsteps.'

The words rang slightly hollow in Xavier's ears.

They parted on the front steps of White's, heading in opposite directions.

Xavier supposed he should be grateful for Charles's frankness about his sister-in-law, and perhaps he would have been, if he did not have the sense it was not as altruistic as the other man professed.

In some ways, Barbara seemed like two different people. The audacious widow who blatantly broke Society's rules and the sensual, intelligent woman who made him laugh and who brought him joy, and that he...what?

Liked?

'Liking' was too weak a word for how he felt about Barbara. He admired her *joie de vivre*, her spirit, her lack of concern for petty rules, and the way she stood up to him like no one else. She seemed free, somehow.

Dangerously free.

It was her lack of concern for rules, or titles, or wealth that had made him frame his marriage proposal the way he had. His need for control over his life.

Clearly, she had balked at his conditions.

But should not a wife make accommodations for a husband? Or would those rules crush the spirit he so admired?

And now this brother-in-law of hers had made a point of putting her past in as bad a light as possible. To what purpose?

To drive him away? If so, why? What did it matter to Charles?

An instinct he rarely ignored told him *something was rotten in the State of Denmark*.

He intended to find out why it was.

* * *

Barbara stalked into the drawing room where she had been told she would find her aunt.

The dear lady was stretched out on the chaise longue, her embroidery in her lap and the pages of a newspaper over her face. The rhythmic rise and fall of her chest indicated she had nodded off as she so often did after luncheon.

She still wasn't sleeping well, not even at the back of the house. Not since the burglary.

Barbara huffed out a breath and sat down in the chair opposite. If she woke her, the poor dear would be out of sorts for the rest of the day and likely Barbara would not get the answer she wanted.

She rummaged through her workbag beside the chair and pulled out the fabric for a footstool she had been working on. It was something Aunt Lenore had started many years before, but had abandoned. Barbara had promised she would try to finish it.

She sorted through the wool threads and picked out a dark red for a rose. Red suited her mood. She was angry.

Angry at Father. As usual.

With an occasional glance at her aunt, she plied her needle in short, swift jabs. But as she settled into the rhythm, her stitches became longer and began to flow.

Her anger, while it did not disappear, seemed to ease to a manageable level. She had almost finished the inner petals of the rose when her aunt stirred. The newspaper fell to the floor and her eyes blinked a few times.

'Shall I ring for tea?' Barbara said quietly, putting her embroidery back in her workbag.

Aunt Lenore smiled. 'Yes, dear. That would be lovely.'

Barbara got up and rang the bell. By the time she turned back, her aunt was upright and patting at her hair. 'I must have dropped off,' she said.

'I think you must have.'

'Dear me. Dear me.' She looked down at the handkerchief she had been embroidering. 'And not a stitch done. And I had hoped to have this ready for your father's birthday.'

'Speaking of Father, do you have any idea where he has gone or when he is likely to return?'

Aunt Lenore turned the embroidery hoop over and peered at the back of her work. 'Gone? Has he gone?'

Barbara stifled her impatience. This was her aunt's way of putting off unpleasant discussions. Answering a question with a question.

'I walked over to his townhouse this morning. His butler said he has left for parts unknown. He took his valet and packed an overnight bag.' And as usual had not left a single word of explanation for his daughter.

'I hope you did not go without a footman?'

'I did not. Do you know where he went?'

'Do you need him for something, dear?'

Yet more questions. 'I do.' She was going to make it very clear to Father she did not intend to marry anyone. Not Derbridge. Not anyone. Crystal clear.

If he hadn't already grasped that fact.

All she had to do was remain single until she was twenty-five, in a month's time, then she could live the rest of her life in relative comfort and on her own terms.

When she did not explain, her aunt sighed. 'I have no idea where he went.'

'But you did know he was leaving London.' It wasn't a question.

Aunt Lenore adjusted her shawl around her shoulders, tied and untied the ends. 'He did mention he planned to visit a friend. Said he would be gone for two or three days.'

'And no one thought to mention it to me?'

'He visited when you were out yesterday afternoon. I forgot all about it.'

'Perhaps the Foreign Office knows where he is?' Barbara mused.

Her aunt looked scandalised. She sniffed. 'They wouldn't tell you even if they knew, and you can wager your best handkerchief they will tell him you enquired after him upon his return.'

Her aunt did not like 'the ministry types,' as she called them. They never revealed Father's whereabouts, no matter the need.

Barbara was pretty sure that he left instructions that no one, except perhaps the minister, was to be informed where he could be found.

'Bother,' she said.

The butler arrived with the tea, and there was nothing more she could say until the tray was placed in front of them and the butler left.

'Petit fours,' her aunt exclaimed. 'So dainty. Do try one.'

Barbara took a bite from one. She tasted lemon icing with raspberry jam filling between the layers of cake.

They were indeed delicious.

Xavier would like these. She had noticed he had a sweet tooth.

Dash it! It didn't matter to her one whit what Xavier liked.

Perhaps it was for the best that Father had disappeared. If Barbara could not speak to him, neither could Xavier.

If he even still wanted to. Barbara had already sent round a message containing the good news. He did not *have* to lower himself to marry her after all. The pains in her belly that morning had made that clear enough. A baby was not in the offing.

Now all she needed was to continue to make herself completely ineligible—and useless to her father—and she could continue on with her life as planned, as if she'd never met Xavier.

She tried to ignore the painful squeeze of her heart. It was a foolish organ, and it did not help her in the least.

'Oh, Barbara,' said her aunt. 'I almost forgot. You received this this morning.' She held up a sealed letter.

Barbara broke the seal. 'An invitation to a ball on Thursday. From a Lady Wells. Do you know her?'

Her aunt frowned. 'No. I do not recall her at all. Thursday, you say? Why so late an invitation? I can't possibly go. My friend Mrs Thursk invited me to play cards that evening. I have been looking forward to it. You will have to decline.'

She didn't *have* to do anything. 'She offers an overnight stay and a grand ball under the stars. It sounds quite charming.' It might be the perfect opportunity to escape from London, if she could only find a way to accomplish her utter ruin in the meantime.

She sighed. 'I may go, if I can find a suitable escort.' She put the invitation aside.

She picked up the newspaper from the floor and glanced at the advertisements.

It was open at the results of the horse races at Epsom Downs. 'Are you gambling on the horses, Aunt?'

Her aunt gave a little snort of scorn. 'Certainly not.'

'Hmm.' Barbara glanced down the list of horses but did not see a name she recognised.

Men loved their horse racing because it involved gambling. As did several other of their sports, cockfighting and bullbaiting and boxing. Blood sports they were called. Unsuitable for a lady's delicate sensibilities, according to Xavier's list of rules.

She lifted her head and stared unseeing at her aunt. Well, maybe that—

'Barbara?'

She came to. 'Did you say something?'

'You are wool-gathering. I said, would you like another cake? Or shall I ring for them to take the tray away?'

'Oh. No more for me. I will ring.'

She got up and pulled the bell. A cockfight would

do nicely How would she find out where such things were held? It would be common knowledge among the men, of course. But who could she ask?

Charles, naturally.

'What are you smiling at, my dear?' Aunt Lenore asked.

'I believe I may have solved a problem.'

'What problem?' She looked anxious.

'Nothing to worry about, I can assure you.'

Not yet, anyway.

Chapter Seventeen

Barbara glanced at the clock. It was almost time for Charles to arrive.

He was due to take her to a cockfight today; he had promised to call for her at ten. She had told him that this desire of hers to witness a blood sport was to win a wager. She had bet a woman's stomach for blood sport was equally as strong as any man's.

A ridiculous wager. But just the sort of thing people did.

She could not rid herself of the sinking feeling in the pit of her stomach. Xavier would never speak to her again, once he heard about today's escapade. Something in her chest squeezed the breath from her lungs. It hurt more than she cared to admit.

The only good part was that after this Father would have to cast her off. Wouldn't he?

While she had not yet heard from Charles, she had absolutely no doubt he would keep his promise.

He always had.

Even on that fatal day when Helmut had been killed

in a duel. Charles had told her about her husband's folly and taken her to the site of the duel in hopes of putting a stop to it.

They had been too late.

The men had been duelling with rapiers. When Helmut caught sight of her, he had been furious, and in his temper had left himself open to his opponent.

The rapier had pierced his heart.

As his infidelity had pierced hers.

But she hadn't wanted him to die. It had been quite awful. For everyone. Especially Charles.

Dressed and ready, she waited in the drawing room, hoping her needlework would settle her nerves, but her fingers shook so much she couldn't thread her needle.

Finally, the butler announced Charles, who strode in looking distinguished in a flower-embroidered waistcoat and navy blue coat. The serious expression on his face boded ill.

She gestured for him to sit on the sofa and gripped her hands in her lap. She took a deep breath. 'I am ready to leave whenever you say.'

He frowned. 'I am not saying you do not look beautiful, because you do, but that attire would not do at all. You would stand out like a cat in a kennel.'

Exactly as she had planned.

He leaned back against the cushion. 'It is as well we cannot go.'

'What?'

'I am sorry, my dear, but there is no cockfighting today. Or tomorrow. Not until Saturday.'

Today was only Thursday. 'Why not?'

'It is a sport of the common classes who are working. Not until Saturday afternoon do they spend time on such pastimes.'

How stupid not to realise that. She rose and went to the window, trying to hide her disappointment. She looked down into the street at people hurrying along beneath umbrellas.

Grey and rainy. Again. Fitting, given the way she felt.

Now what was she going to do? Dance naked down Bond Street? In the rain?

Something like that and they would put her in Bedlam. Not what she wanted.

'Nothing this evening?'

'No. And besides, we are going to Lady Wells's ball this evening. You promised you would go with me.'

Since Charles had told her he was also invited, she had decided it would be the perfect way to make her escape following a scandalous appearance at a cockfight. Now it seemed all her plans had gone awry.

'Two days to wait is not such a long time,' he said, clearly trying to ease her disappointment.

If there was any way of knowing that her father would be out of town until after Saturday, she might take the chance.

It was too risky. She shook her head. 'I will lose the wager.'

'Unless...' He hesitated.

'Unless what?' She sat down beside him on the couch. 'What have you thought of?'

'Did it have to be cockfighting? You said a male blood sport.'

'I did.'

'Pugilism is a male sport. Boxing. It is quite bloody and violent.'

She clasped her hands in her lap. Boxing. 'There is a boxing match?'

'Not a match. Sparring.'

At her blank look he added, 'Practice. Gentlemen practise boxing every day at Jackson's saloon.'

'Oh, practice. Like fencing.'

'Nothing like fencing. Well, perhaps a little. It is not an actual match, but the men do hit each other. More often than not there are bruises. And sometimes a bloody nose or two.'

'Do ladies attend this practice?'

'I have never seen any. I would think it is far too violent for the fairer sex. At least, those who are ladies.'

It sounded perfect. 'And when do these practices take place?'

'All the time.'

'You mean we could go now?'

'We could. Do you think it will satisfy the requirements of your wager?'

'I believe it will. Let us go.'

'Are you sure? I think you will not enjoy it.'

She gave him a bright smile, while inside she felt a little nauseous. 'I am sure.'

'You will need a hat and a veil. We would not wish anyone to recognise you.'

She smiled inwardly. 'Naturally. I will fetch my hat and coat at once.'

Xavier tried to focus on his opponent in the ring. Thinking about Barbara's refusal of his offer and what to do about it kept spoiling his concentration.

He had to find a way to prove to her that she was making a mistake by turning him down.

Because he wanted her as his wife? Was want even a strong enough word?

He had the feeling that if she did not marry him, he would regret it for the rest of his life.

And that was ridiculous. Wasn't it?

Oh, Lord, what a mess. He seemed to be going around in circles. Anger rose like a hot tide.

Thwack! A blow from his opponent to his head made his ears ring. He refused to feel the pain. He danced back and looked for an opening.

Focus.

He landed a flush hit to his sparring partner's chin that rocked Pimm back on his heels and earned Xavier a glare of anger.

Xavier reined in his temper. Boxing was a science not a brawl.

They closed in a flurry of fists.

A stir among some of the patrons watching him spar caught his attention. He glanced in that direction. A woman?

A glancing punch to his ribs made him wince and knocked the breath from his body. His sparring partner shook his head at him. 'Keep your guard up, Your Grace.'

For a second, his brain did not believe what his eyes had seen.

Not just any woman. Barbara.

He took a blow to the stomach and went down to his knees. Pimm landed a blow to the side of his head. The room darkened.

Above all the other voices, he heard her cry of shock.

Someone shouted. 'Bloody hell. The black widow.' There were whistles and cat calls.

Xavier shook his head to clear his vision.

The trainer leaped forward and started the count.

Breathing hard, Xavier waited until the count nine and got to his feet.

There was blood dripping on his chest from his nose. Anger welled up in his chest in a hot tide.

His sparring partner put up his hands and backed away. 'No more, Your Grace.'

The trainer, Able, a wily old pugilist long retired, climbed the ropes. 'It is over,' he said firmly. 'I'll be having no temper tantrums, Your Grace.'

His anger had nothing to do with boxing and everything to do with Barbara, who stood wide-eyed among the sporting men at the edge of the ring, a hand covering her mouth. Most of the men were looking her way, either in surprise or with vulgar leers.

'I apologise, Able. I was distracted.'

Able's eyes followed the direction of his glance. 'Women.' He spat out a curse. 'Who brought her in?'

Charles. He was already pulling her by the arm, trying to drag her away. Didn't he realise the damage bringing her into Jackson's would do to her reputation? Xavier was going to have strong words with the fellow. Very strong words.

As his temper subsided to dull rage, the pain from his bruised and battered body made itself known.

He accepted that pain as his due for his own lack of skill. But there was another pain in his chest he didn't recognise. A tightening around his heart that was somehow more painful that any of the blows from his opponent's fists.

Put there by the horror he had seen in her expression. Horror at seeing what sort of man he really was. The brute.

How could any woman understand that the only thing that kept him from being the brute he could be if he lost control was the give and take of blows he received in the ring?

Even he didn't understand it.

He wiped his face on the towel Able handed to him and made his way to the changing room, where he allowed Able to minister to his cuts and bruises. He hardly noticed the sting of the ointment applied to a cut on his cheek.

'Careless, Your Grace. Very careless. If I didn't know better, I would say you had never set a foot in the ring before. Mr Jackson, he's gonna ban you again. Good thing Pimm kept *his* head after that nasty hit to the jaw.'

'Tell him I apologise.' He pulled a few guineas from his pocket. 'Hopefully this will make it right.'

'Ah. It might do at that. Though I think that hit to your ribs gave him considerable satisfaction.' Able chuckled.

Devil take it. The thought of Barbara watching all of that made him shudder.

By the time he was cleaned up and dressed, there was no sign of Barbara and the Count, but the gossip hadn't ceased.

Julian, who had not been there earlier, approached him. 'Did I hear aright? The Countess came to watch you box? What the devil were you thinking to invite her here?'

He glared at his friend and clenched his fist. Then slowly released his fingers. Control was everything.

He'd already let his control slip once today. It wasn't going to happen again.

'She was here?' He hoped he sounded as dismissive as he intended. 'Not at my invitation.'

'Once this gets out, she won't be accepted anywhere.'

He inhaled a deep breath and enjoyed the sting of pain. 'No.'

Julian looked puzzled. 'Don't you care?'

Of course he cared. Deeply. Far more than he should, given that he had already decided that she was not the wife for him.

And yet…

He pushed the thought aside. He needed to get to the bottom of why the blasted Count would knowingly ruin her. Because he must have known it would.

'No. I don't care.'

Julian's eyebrows shot up. 'And here was me thinking you had finally met your match.'

'Why the hell would you say that?'

'Because she is the only female you have ever looked at with any kind of interest and the only one who seemed to stand up to you.'

She was. She had been. And she was the only female he had actually wanted to offer for, if he told himself the truth.

If only she hadn't had such a scheming unpleasant father and a tendency to do things that put her beyond the pale.

How could she not know that attending an all-male preserve such as this was just as scandalous and trying to enter a gentleman's club in St James?

He stilled.

Barbara was no fool. Was it possible she had known what she was doing all along? That she intended to ruin herself utterly?

Why on earth would she do such a thing?

Because she thought to make sure Xavier wouldn't marry her? Would she go so far?

He recalled the things he had demanded with a wince.

'Sorry, Your Grace.'

'No, no. Not you. A thought.' A terrible realisation. He needed to talk to her and see what he could do to make things right.

Chapter Eighteen

Aunt Lenore appeared at the doorway of Barbara's chamber. She stared at the trunk in the middle of the room and the half-filled portmanteau.

'What are you doing?' she asked.

'Packing.'

'Where are you going?'

'To Lady Wells's ball. Charles will accompany me.' She needed to leave before the news of her attendance at the boxing saloon reached her aunt's ears.

Aunt Lenore flitted into the room and perched on the chair at the dressing table. 'This is very sudden, Barbara. You said nothing to me about going to this ball alone.'

'I most certainly did. I told you I would go if I could find a suitable escort.'

'I should go with you.'

'No, no. You go and enjoy your game of cards. I will be perfectly safe with Charles. You know I will.'

'But why are you packing? Will you not return tonight?'

'It will be very late when the ball is over and Charles was worried about footpads. I might even stay a day or so longer. I have never been to Greenwich. I would like to see the observatory.'

Her aunt looked doubtful.

Barbara gave her a quick hug. 'Do not worry. Everything will be fine.'

'If you say so. But you will take your maid?'

'Naturally.' She just hoped her maid wouldn't object to country living, because after today, Barbara could never return to London Society.

'Have you heard from Derbridge?'

The sound of his name was like an arrow piercing her heart.

She took a deep breath. 'The Duke and I agreed that we were not suited and he will pursue a bride elsewhere.'

It hurt to say it.

It hurt to think it.

After what she had done, she knew she would never see him again. Could never. It would be far too painful. For her.

Because now he must despise her utterly. She had seen it in his eyes in that brief second when their gazes met in that horrible place full of men and smoke and... She shuddered.

She never wanted to see that look from him again.

She was not the right wife for him and he had only offered marriage because he saw it as his duty.

Marriage under those circumstances was out of the question.

'Oh, dear,' Aunt Lenore said vaguely. 'I thought you two were getting along well. The way he looked at you at the theatre. And you him. April and May, I thought for sure—'

'Aunt! Please. Stop.' She threw her toiletries in the portmanteau.

'Your father needs to hear about this.'

'Father is not here.' As usual. 'You can tell him all about it when he returns.'

Her maid came in with her hat and coat on and with a footman. 'The hackney is outside, my lady, and James is ready to take your bags down.'

'Thank you.'

'A hackney?' her aunt said. 'Why is Charles not coming to fetch you?'

'Because he needs to hire a carriage and I am meeting him at the livery.' In fact, she had hired the coach, since she would need it for her onward travels, but she did not want her father to know which stable she had used and trace her whereabouts. She had arranged for the hired coach to meet her at Charles's lodgings.

'Excuse me please, Aunt, I am already somewhat late, and if I delay further this hackney will cost far more than it should.'

She stepped back to allow the young man to pick up her trunk and followed him downstairs with her maid carrying the bag.

At the front door, she bid her aunt farewell. She gave

her only a brief kiss on the cheek, and felt terrible, because likely she would never see the woman again. She had grown fond of her.

Unexpectedly, tears burned at the backs of her eyes. She was going to miss the old dear. She turned away quickly in case she revealed too much.

Her aunt was her father's creature and would always take sides with him. Barbara could never trust her with her secrets, at least not anything important.

Out of her aunt's hearing, she directed the hackney driver to Charles's lodgings and climbed aboard with her maid.

Charles was waiting for them on the pavement when they arrived.

'I was beginning to think you would not come,' he said. 'Or that I had misunderstood and I should come to fetch you.'

Barbara lowered the veil on her hat. For once, she did not want to be recognised. 'You are sure you do not mind staying overnight?'

'Positive.'

There was an odd note in his voice.

She frowned.

'Do not worry, my dear. All will be well. By tomorrow your little mistake will be old news and everything will be as before.'

He clearly did not understand English Society. 'You are such a good friend to me, Charles.'

He beamed. 'Please. Get in the coach and let us be

on our way. I will ride with the coachman if you do not mind. The confines of the carriage upset my digestion.'

They climbed aboard.

Barbara leaned back against the squabs as the coach started off. She had done it. Finally she had escaped the machinations of her father.

The fact that she would never see Xavier again carved a hole in her chest. The pain of it was almost unbearable. But it would heal. It had to. While she had been unable to prevent herself from falling in love with him, he did not love her back.

He saw her only as a duty or a burden that needed to be moulded into his idea of a perfect wife.

That horrible list of his had made that perfectly clear.

She glanced over at her maid, who was staring out of the window. 'Have you ever been to Greenwich?'

'No, my lady. I cannot say I have.'

'Nor I.' Charles might say she should not worry, but the chance was very high that someone among Lady Wells's guests would have heard of her supposed faux pas this afternoon and in short order she would be *persona non grata*.

Which was why she planned to plead illness once she arrived and remain in her room until she could sneak away.

She hoped Charles would not be too annoyed when he discovered her gone tomorrow morning.

She felt terrible about taking advantage of his friendship. Dishonourable.

She would leave him a note and hopefully he would understand, the way he always had.

As to where she would go? She had decided on a small village near the coast. She had enough funds to last her for a few months. She did not know how long it would take for Father to hand over her widow's portion from her first marriage after her birthday, but hopefully not longer than that. But if it did, she had the Lipsweiger jewels to fall back on.

She took a deep breath.

She could do this.

She really didn't have a choice.

'The Countess is not at home,' the butler declared.

'The same way she wasn't at home the last time I called?' Xavier said.

'Your Grace, she has left the house.'

Damn it. The man was telling the truth. Xavier could tell. He contemplated leaving it at that. But could not. He needed some sort of explanation for her behaviour and to help devise a plan to deal with it.

'Is Miss Lowell at home?'

'I can ask.'

Xavier handed the man his card. He wasn't going to storm in on the elderly widow. It wouldn't be right.

Barbara was a different matter.

He paced the hall, waiting for the butler's return. It seemed like a long time, but probably wasn't.

'Miss Lowell will see you in the drawing room,' the

butler said when he reached the bottom of the stairs, and with a sigh he turned to go up again.

'Don't bother to show me up,' Xavier said. 'I know the way.'

The ancient butler stepped back with a relieved look. 'Thank you, Your Grace.'

He found Miss Lowell sitting stiffly on a sofa with the air of a person about to be sent to the gallows, or worse.

No doubt she had heard of her niece's latest *mistake*.

'Good evening, ma'am,' Xavier said, bowing.

'Your Grace.' Her voice was barely audible. 'To what do I owe the pleasure? I believe my butler informed you my niece is not at home.'

'Do you know where she is? I wish to speak to her.'

Startled, she stared at him.

Xavier reined in his impatience. He did not want to scare the poor lady out of her wits. He wanted answers.

Miss Lowell adjusted her shawl as if trying to decide what to tell him. 'She went to a house party in Greenwich, with her brother-in-law, the Count of Lipsweiger and Upsal. I do not know when she will return. She planned to stay the night.' The words came out in a breathless rush.

He frowned. After all the Count had said about his widowed sister-in-law and the way he had participated in her ruin, why had the man taken her off to Greenwich?

'A house party?'

'At the home of a— Hmm… Let me think. It was

not someone I know, but Barbara was determined to attend. The strange thing is, no one else I have spoken to seemed to have received an invitation. I wondered if I had made a mistake letting her go. Her father will be very annoyed if so.'

He could not imagine this frail little spinster being able to stop Barbara doing anything once her mind was made up.

No one could.

'Can you recall who it was?' Was he mad? Did he think to follow her like some mooncalf? Just because he had the strange sensation that something wasn't right. Simply to make sure she was safe.

It would be an idiotic thing to do. The sort of thing his father had done. And the sort of thing that had got his father killed.

But the thought of doing nothing, of leaving Barbara to her own devices, was untenable.

For once he had a strong feeling of sympathy for his father, if the man had felt half as strongly about his wife as Xavier did about Barbara.

It was a madness he couldn't seem to quell.

'I am trying to think, Your Grace.'

Xavier bit back his impatience. 'Take your time.'

The carriage pulled to a halt and Charles opened the door.

When she got out, Barbara was surprised there weren't any carriages in the imposing circle in front of the house.

There was a light at the front door, but it seemed rather too quiet. And no one came out to meet them.

'Are we here on the right day?' she asked.

Charles took her arm. 'I think perhaps we are a little early.'

It was past nine, but then some parties did not start until eleven. She tried to recall the time on the invitation.

'I hope Lady Wells isn't put out, if so.'

'It will be fine,' Charles said cheerfully, urging her forward with a little more enthusiasm than was warranted.

They marched up to the front door and a footman opened it.

He did not seem surprised to see them.

'Send a man out for our bags,' Charles said.

'Yes, my lord. Her Ladyship said to bring you to the yellow drawing room.'

He led the way down a long corridor to the back of the house.

Well, at least they were expected.

The drawing room was most tastefully decorated in gold and red after the Chinese style.

'How elegant,' Barbara murmured.

'Wait here, please,' the butler said. 'Her Ladyship will join you shortly.'

Barbara looked at Charles as the butler departed. 'This doesn't seem like much of a party. We cannot be the only guests, surely?'

'As I said, I think we are a little early.'

Barbara wished she had kept the letter of invitation, to see exactly what time they were expected. But she hadn't.

The minutes ticked by.

'We are going to have to apologise for our mistake,' Barbara said. 'I am going to put all the blame at your door, Charles,' she teased.

He looked a little grim.

'I am jesting.'

The drawing room door opened. Barbara turned to see who the butler would announce.

She stumbled back as she realised she was face to face with—her father?

'What are you doing here?' she said and looked at Charles.

Guilt had replaced grimness in his expression.

'You knew he would be here?'

Her father regarded her with hooded eyes and pulled at his bottom lip.

'You have been behaving very badly, my girl. It is time you saw sense.'

She glared at him. 'What I do is none of your business. I am a widow and independent of anyone. I suppose you want me to marry the Duke. Well, be assured, he wouldn't marry me if I was the last person on earth.'

Her father's eyes narrowed. 'And why is that, daughter?'

'Because I made sure he won't.' By her visit to the boxing saloon. Her heart ached with the knowledge, but she could not help but feel a tingle of gladness.

Xavier did not deserve to have her father as part of his family. Or her.

She breathed deeply against the burning sensation at the back of her nose. She would not let her father see her cry.

Charles rose to his feet. 'Good evening, Ambassador. Your daughter has managed to break every social rule possible by attending a boxing match today.'

'It wasn't a match,' she said. 'It was sparring.'

'No difference,' Charles said. 'You are ruined and you know it.'

He actually sounded self-congratulatory.

She stared at him, puzzled by the expression on his face, a sort of triumphant look.

'Well, if the Duke won't marry you, we have to find a different suitor.'

Father looked at Charles with a smirk.

The back of her neck prickled. 'Charles doesn't want to marry me any more than the Duke does.'

Father raised his eyebrows. 'Charles?'

'This is nonsense,' Barbara said.

'You wrong me, Barbara. I would very much like to wed you. And you need have no fears for your reputation in my country. No one will know or care about what has happened in England.'

'I care,' she said sharply. 'And even if I did not, I won't marry you, Charles.'

'You will,' Father said with a smile that was all teeth and a hard expression in his eyes.

She had never heard her father sound so implacable.

She stiffened. 'No one can force me to marry. Not here in England. It is against the law.'

Her father shrugged. 'So they say.'

She looked at her brother-in-law. There was a smidgeon of regret amongst the triumph. 'I am sorry, Barbara, but I need my family's jewels, and this is the only way to be sure of them.'

An awful thought occurred to her. 'Did you arrange for someone to enter my aunt's house, to try to steal them when I first arrived in London?'

He winced. 'It was not my best idea. As your father pointed out, if I stole them from you, I would never be able to use them as collateral. So, while I would have preferred another way to regain my family property, this is the only option.'

She backed away from him. 'Of course it is not. Take them. They are yours for the asking.'

He prowled closer. 'I cannot risk you trying to take them back at some later date, because of that ridiculous settlement my brother made.'

'I won't. I swear it.'

'Well, if it was only you, I might trust your word, but your father is another matter.'

She wouldn't trust her father either.

She eyed the door. Father was standing in front of it. She would not get past him.

Perhaps a window?

Charles took another step closer. 'It is a fair offer, my dear. You will have everything you need. We are friends. You will not find me a bad husband; I am not like my brother. I will not disrespect you. And you will not have to face the consequences of your terrible behaviour.'

'I do not have to face anything. I have no intention of returning to London.'

'And how will you live?' her father asked.

'I have saved up some money. And I will receive the settlement from my first marriage in four weeks' time. On my twenty-fifth birthday. You know this.'

Her father grimaced. 'That money is spoken for.'

Her gaze focussed on him and his defensive expression. 'How can it be spoken for? You have no right to use that money. It is set aside for me.'

'Whatever I have done has been for your benefit. You should be thanking me.'

She glared at him. 'When did you do anything that was for my benefit? Never.'

Father's face reddened. 'That is no way to speak to your father, girl.'

Charles put up a hand. 'Enough. You squabble like children.'

She turned on him. 'This is nothing to do with you.'

His expression darkened. 'It has everything to do with me. I have agreed with your father to relinquish any claim to that money, in return for your hand in marriage and my family jewels.'

She stepped backwards, trying to get closer to the window. 'Are you saying that you stole my money, Father?'

Her father's face reddened. 'I used it to better our lot in life. It is expensive being a diplomat.'

'Your lot in life,' she muttered. 'You never gave a fig about me.'

What was she to do now? Take in washing, as her aunt had suggested?

She stared at Charles. 'You actually believe my claim to be legitimate.'

His mouth hardened. 'I did not say that.'

'If it is not, why would we need to marry? You could take me to court and get them back.'

He glanced over at her father. 'I am sorry, this is the safest way. The best way.'

'Well, I won't marry you and that is final.'

A woman walked in, followed by the footman who had let them in. This was the woman who had been sitting with her father at the theatre. *She* was Lady Wells?

Barbara's stomach dipped. There would be no help coming from that direction. How dare Father plot against her in this way!

'I am leaving.'

'I think not,' Father said.

'Let me show you to your room,' Lady Wells said in an infuriatingly patronising voice. 'You can freshen up while you await the vicar.'

'You cannot force me to wed,' Barbara said.

The young footman took her arm in a hard grasp. 'This way, miss,' he said.

Where on earth had they found such an awful man? 'Countess,' she said, glaring at him.

Glaring did no good. He pulled her out of the room and up the stairs.

'Go with her, darling,' she heard her father say. 'She might as well wear the jewels so Charles knows he is getting what he wants.'

The sound of Charles's crack of a laugh was like a slap across the face.

Chapter Nineteen

As Xavier left Miss Lowell's presence, he could not rid himself of the feeling that something was wrong. Yet why would it be? Lady Wells was the woman with March at the theatre, he recalled, and must be a family friend.

Damn Barbara for making such a spectacle of herself and then running away without giving him a chance to talk to her!

It was partly his own fault. He should have known she'd balk at all those rules and conditions. Rules and conditions he hadn't a hope of enforcing.

Well, he couldn't force her to talk to him any more than he could force her marry him. And if she needed his help, surely she would have asked?

In his gut—no, in his heart, if the tightness in his chest was anything to go by—he knew he'd been dishonest with himself and, worse, dishonest with Barbara. He had been too cowardly to tell her that he didn't simply want to marry her out of duty. He wanted to marry her because she made him…happy.

Happier than he could ever remember feeling.

Had his idiotic proposal really led to her extraordinary appearance at Jackson's earlier today?

The expression he'd glimpsed on her face, guilt tinged with desperation, haunted him.

And now she was gone?

And she had gone with the Count. For some reason, the longer Xavier knew the Count, the less he trusted him. It was he who seemed to lead Barbara from one scrape to the next.

What was it that troubled him about her departure? For one, he had never heard of this Lady Wells until she had appeared with Ambassador March, so clearly she wasn't the best of *ton*.

Barbara's aunt had, after several long minutes of searching, found the woman's invitation and thus her address. She did indeed reside in Greenwich.

And Greenwich wasn't a terribly long way from Mayfair.

Despite all Xavier's good intentions not to interfere in Barbara's affairs, he changed course and headed home. By hell or high water, he intended to know that Barbara was safe. If she was safe and happy, he would have nothing more to say about it.

But he could not disabuse himself of the notion that he needed to make haste.

Which meant driving his curricle at speed.

When he arrived home, it did not take long to have his horses set to, his overnight bag packed and to yield to the insistence of his groom, Dirk, that he must come along too, despite being told he wasn't needed.

Xavier did not have time to argue.

Of course it was raining, more a light drizzle, but his driving coat was waterproof, as was Dirk's, and once clear of town traffic, he made reasonably good time.

Even so, it was past eleven when he arrived at Lady Wells's address.

There was no sign of any sort of ball going on, though there was what looked like a hired coach standing on the drive, clearly ready to leave. The coachman was likely somewhere indoors taking refreshment.

Strangely, there were also no lights showing in the windows, though perhaps this was because the shutters were closed...

Odd.

Worrisome.

Xavier pulled up well before he reached the front entrance of the house. 'Turn the carriage around, please, Dirk,' he said. 'We will not be staying long.'

Dirk, already at the horses' heads, touched his cap.

'Try not to attract anyone's attention.' He wasn't sure why he added that, but it felt right somehow.

'Right you are, Yer Grace.'

Perhaps the party was at the back of the house, he mused. Instead of knocking on the front door, he made his way around to the rear.

It was equally as silent back here. A light emanated from a room overlooking a stone terrace.

He could hear voices from within. Nothing like the

sounds one would expect if there was a ball going on, however.

Remaining in the shadows, he walked quietly up onto the terrace and discovered the French doors slightly ajar. He peered into the room.

'He should be here very soon,' the man with his back to Xavier said to someone else hidden by the drapery from his view.

Xavier shifted to see if he could get a better look at the occupants.

Something hard pressed into his back. A gun?

'Don't move,' a rough voice said. The owner of the voice reached around Xavier and pulled the French door open.

'Guv,' he said loudly. 'We got an intruder.' He pushed Xavier across the threshold.

Xavier cursed his carelessness.

He strode into the room, removed his hat and looked around with a frown. 'What the devil is going on here? Where is Barbara?'

'Thank you, Ball,' Charles said. 'Please see that His Grace does not cause any problems.'

Xavier turned his glare on the burly man who had followed him in. Ball, dressed like a groom, was indeed holding a pistol. A cocked pistol. The man kept a wary distance, but did not lower his weapon.

In the meantime, March was staring at Xavier in horror. As well he might. Holding a Duke at gunpoint was not exactly a good career move for a diplomat.

'Your Grace. I— Well—' the Ambassador stuttered, apparently at a loss for words.

Charles stepped forward with a smooth smile. 'Good evening, Xavier. We were not expecting you.'

'So why post a guard? Tell your man to put his weapon down so we can talk in a civilised manner.'

Charles winced as he glanced over at the groom and back to Xavier. 'Perhaps once I have explained, Your Grace, you will be content to return to your carriage and to London and forget all this unpleasantness.'

He did not, however, ask the groom to lower his gun.

Xavier gritted his teeth. 'Then explain quickly, for I find that my patience is short. Where is the Countess?'

'Now, now, Your Grace,' March said, clearly having regained some of his wits. 'This is a private family gathering. Nothing that need concern you.'

'Indeed,' Charles said quickly. 'In fact, I rather think I am doing you a favour.'

Xavier looked down his nose at the fellow. 'I have no idea what you are talking about.'

'Really?' Charles spread his fingers and looked at them quizzically before raising his gaze to meet Xavier's. 'I would say that the Countess was about to find herself at the centre of a major scandal when your rather sordid affair became common knowledge. Especially after her appearance at Jackson's saloon. By wedding her, I will relieve you of that embarrassment. Indeed, it seems your arrival is most fortuitous: instead of Ball here, you can stand as witness. No one will argue the validity of a wedding if witnessed by a Duke.'

Wedding her? Xavier's chest felt as if it was bound in iron. He forced himself to take a breath. 'You and Barbara are getting married?'

'As soon as the vicar arrives.'

That Barbara liked the fellow, Xavier knew, but he had never seen her show him any sort of warmer emotion.

If it was so, then everything between her and Xavier would have to have been a lie. His stomach dropped.

He could not have been that stupid, surely?

'And she has agreed to this wedding?'

March shifted his feet. His hands shook as he tugged at his cravat and smiled reassuringly. 'My daughter has always been headstrong, but she knows it is the best solution.'

The words rang patently false, and Xavier's heart seemed to lighten.

'The best solution for whom?' he asked.

'Let me find Lady Wells and make sure all is ready,' March said. He left rather hastily.

'Sit down, Your Grace,' Charles said. 'We will not take too much of your time.' He gestured to Ball. 'Give me the pistol and go ready the horses. We leave within the hour.'

His henchman handed over the weapon and left.

Xavier eyed the gun.

Charles shook his head. 'Do not think about it, Your Grace. Killing you will make everything extremely difficult. But I will do it if I have to.' He gestured for Xavier to sit. 'While we are waiting, allow me to explain how the dear Countess stole my family jewels. Then you will understand why this is necessary.'

Xavier sat and leaned back casually against the chair back. Sooner or later the fellow would make a mistake, and he would be ready.

Because whatever Barbara was, one thing he knew, she was no thief.

Barbara's heart raced uncomfortably in her chest. She still could not believe this was happening, and with her father's approval. This was beyond anything he had done to her in the past.

She glared at Lady Wells standing at the dressing table opening the jewellery box. 'I will not marry Charles,' she said, for about the tenth time.

Lady Wells shrugged. 'Stop making such a fuss and do as your father bids.' She picked up the necklace. 'It is so beautiful. Do you not realise how fortunate you are? Come here. I will fasten it for you.'

Barbara glanced at the door. Lady Wells had asked the footman to wait in the hall. There was no point in making a run for it that way. At least, not until the woman left. And Barbara needed her to leave.

She tried to look meek. 'You think I am fortunate?'

'I do. The Count is as handsome a young man as you could wish for, and very pleasant.'

Hah! That was what she had thought about his brother. 'Well…' she said doubtfully.

'All will be well. Did your father not say so?'

Her father only cared about what he wanted. 'I suppose so.' Barbara joined the woman at the dressing table.

'That's better.' Lady Wells smiled at her, draped the necklace around her neck and fastened it. Then Barbara put on the rest of the parure, the bracelet, the tiara. It was a beautiful set. No doubt about it.

Together they looked at her image in the mirror.

'Lovely,' Lady Wells said.

All Barbara could see were bonds where once she had seen the chance to live her own life.

Her stomach felt hollow, her chest empty. Would she ever be free? Rage rose up like a hot tide.

How could Father do this to her? Again.

She would not let him.

'Wait here until we are ready for you,' Lady Wells said. 'Do not try to leave—Jack will remain outside until I come for you.'

Barbara nodded and sat on the chest at the foot of the bed, hoping her anger was not visible on her face.

The moment Lady Wells closed the door behind her, Barbara ran to the window and quietly pulled back the curtain.

Aha! Not a window. A French door leading out to a balcony. She pushed the handle down. The door did not budge and there was no key in the lock.

She glanced at the door out to the hallway. She would have to be very quiet if she did not want to arouse her guard's suspicions and have him poking his nose in here.

She glanced around. Would the key be in the room,

or would it be with the housekeeper? In her experience, because maids had to sweep down the balcony when they cleaned the room, the key was likely to be somewhere handy for the maid as well as for any guest using the chamber.

She opened the drawers in the dressing table. Nothing.

Then she checked the mantel above the fireplace. And there was a key sitting in the drip tray of a candle holder.

It fit the lock.

Quietly, she unlocked the balcony door and crept outside. Blast! It was still raining. She went back inside and covered her head with her shawl. It wasn't much but it would help.

She stared down over the balustrade. It was a long drop. But one didn't live most of one's life at boarding school without learning the make-a-rope-from-bed-sheets trick in order to leave by way of a window.

Not something Father would think of, since he never had a ha'p'orth of interest in anything Barbara had ever done.

One thing she did know, she would not have long, and she would need to get as far from here as possible before they noticed her missing.

She stripped the bed, used the nail scissors in her reticule to snip the hem, and tore both top and bottom sheet into three lengths that she tied together.

She secured the end to one of the stone balusters and tossed the rest of the linen over the top of the rail.

It didn't quite reach the flower bed below but was not far off.

Climbing in skirts was never easy, and already the sheets were becoming sodden, but she carefully balanced on the railing and eased herself over. Having lowered herself down hand over hand, she dropped the last little bit.

The thump of her landing sounded shockingly loud in the quiet of the night. Hopefully the patter of raindrops would hide the noise.

She stood still listening but could hardly hear much more than the pounding of her heart.

She was at the side of the house.

Which way to go?

If she went around the front and tried to walk down the road, they would likely catch up to her very quickly.

She headed for the back of the house.

As she rounded the corner, she could see a large terrace and beyond that darkness. Hopefully lawns, not a maze of formal gardens.

The sound of voices wafted out of a window. Not voices. A voice. A particularly well-known deep voice. Xavier?

'Explanation?' he said. 'Or an excuse?'

Was he also part of her father's plot? Her heart sank.

'Where is the Countess? I shall not be pleased if she has come to any harm.'

Had he actually come for *her*? It wasn't possible.

'My dear Xavier, do not be fooled by a pretty face,'

Charles was saying. 'Think. You will make yourself a laughing stock.'

Barbara wished he was wrong. She dashed raindrops out of her face and looked longingly at the darkness. Within a very few minutes she could be far from the house, and they would never ever find her. But Xavier...

'I want to hear Barbara say she is here of her own volition. That marrying you is what she wants.'

No one before had ever cared enough to ask what she wanted.

Her eyes blurred.

No one but Xavier. She took a deep breath and slowly mounted the steps to the terrace. Silence had fallen in the room.

Xavier was facing her direction, looking extraordinarily handsome with his rain-soaked hair sticking to his face. He seemed bored. And yet... No, there was anger in that bright blue gaze. Fury.

She altered her position until she could see the other occupant of the room. Charles. Sitting with his back to the window. All she could see of him was the back of his head and a pistol in his hand.

Pointed at Xavier.

Xavier gave him one of those dark looks of his. 'You do know that kidnapping a peer of the realm is a hanging offence, don't you?'

'Then perhaps I really would be better off getting rid of you,' Charles said with one of his charming little chuckles. 'After you sign the wedding lines.'

Barbara swallowed a gasp of shock.

Why would Xavier stand as a witness to her marriage?

The sound of wheels on the gravel drive caused her heart to rise higher in her throat.

The vicar. It must be.

Any moment Lady Wells would come to fetch her down. If she remained here another minute, she would be caught.

Xavier could look after himself. Couldn't he? Charles wouldn't dare kill him.

She wished she could be sure. Her mind went back to the day Helmut died. The way Charles had shouted a warning, distracting her husband at the worst possible moment.

She had always thought it strange. Now...she wondered if it might have been deliberate.

Had he meant for Helmut to die that day?

She glanced around wildly. A gardener's rake leaned against the wall.

It wasn't much of a weapon, but there was nothing else.

A ball of anger sat in the middle of Xavier's chest, hot and ready to explode.

Every word out of the Count's mouth fed the furnace. The mask of affability was a complete lie. The man was as ruthless as they came. The thought of him having power over Barbara, turned anger to fury.

He forced himself to remain still, outwardly calm, ready to spring when the opportunity arose.

It would have to be when Barbara arrived in the room. Once he knew for certain that she had no wish to marry this man.

Somehow, he would have to get her away, but the odds were not good. He would be facing at least three or four men, including the Count. March he could discount. He was elderly and unfit. Unless he also was armed.

The curtain behind the Count moved. Not as if blown by the wind, but as if edged aside by someone looking in.

One of the grooms?

It hardly seemed likely.

Had Dirk decided to follow him? Xavier couldn't think why he would.

The curtains parted. The bedraggled, bejewelled figure of Barbara dashed in and struck at the pistol with a stick.

Xavier leaped from his chair to tackle the Count who had risen with a curse. Xavier grabbed for the pistol, which went off with a loud bang.

Plaster sprayed down from the ceiling.

Barbara shrieked.

The Count cursed.

Xavier landed a punch flush on the other man's jaw. He collapsed. The gun slid across the floor.

Barbara made a dive for it and stood up with it in her hand, flushed and triumphant.

Xavier stood looking down at the Count, who was

feeling his jaw and slowly coming to his senses. He groaned.

March burst into the room with Lady Wells.

'What the devil is going on?' March said. He looked at the Count on the floor and at Xavier and Barbara standing side by side. 'Good God.'

'The jig is up,' Xavier said dryly. 'It is my guess that Lady Barbara has no wish to wed the Count here and I intend to see that her wishes are observed.'

Barbara looked at him, her gaze misty. She blinked as if to clear her vision and dipped a curtsey. 'Thank you, Your Grace.'

Her formality chilled him. Well, it was no more than he deserved.

He hauled the Count to his feet and thrust him into the nearest chair. 'Sit there, until I decide what to do with you.' He glared at March and Lady Wells. 'You also.'

They sank down onto the nearest sofa.

Xavier took the pistol from Barbara. 'Thank you,' he said softly.

She met his gaze, her expression impossible to read. 'Why are you here?'

Puzzled, he shook his head. 'I apologise for interfering. Something just smelled wrong. I had to make sure you were all right.'

'You came. For me.' Her voice broke slightly. She looked away. 'I—I didn't deserve that you should. After all I have done.' Her voice was little more than a whisper. She looked lost somehow. And something painful dug at his heart. 'And my father and his schemes—' She gave a wry little laugh. 'So embarrassing, but I thank you for coming to my aid.'

He glanced at the wary-looking Count and the sheepish Ambassador and grimaced. 'It's a pretty kettle of fish, but I am sure we will come about.'

'You will,' she said softly.

He rubbed his knuckles, bruised from where he had hit the Count. 'We need to talk, but first I have to deal with them.'

'What will you do with them?'

'Pack them off where they came from, I suppose. After they sign a confession regarding kidnapping and other felonies. That should keep them both in line.'

She nodded. 'And it won't cause another scandal.'

'Exactly. We will stay here tonight, while I get it all sorted out, and then we will talk in the morning.'

The door opened to admit a small dark-coated fellow wearing a starched white collar at his throat.

'Ah,' Xavier said. 'The vicar.'

The vicar put on a pair of *pince-nez* and glanced around. 'Where are the bride and groom?' he asked.

Xavier stepped forward. 'Your services are no longer required.'

'What? You get me out on a night like tonight for no reason? I demand to be compensated for my time.'

'So you shall be,' Xavier said. He handed the man his calling card. 'Write me a note and I shall see to it when I return to London.'

The burly groom who had captured Xavier came in through the French doors. He looked startled.

Xavier rolled his eyes upward. How many more people was he going to have to deal with?

When the groom's gaze fell on the gun Xavier still held in his hand, his eyebrows shot up.

'Like that, is it? Well, guv, let me know what you want to do. I'm your man.'

Charles glared at him.

Xavier laughed. 'No honour among thieves, I see. You can go and fetch my curricle and my tiger, Dirk, and see that they are looked after. Make sure you do exactly as Dirk says and all will be well.'

The man touched his cap and left.

'If you don't mind, Xavier, I shall retire,' Barbara said.

'As you wish. It has been a long day.'

She slipped quietly out of the room. He had never seen her so crushed.

But she didn't want to wed Charles and she didn't have to, and that was all that mattered.

He opened the drawer of the writing desk in the corner and pulled out quills, ink and paper. 'Now, let us see about these confessions so you gentlemen, and Lady Wells, can be on your way.'

'This is my house,' Lady Wells said stiffly.

'And you may return in a month or two, if you wish. But tonight, you will leave. Now, who is going to be first?'

* * *

Barbara eyed Xavier across the breakfast table. He looked so handsome, if a little tired.

She felt guilty about leaving him to deal with Charles and her father, but last night she had simply been too emotionally drained to do anything else.

Truthfully, she had been afraid of what she might do or say should Xavier say one kind thing to her. She had felt like bursting into tears.

Today she was ready to face whatever might come and be strong and resolute.

He smiled at her and her heart tumbled over. She hoped that he did not notice how her hand shook as she put down her cup.

'Would you like more tea?' she asked, proud of how calm she sounded.

He leaned back in his chair. 'No, thank you.' His face softened.

She knew that expression. It was the way he looked at her after they made love.

She had half expected him to come to her last night, and she'd lain awake and listen to the carriages departing. But he hadn't come. And she hadn't blamed him. It was better that they make a clean break of it.

'Barbara—'

She couldn't bear to hear him explain why they must part. She knew all the reasons why she could never be his duchess.

She put up a hand to stop him saying more. 'Please.

I will leave right after breakfast. As soon as a carriage may be hired.'

'My love,' he started.

No. No. She shook her head. She could not, would not be his love. How could she bear to share him with a wife?

She started to rise.

He got up and came around to her side the table, moving her chair for her as she stood and then capturing her hand.

'Dearest, I will speak. And you will listen,' he said with a touch of laughter in his voice.

She braced herself. 'Very well, say what you must.'

'First, I must thank you for coming to my rescue last night. It seemed you had already made your escape and did not need my help after all.'

He had come to her aid. Something twisted in her heart, such a sweet pain. She forced herself not to feel it. 'I could not leave you sitting there with a pistol pointed at your head. Who knows what Charles might have done once he discovered I had gone?'

'Indeed, the man is an absolute bounder. Come with me.'

He escorted her out of the breakfast room and into the drawing room where last night's drama had played out. Someone had cleared up the plaster, though a hole remained in the ceiling.

Xavier seated her on the sofa and sat at her side. Her heart picked up speed. He must be expecting her to say something.

'Did—did my father leave willingly?'

'"Willingly" is a bit strong, but he promised to return to Lisbon. I will see to it that he receives a posting to some far-flung outpost where he and Lady Wells will never trouble you again.'

It was what she had always wanted. To be free of Father and his machinations. In spite of that, the future seemed somehow very lonely. 'Thank you.'

'I am afraid that the money you were supposed to receive from your first marriage is all but gone.'

Her stomach sank. But she had known as much already. Still, she had the jewels.

'And Charles?'

'Charles is another matter. He believes the jewels are his and, no matter what he says, I do not think he will rest until he has them back.'

A cold sensation ran down her back. 'I believe he had someone try to steal them when I first came to London. They entered my aunt's room instead of mine.' She shivered. 'Who knows what he will attempt next? Perhaps I should sell them.'

He regarded her for several long moments. 'Despite how little I like the fellow, I think there is a good chance they are rightfully his.'

She let go a breath. 'Father cheated.'

He nodded.

'So I will be penniless.'

'Not if we wed.'

The words took her breath away. Her heart filled with joy for one brief wonderful second. Reality brought her down to earth. After all she had done, how could she let him sacrifice his reputation?

'No. Xavier. I could never be the sort of proper duchess you want. You know I could not.'

He grasped her hand in his and would not release it, though his touch was gentle, it was exceedingly firm.

'I do not want a proper duchess,' he said. 'I want you.' He shook his head ruefully.

'That did not come out the way I meant it.'

He slipped off the sofa to kneel on one knee, kissed the back of her hand briefly and gazed into her face.

As he spoke, his voice became husky with emotion and his eyes were sincere and open and full of love. 'You are the *right* duchess for me. You are kind and generous and loving. You are clever. You make me laugh at myself. You make me see the world with kinder eyes. I need that. I have been angry too long. I want to be happy.'

She peered into his eyes. 'You aren't angry any longer?'

'All this time, I was angry at my father for marrying my stepmother. She took him from me first, because he loved her and then because he died trying to save her life. I never forgave him for dying. He should have stayed with me instead of following her.'

'She made him happy.'

'More so than my mother, who was by all account shy and very reserved. My stepmother was vibrant and young and yes, reckless. But she made him happy. Happier than I made him. I resented her for that, bitterly. Until I met you. Now I know what he felt for her. I want that.' He hesitated. 'But only if you want it as well. If you do not then I will arrange for you to live comfortably wherever you desire. No strings attached, I promise, and you would never have to see me again, even though I know it would break my heart to lose you.'

He *had* come for her last night. The only person in her life to come to see if she was all right. The only person to offer her protection without expectation. How could she not want him? She loved him.

But for him to marry her... 'You will be ruined. After what I did, I will be *persona non grata.*'

'Ruined? No. I will be a new man. A happy man. And to the devil with Society. I don't care a damn what they think. I need you, Barbara.'

Emotion filled her eyes with foolish tears. She could not speak around the hot hard lump that had lodged in her throat.

'I need you too, Xavier,' she managed to say.

'I love you,' he said.

'But *I* love you too well to—'

He touched a finger to her lips. 'Don't. If I lose you now I have finally found you, I don't know what I will do.'

'Oh,' she whispered. It was the nicest, sweetest thing she had ever heard. How could she deny her feelings any longer?

'I love you,' she said. 'I love you terribly, awfully, wonderfully. But best of all, I trust you.' For the first time in her life, she had someone she could trust.

He kissed her.

Epilogue

'The carriage is waiting, Your Grace,' the butler announced when the wedding breakfast had been cleared away.

'Shall we?' Xavier asked his bride. Barbara looked radiant in a gown the colour of a summer sky. The diamond tiara gleaming on her brow did not sparkle as brilliantly as her eyes when she smiled at him.

Somehow, Xavier had managed to convince her that they had no need to run off to Gretna Green. A wedding by special licence at Woodburn House, witnessed by only Julian, her aunt and a few of the servants was equally as scandalous. After all, anyone who was anyone among the *ton* would expect to be invited to the *wedding of the Season*. Fortunately, although a duke, he wasn't a royal one, and he hadn't been required to ask the King's permission.

As they rose from the table, Xavier gazed into Barbara's face and felt his heart stir at the joy he saw in her expression. A joy that infused his very being. He brought her hand to his lips. 'I love you,' he said softly.

'I love you too,' she murmured. 'Husband.'

His blood ran wildly through his veins at the heat in her eyes.

On Xavier's right, Julian groaned theatrically. 'I see it is time we left you two to your wedded bliss.'

'As soon as possible, if not sooner,' Xavier replied, unable to pull his gaze away from his wife's face.

Julian laughed.

Aunt Lenore pretended not to see or hear, but she too rose to her feet and fiddled with her shawl. 'I am only sorry that your father was not here to witness your marriage, Barbara.'

Barbara tore her gaze from Xavier's and smiled gently at her aunt. 'I will write to him and let him know of it. He should receive the letter in about six months.'

And he would not return to England for five years if Xavier had anything to say about it. Which he actually did.

Barbara leaned forward and kissed her aunt's cheek. 'Please, do not worry about Father. He won't come to any harm. And thanks to Xavier, you will be well taken care of despite his absence.'

Aunt Lenore's eyes misted. 'Duke, you have my gratitude. Your kindness—'

He raised a hand. 'Please, call me Xavier. I do this because it makes my wife—' how he loved saying those words '—it makes my wife happy. Please, be assured, you are as dear to me as you are to her.'

Aunt Lenore dabbed at the corner of her eyes with her handkerchief. 'Thank you.'

'Julian,' Xavier said, putting an arm around his friend's shoulders as Barbara accompanied her aunt to the front door. 'You will see Miss Lowell safely home?'

'Of course I will.'

They shook hands. 'I hope you will soon find yourself in wedded bliss,' Xavier said, half joking, half not.

Julian gave him a horrified look. 'God, no! What the devil would I want with a wife?'

It hadn't been long ago that Xavier had had those same feelings, despite knowing it was his duty to marry. And look at him now. Perhaps Julian would be as fortunate.

The butler sheltered Aunt Lenore with an umbrella as she walked out of the front door and climbed into the carriage. Julian hopped in after her.

'I am so glad you convinced me to marry you here at Woodburn,' Barbara said, as they held hands and watched their guests' carriage depart. 'I know you love this house.'

'So am I. I don't think there is anything worse than northern roads, unless it is Scottish inns.'

'Are you saying you wish to spend the rest of your wedding day in a comfortable bed?'

He looked at her sharply and saw a very naughty twinkle in her eye.

'Did you have something else in mind?' He took a deep breath. Whatever it was, he would do it, if it would bring her pleasure.

She laughed. A sound that made his heart sing with

anticipation. 'Oh, no, that is exactly what I have in mind.'

But there would be other days. And other nights. And other ideas of where to spend them. And he could not wait to enjoy them all, with his beautiful, exciting wife.

He swept her into his arms to the sound of her laughter and carried her up the stairs to their chamber.

* * * * *

If you enjoyed this story, be sure to read
Ann Lethbridge's previous historical romances

The Viscount's Reckless Temptation
A Shopkeeper for the Earl of Westram
The Matchmaker and the Duke
A Family for the Widowed Governess
A Cinderella to Redeem the Earl

MILLS & BOON®

Coming next month

CINDERELLA'S CHARADE WITH THE DUKE
Jeanine Englert

'I would like to extend your offer of employment not only as Millie's governess, but also as my fake betrothed. I think a Lady Penelope Denning would do nicely,' he said, his words rushing out. 'But if you prefer another name, I am open to such possibilities. Do you think you could do that?'

She could have sworn he said something about pretending to be his betrothed, but surely she had misheard every word. 'I am sorry, Your Grace. I do not think I understood you properly. I would love to remain on as Lady Millie's governess, but that last part... Did you say you wish for me, an orphan from Stow, to also pretend to be your betrothed as some other person entirely?'

A beat of silence passed and then His Grace sat back in his chair, his hands sliding down the curved wooden armrests before covering the painted gold flowers at the ends. He met her gaze. 'Yes, Miss Potts, that is *exactly* what I wish for you to do.'

Not even Ophelia would have anticipated this request. Hattie was torn between the shock of silence and the wild laughter of disbelief and confusion. He stared at her and waited.

She asked the only thing she could think of. 'Why?'

'A fair question,' he replied.

This whole scene was ridiculous. Why would *this* man need a woman like her to be his pretend betrothed? He was a duke, he was handsome and had all the time and wealth in the world at his disposal. He could find an eager wife in the time it would take him to blink.

He paused in front of the portrait of the late Marchioness and faced Hattie. 'In the simplest terms, Miss Potts, I cannot take a new bride, but the *ton* will give me and my daughter no peace until I am adequately…unavailable to help quash the rumours they create to sell their gossip sheets. I cannot ask a woman of high Society to fill such a role as they all know one another and will talk about such a ruse and embarrass me.

'So, my hope was that you being from Stow and far removed from here and someone who cares for my daughter and whom my daughter adores would help me with this…endeavour.'

'You mean lie to everyone?'

'Yes.'

Continue reading

CINDERELLA'S CHARADE WITH THE DUKE
Jeanine Englert

Available next month
millsandboon.co.uk

Copyright © 2025 Jeanine Englert

COMING SOON!

We really hope you enjoyed reading this book.
If you're looking for more romance
be sure to head to the shops when
new books are available on

Thursday 23rd October

To see which titles are coming soon, please visit
millsandboon.co.uk/nextmonth

MILLS & BOON

MILLS & BOON TRUE LOVE IS HAVING A MAKEOVER!

Introducing

Love Always

Marrying a Royal
Nina Milne
Suzanne Merchant
2 BOOKS IN ONE

Summer with the Billionaire
Rachael Stewart
Justine Lewis
2 BOOKS IN ONE

Swoon-worthy romances, where love takes centre stage. Same heartwarming stories, stylish new look!

Look out for our brand new look
OUT NOW
MILLS & BOON

FOUR BRAND NEW BOOKS FROM
MILLS & BOON MODERN

Indulge in desire, drama, and breathtaking romance – where passion knows no bounds!

Demand from a Greek — Lynne Graham / Jackie Ashenden

CRAVE ME — Michelle Smart / Lorraine Hall

DARING CONFESSIONS — Lela May Wight / Clare Connelly

With his Ring... — Lucy King / Millie Adams

OUT NOW

Eight Modern stories published every month, find them all at:
millsandboon.co.uk

OUT NOW!

BUSINESS WITH PLEASURE

THE TYCOON'S AFFAIR COLLECTION

MAYA BLAKE

Available at
millsandboon.co.uk

MILLS & BOON

OUT NOW!

In the Spotlight

FAME'S TEMPTATION

RACHAEL STEWART · SOPHIE PEMBROKE · ABBY GREEN

Available at
millsandboon.co.uk

MILLS & BOON

LET'S TALK
Romance

For exclusive extracts, competitions and special offers, find us online:

- **f** MillsandBoon
- **X** @MillsandBoon
- **◉** @MillsandBoonUK
- **♪** @MillsandBoonUK

Get in touch on 01413 063 232

For all the latest titles coming soon, visit millsandboon.co.uk/nextmonth